TRUCK STOP EARTH
by
~~Michael A. Armstrong~~

by
James Ignatius Malachi Obadiah Osborne

Perseid Press
P.O. Box 584
Centerville MA 02632

Truck Stop Earth

First Perseid Press trade paperback edition, 2016
First Perseid Press hardcover edition, 2016
First Perseid Press ePub edition, 2016
First Perseid Press Kindle edition, 2016

Cover Design, Roy Mauritsen
Interior Design, Sarah Hulcy
Book Cover Image copyright © 2016, Perseid Press

Paperback version ISBN-13: 978-0-9975310-1-5; ISBN-10: 09975310-1-0
ePub version ISBN-13: 978-0-9975310-0-8; ISBN-10:09975310-0-2
Kindle version ISBN-13:978-0-9975310-3-9; ISBN-10: 09975310-3-7
Hardcover version ISBN-13:978-0-9975310-2-2; ISBN-10: 09975310-2-9

Printed in the United States of America

10 9 8 7 6 5 4 3 2 1

TRUCK STOP EARTH
by
~~Michael A. Armstrong~~

by
James Ignatius Malachi Obadiah Osborne

TABLE OF CONTENTS

AUTHOR'S NOTES

Everything in this book is true and really happened to me, at least as well as I can remember.* At the advice of my editor and coauthor, Michael Armstrong, as well as our lawyers, and, OK, at the insistence of those goddamn corporate publishing suits, certain names have been changed. Also, Mike suggested—because a certain class of person might actually seek out Della on the premise it could be a cool place to live—that we change the name of the actual Alaska town where this happened. We've given the average intelligent reader enough clues that she can figure out its location, but the really brain-damaged aren't likely to guess. Besides, Mike says Della has enough problems of its own without importing more. Since he's lived there longer than me, I have to respect his wishes.

I might have used more exact names of people and places I've met and mention here, but to tell you the truth, I have a lousy memory for names anyway. It's probably just as well. Some of those assholes might not have a good sense of humor.

---

* OK, I might have made a few things up.

Other than that, this is totally true. It's kinda a crap shoot how our publisher will slot this, and you never know about those Gen Z clerks working in big chain bookstores who can't even count change. Drop us an IM and let us know where you found this, and if you think it's true.

A lot of other people just kissed me off. You know who you are, you shits, and I hope that when the Grays abduct you up on the mother ship, they don't use KY jelly on the anal probes.

I'd also like to thank the social workers of the world, particularly the ones who made brave attempts to treat me and cure me of my delusions. Folks, I wish it had been that simple. As you'll read here, reality is what happens when therapy and really cool psychoactive drugs don't quite work as advertised.

But mostly I'd like to thank the Grays, the invaders from space, and the Alien Occupation Government, because you gave me a purpose in life. I kicked your butt in Della, we and the Resistance, and though I know I didn't send you whining all the way back to whatever ass-pit corner of the universe you came from, I do think I've taught you a thing or two about messing with humans. Someday we're gonna zap you off the planet and bring you to justice.

And you, dear reader, I thank you for taking a risk and reading this book, or at least buying it. Poor Mike has been hustling for over 25 years trying to make a living from writing, and I really hope that his modest profits from this book will help him live in the style he'd like to become accustomed to.

—James Ignatius Malachi Obadiah Osborne
("Call me Jimmo")

*

When, while out walking on the beach one day, I ran into this strange-looking guy with dreadlocks, I knew my life would be changed. He spun this really odd story about alien invaders, GETS, RATS, searing butt chips, and other bizarre stuff. Jimmo couldn't get others to bite on his story—I won't name names, but you know who you are, you unimaginative dicks—but I knew not only did he have a good story, but it was true.

For over 30 years I've been writing science fiction, and the one thing you learn writing science fiction is how to tell the difference between reality and fiction. Like they say, reality is what happens when science fiction breaks down. The more Jimmo talked to me—because I was the only one who had the patience to listen to him—the more I realized his story was so disjoint, so scrambled, so damn bizarre, it couldn't possibly be false.

I believed him.

As we got to talking, I realized that some 60-inch story in Alaska's best weekly paper wouldn't possibly do justice to his tale, which is all he'd asked for in the first place, my having let slip that I worked for Alaska's Best Weekly Newspaper, herein called the Della News. He'd have to write a book.

Or rather, I'd have to.

It quickly became obvious that while Jimmo had a great story, he couldn't write his way out of Grunt English, the kind of class I used to teach, where the only requirement was that you be able to print your name and have a pulse and a core body temperature above 95 degrees. Someone would have to write his story for him.

So we made a deal: Jimmo would tell his story as best he could, and I'd fix it up and make it semiliterate, all the while preserving his unique voice. I wrote up a grant and got the Della Starving Artists Fund to buy him a laptop computer with voice-recognition word-processing software. In his spare moments he'd dictate his story, send me the disks, and I'd clean it up. Every couple of weeks we'd get together somewhere—we kept having to move around because of the fear of a Gray assassination—and discuss various points in the book. After about six years of this, we had a book, and here it is.

Whether or not you believe it is true, frankly, we don't give a damn. You can use this information to resist the Alien Occupation Government, or you can be a spineless tool of the Grays. We don't care. All we want to do is tell a story and maybe in the process make a whole hell of a lot of money.

I think we've done the former, and with your help, we'll also achieve the latter.

—Michael Armstrong, "Della," Alaska

Chapter 1

So like I came into the country over this long crummy-as-shit road, and right away I saw the black helicopters. What did I expect? I knew the bigheads had followed me all the way up from Canada and into good ol' Truck Stop Alaska. "James Ignatius Malachi Obadiah Osborne (call me Jimmo)," I said to myself, "those black helicopters are gonna dodge you until the day you die." That's what I said, and let me tell you, it's the damn truth.

Should I of been surprised to see the black helicopters at the border? Not I. Not you, either, if you hadn't been duped by the big Cosmic Gray Conspiracy to mind your own damn business and just pay your taxes to the Alien Occupation Government, but you have been, that's why I'm telling you this story.

Sure, some Rational Thinking Straight who isn't on anti-psychotic drugs would say, "Those were Blackhawks, it's the damn border, Alaska is crawling with military, that's why you saw black helicopters." And that damn RATS would be right, he would, in the particular reality he happened to inhabit. I don't play in that reality, not since years ago oh never-mind, because I have seen the absolute all and everything and what-the-hey of the Universe, my dear reader, I have, I have. And I tell you, those black helicopters are real, they're everywhere, and this whole planet is run by alien Grays, and you know what I found out? God's truth.

Alaska is like the main pump island of a filling station on the Outer Milky Way Throughway. Truck Stop Earth, you betcha.

But I'm getting ahead of myself, and giving away the kicker, when I have exactly 323 pages (it's in my contract, no more, no less) of double-spaced, Times New Roman font, 12-point typewritten text to go. So bear with me.

Let me start over.

*

First, I didn't see the black helicopters right away. When I was coming into the country, on that rutted gravel road between Beaver Creek, Yukon Territory, and the Alaska border, first I saw the couple in the black jumpsuits. I had hitched a ride to Beaver Creek the night before, a nice midsummer night, clear and hot and with sunset about six minutes past oh-dark-hundred, only I guess you called it "oh-light-hundred" up there in the far north. I had had pretty good luck coming up the Alaska Highway. After a little unpleasantness at the border, which I solved by showing the customs guy my red-jacket US Passport, the one I got from when I was in the Foreign Service, and flashing him five big Dead Presidents, after that I got some good rides. A bunch of Coasties on their way to Kodiak, who told me about Della, God bless 'em. Then, a trucker hauling Snap-on-Tools to Fairbanks—that got me as far as Whitehorse. Then this really choice blonde babe who turned out to be a born again, sorta like me, who picked me up because I had a sign that said JOHN 3:16.

Hannah, the blonde, took me to Beaver Creek because I had some rare choice Plankeye minidisks, bootlegged from their Mark of the Beast tour. Plus, I think she wanted someone to talk to, on account of she was on her way to join this religious commune out of Big Delta up there where the Alaska Highway ends. Hannah had been betrothed and saw her youthful life fading away into babies and stacking hay.

OK, we did the beast with the two backs, too, but we prayed for forgiveness afterward. Of course we used raincoats, some nubbly glow-in-the-dark condoms I had bought in the restroom at a Texaco in Whitehorse. ("Watch it glow as you grow," the package said.) So Hannah got me to Beaver Creek, har-har, but she dropped me out before the Canadian customs shed, right there on the edge of town, tellin' me I'd have "to trust to the Good Lord" for my passage out of Canada. I understood. I wouldn't cross a border with a hitchhiker, either. Hannah laid a big sloppy kiss with a wad of tongue as a farewell. God bless the lucky Delta dick who gets her for a wife, he's going to wear out his johnson if Hannah keeps that up.

So I left Canada in the sense that I said good-bye to their customs, some surly fat bitch who made real sure she punched my SSN into her computer, so the Canuckadians would know they were rid of ol' Jimmo, farewell. But it's a long haul between the spanking new Canadian customs building outside of Beaver Creek and the big concrete building of US Customs right at the border, about twenty miles of road, and there isn't a town, village, gas station, or anything the whole way. It's just open country, a real no-man's land.

The guys in the black jumpsuits wanted to give me a ride.

I was walking along the side of the road six miles out of Beaver Creek, real peaceful like, digging the wildflowers and the beer cans and the little shreds of filter fabric sticking out of the edges, when I turned at the sound of a car coming from down the road. Not even thinking, I stuck my thumb out, but before I had a chance to pull it back in, the white Jeep Cherokee stopped. At first I thought they were camo dudes, like the ones who patrol around Area 51 at Groom Lake. Man, I hate those rent-a-grunts, but I guess they made it personal after that little incident when I blew their cover and listed their names and home addresses on the Web. 'Nother story.

I didn't even have to look at their plates—Alaska blue 'n' gold NRG lettered plates, and in Alaska they only go up to the J's—to know who they were: AOGs, Agents of the Grays, Alien Occupation Government. They looked like bat-fags, Bureau of Alcohol, Tobacco, and Firearms goons, right down to the thin Kevlar vests. Two of 'em, though, in the slick black jumpsuits.

"Need a ride, son?" asked the guy in the passenger's side as he rolled down the window. Tinted windows, thick windows: armored, I knew.

"Just hiking, sir," I said. Old habit from when I was in Delta Force. Any guy calls you "son," you call them "sir." I'd of saluted, but when Delta kicked me upstairs on special assignment as a deep cover agent in the Foreign Service, I swore off saluting. With my dreadlocks tucked up into my baseball cap, and the hair buzzed on the side of my head, that guy might of thought I was military with a high and tight, in civvies.

"We can give you a ride up to the border, son," the guy went on.

"Only a couple of miles. I'll walk the rest of the way."

Then they got out. Right then I knew they were Grays because they had the mirrored sunglasses and the jerky legs.

The Grays on bottom duty get face surgery so they look normal—real noses, mouths, and ears—but the big triangular eyes are hard to fake. Takes a lot of bone surgery, so most of them just wear big sunglasses. And the Grays have long torsos but stumpy legs, kind of like that Frog painter Hangin' Too Loose Lowtrec, so to look human, they walk on these like stilts. Our high gravity really messes them up, though, so they never get good at it. You learn these things when you become an enemy of the bigheads like me.

The driver was a wymmin, I mean, I knew the type, feminazis: big broad shoulders and almost no boobs, and fat hips. She had short hair just over her ear flaps and long bangs. Female Grays don't like to alter their ear flaps. They're really weird that way: they think those vestigial flaps are the sexiest thing. For all I know, that's how they screw. Go figure. Aliens are really strange.

So the wymmin Gray got out, same klutzy walk, and they both gimped over to me, looking real tall, but I knew I could kick their legs out from under them. 'Course, iffen I did that, they'd blast me to cinders, but it's nice to know I had the option to damage them before I died. They leaned up against that white Jeep Cherokee with the funny windows, hooking their thumbs in their belts. Those Grays watch too many of our Western movies, if you ask me. Someone ought to tell them, or at least turn 'em on to some Mel Gibson thrillers so they can learn a new attitude . . .

"You're kind of out here in the middle of nowhere," the wymmin says. She had one of those squeaky high voices their females have. It always flips me out. You see a big momma like that, and then she has this high voice.

"Yes ma'am," I said. "I'm used to walking."

"So we'll give you a ride to the border," she said. "Across the border, make it easy on you. Into Tok. You must be going that way."

"Might take a right at Tositna and go up to Chicken," I said. "Do some gold mining."

"Yeah." The guy scratched his balls, in that sympathetic gesture guys make to each other, sort of like saying, Balls, what a pain, huh? Only I knew he was readjusting the servos on his stilts.

"So you sure you don't want a lift?" The wymmin Gray glared at me through her glasses. I knew she was scanning me. Hell, I knew they had me pegged already. They'd put a chip in my butt after my first abduction near Cedar Key (see Chapter 16), so they could track me like that, you bet.

"Don't wanna trouble you," I said.

"No trouble," the guy said.

"Still . . ." I stared off into the distance, thinking of Hannah. I figured if they were scanning me, they'd pick up the increase in blood pressure and the little woody I was working up. "I'm sort of hoping for a ride with this babe I met in Beaver Creek." I grinned, and the guy Gray grinned back, showing me his stumpy little tongue.

"Gotcha," he said, winking and making a little gun with his fingers and shooting it at me. Really. They ought to watch some old Bond movies if they wanted some better clichés.

"Dude," I said.

The wymmin nodded and the guy nodded and they got back in the white Cherokee and drove over the hill and probably to one of their shuttle crafts. A few minutes later, the Coasties who had given me a ride 500 miles down the road picked me up again.

When the Coasties dropped me off just before the border, I saw the black helicopters.

Welcome to Alaska, I thought. Now go home.

*

But I wasn't going home. Alaska had to be home. I couldn't go anyplace else. You want to hear the whole crap of my life? I didn't think so, not one big hunk of shit-ass exposition infodump, so pardon me if I go on. I'll give it to you in dribs and drabs, iffen you like, or you can just deconstruct it out of the hidden semiotics of my prose, like that Doo Ruda guy would do.

You talk to any Alaskan who wasn't born here, anyone who had to come from someplace else, and had set down roots—which is about two-thirds of the state—and every damn one of them has this cornpone "coming into the country" yarn about how they came up here with six dimes in their pocket, a Swiss Army knife, and a good idea and a strong back, and it's all hooey, I say. Hooey. Most of them got transferred up here by some oil company, with a big moving allowance, and they did a six-year shift, and got laid off so fast they didn't have the brains to move on to Kazakhstan or some other hot-shit oil prospect, and they got stuck, like starfish laid high after a minus-six tide. Most of 'em came into the country on a 747 into Anchorage, not the hard way, hitching up the Alcan humping a ruck, 500 dollars stashed in their boot, a roll of Krugerrands in their money belt, and a 'scrip for Paxil in their wallet.

But if you came up the road, you know the story. Rattled as I was, that country still sucked me in. I walked over the border, the customs agents hawk-eyeing me the whole way, their videos trained on me, and I was still overwhelmed. The Yukon's cool, you know, a lot of the same scenery. If you think about it, the only difference is this bare line kept clear in the wilderness, from the Gulf of Alaska to the Beaufort Sea. Only Alaska seemed different, somehow, God's promised land for the freedom lovin' and the freedom fightin', none of that namby-pamby socialized medicine crap you get in Canuckada.

You could smell it, that freedom. I know I sure did.

As I came up that gravel road, and stepped onto pavement, the sound of the big American flag slapping in the breeze, and the beauty of those eight stars of gold on a field of blue of the Alaska flag flying just as proud below it, I said to myself, Jimmo, this is it. This is where you make your stand. You ain't never going back Outside, you ain't never going to be subjugated by the Alien Occupiers.

Those big mountains spread before me, the air so clean and clear. Fresh snow glinted on the high peaks, glaciers stabbing down like the sword of Jesus, praise the Lord, the slopes purple-blue with forests so thick and vast you could cut 'em when Christ came down from the cross and they'd still be there come Armageddon. Scarlet waves of fireweed high in bloom rippled across the taiga, high up there in the open country at the heart of Alaska. God Almighty, it was absolutely beautiful.

So I walked into it, ass to Canada, so caught up in the majesty of it all that I didn't even hear those black helicopters thuck-thucking their way south. Alaska. Ever since I left Florida, the voices had been telling me to go north, just like my Uncle Obie, and north I had gone, until here I was.

That was my coming into the country yarn, and one of those beats a jet plane into Anchorage, hands down, you slimy oilie.

*

Now the thing about Alaska from the traveling vagabond hitchhiker's perspective is that there are only a few roads, not many towns, and miles and miles of open country where a guy can get stuck for fucking days. Weeks. In the Alaska tourley season—see, I had already picked up a word: "tourley," what some Alaskans call tourists—the traffic over the border to Tok runs a car a minute. I clocked it. Sometimes, two cars a minute. Not cars, really: RVs, recreational vehicles, little alien shuttlecraft, if you ask me, full of oldsters trying to cram in one last adventure before it's Reagan Time, drooling on your pajamas.

RVs, I long ago learned, rarely pick up hitchhikers.

But I was cool. A few miles over the border there's a gas station. The way you get rides at gas stations, particularly if you wear that shaved-sides, under-the-cap dreadlocks look like me, is you walk up to some guy with a VFW or AMVET cap, and you ask, "Hey, brother, can you give a soldier a ride?" I've got the patter pretty much down pat, how I'm being posted to Elmendorf or Ft. Rich or Greeley—oops, can't say that, they shut it down—and instead of using my moving allowance, I saved my money and hitched. Now vets know that you can get free tickets on MAC flights and stuff, so I'd have to throw in a line about "seeing the country" or "saving my money for my kid's operation." Really, they still swallow that line.

Or maybe they figure it's all bullshit, but they hitched long ago, too, and maybe the wife is bugging the piss out of them, and they figure, OK, this'll pay her back, pick up some spaced-out dude and make her suffer.

God, I love America.

Now the other scam that works is if you see some hip people (which is anyone wearing Birkenstocks), maybe someone without a backpack—this is crucial, because if they have a pack, they're just like you—and you strike up some conversation. If it's a cafe with not a lot of RVs out front, but maybe more than a few VW vans or Subarus, I'll let my dreads down, put in my earrings, and scope out the hip dudes. It doesn't matter if they're young or old, like in their 40s, if they're hip, they'll give you a ride. Single babes get cautious, so like that's when I do the sensitive new age guy—SNAG—thing. Rub a little patchouli behind my ear and they're putty in my hands.

So it was one VFW RV ride to Tok, get stuck there with some Germans for an afternoon, let them scare away the citizens by the road, and by late afternoon I'd scored some lesbians in an orange VW van. They had engine trouble. When you can disable a Gray shuttlecraft with a Swiss Army knife, you can fix a VW engine. With lesbians you don't even have to pull the SNAG trip, because there is not a lesbian in the world—not one I've met yet—who doesn't believe that she can rip the balls off a guy who gives her a hard time. The thing is, they're right. Also, lezzies will pack a rod more often than any other babe.

Now there's a whole lot of country between Tok and Della down there on the tip of the Kenai Peninsula, but Della is the story of this 325-page epic, so let's cut to the chase and get to Della, all right? As it turns out, those lesbians were going there to look up some relative, which I think was pretty fucking cosmic, now that I look back.

But in case you want to know what's between Tok and Della, see Appendix A, OK? I mean, what the fuck is this, an adventure about destroying the AOG, or some goddamn tourley manual? Right. Adventure. I thought so.

Three days after coming into the country, I found Della.

*

The lesbians called themselves Lilly and Margo. Heteros have exacty 27 stereotypes they like to apply to lesbian relationships (May-December, butch-femme, top-bottom, and so on.), some of them true, most clichés. Lilly and Margo had created a new one: retro Beat twin sisters. Oh, they didn't look a bit alike once you got past the long red hair with the dark roots, other than that they were about the same age, height, and weight. Lilly had these dorky retro black-frame glasses and great blue eyes, and Margo had dorky retro purple-frame glasses and brown eyes. Right off I could tell I was supposed to get them confused, so I kept calling them the other's name, which they appreciated. For all I know, they switched names and glasses anyway, and the ones I got stuck with might have been the wrong ones. Lilly could have been Margo and Margo Lilly, if you know what I mean.

They dressed in a style I'd soon come to know as Hip Bush Rat Alaskan, big baggy khaki shorts, tights or poly-pro long johns, and baggy sweatshirts. Lilly had a stud in one nose, nine earrings, and probably a few more piercings I didn't think it my business to know. Margo, on the other hand, had just one pierced ear, with a little emerald stud. She said she'd had a matching stud years ago, but lost it, and took to wearing only one earring. When the other hole grew in, she went to being a pirate, as she put it.

Back in the bench seat of their van they had this huge charcoal-colored dog, half wolfhound and something else, called Bobo. As a general rule, Bobo hated men, Lilly explained, but because he liked me, that's why they picked me up. Right off the bat I figured out Bobo: he was an alien sniffer. Usually the resistance uses purebred wolfhounds, but mixed will do. It wasn't that Bobo hated men, I could have explained to Lilly, but that he hated aliens, of which many were men, particularly the kind that might approach a dog like Bobo. If a guy came up to Bobo pulling that "nice puppy" crap, odds were he was an alien trying to snuff the dog. I could have told them that, but didn't. Since I was with the resistance, Bobo automatically took a shine to me.

Once I got their van going—a bad recharge line fixed with electrical tape—we made like hell for Anchorage, just straight through this roller-coaster land bordered by huge ass mountains to the south and taiga that went on forever to the north, a frost heave every hundred yards. Margo was all for camping out and enjoying the scenery, Lilly wanted to punch it, and I just sat in the back with Bobo and watched the fireworks. Lilly won out, and it was do not stop at Sheep Mountain, do not slow at Palmer, just gas up and go all the way into the city.

Chapter 2

When we got to Anchorage, Margo drove that old van downtown to a hostel, and there we parted ways. I'd tell you the whole huggy-muggy scene, but I'll save you the pathos and sadness at parting. Keep reading. I took a bus from downtown, and wound up at a bus stop across the street from this hospital just for Natives, with a capital N.

That's what you call the aboriginal peoples of Alaska. ("Aboriginal peoples": I picked a few things up in college anthropology.) Not "Indians" or "Eskimos," because in Alaska, you have both Indians and Eskimos and I'm not gonna explain it further. They're all Natives, and when you say "Native," the big "N" is sort of understood. If you've liked lived in Alaska for generations and you're not Native, then you're not a native, you're a sourdough, got that?

Anyway, I got off the bus and sat down on this bench to kind of get my bearings. This old Native guy—see, capital N?—sat down next to me. Old Man Tom confused me even further, said he wasn't just native Native, he was Inupiaq, which meant "the real people." I kinda liked that: the real people, since that's what those of us in the Resistance called ourselves sometimes, as opposed to the RATS and the toadies of the Gray Conspiracy.

Old Man Tom said he came from up north, from Barrow, only he also called it Utqiagvik. "My wife's in the hospital," he said, waving across the street. "She's dying of a bad heart."

I nodded. What can you say to do that?

"I camp over there." He waved behind him. We were on this big five-lane road, with an overpass from the bus stop over to the hospital. Old Man Tom said that in the winter dog teams raced across the overpass. I really love how Alaskans will bullshit you sometimes. The hospital was on the north side of that road, and a police station on the south side, where we were.

"You camp by the police station?"

"In the park beyond it. None of the cops go back there because then they'd have to walk."

He grinned when he said "walk." Old Man Tom either had one fine set of false teeth, or his originals were in amazing shape. I think they were original cuz he didn't have that little click oldsters did when they had false teeth. I don't care what the TV ads say, you just can't glue teeth on that solidly onto gums.

"Isn't there like someplace else you could stay?" It didn't seem right that a guy whose wife was dying had to camp out.

Old Man Tom chuckled. "Oh, my kids have got them a fine home in town, right over there." He waved at a subdivision east of the hospital. "My daughter's a doctor, a really fine doctor. My son works for the corporation. They're rich. There's even a room for me there, and I go stay with them on Saturday night, so I can take a shower before church. But the rest of the time I like to camp."

I nodded. I could understand that. "I like to camp, too."

"You want, I could show you some good places to camp. No one will ever find you, unless they come over in the black helicopters." I must have jerked or something when he said that, because Old Man Tom quickly added, "not that the black helicopters come over very much, just sometimes."

"That's OK." I smiled at Old Man Tom. "I know how to hide from the black helicopters."

"Most people don't believe in them," he whispered to me.

"Most people are fools."

A horn honked, and I looked up. An orange VW van had pulled into the bus stop turn-out lane.

"That your girlfriend?" Old Man Tom asked. "Or your boy friend?" He winked when he said that.

"A friend."

Lilly leaned across the passenger's seat and popped open the door. "Jimmo! Get in."

"Nice talking to you," I said to Old Man Tom. "Hope your wife is OK."

"Oh, she's going to die, and then I will too. It happens." He nodded at the van. "You'll live a long time, though. Guess you won't need to camp."

"Maybe—" I looked up at Lilly waving. A bus was trying to pull into the lane. "Maybe not." I got in.

I sat down and buckled up. Lilly pulled out into traffic. Bobo came up and sat between the two front seats. He put his big head on my thigh and I nuzzled him behind the ears. My buddy.

"Where's Margo?"

"Back at the hostel." Lilly sped up and moved over into the left lane. "We, uh, decided we needed some space." She stuttered a bit on the last word, "space," and bit her lip. Her eyes looked a bit red, and if I hadn't been a sensitive new age guy, I might have thought she had allergies or had gotten high. Nope. She'd been crying.

"How'd you find me?"

"When we dropped you off at the bus center downtown, I saw you get on the Number 75 bus. I looked up the schedule and just followed it out here. Plus some stoners at the bus center told me people camped out in that big park"—she waved off to her right—"and you might have figured that out."

"Where we headed?"

"There's a city campground out this road. I asked around. If you've got a van, there aren't a lot of places to squat."

"Cops drive cars."

"Right."

We followed that road as it headed east, then turned north. Anchorage kind of flipped me out. It had these like really huge mountains to the east, most of them forested and undeveloped, and then on the flat lands, it was all grown up like shit. They could of done something interesting with that land, but near as I could tell, the way people developed it was to chop down all the trees, flatten the land, fill it in if they had to, and put up crap that could have been built anywhere in the US of A. Big box stores. Strip malls. Steel buildings.

Only, in a lot of places the trees had come back, or people had planted them, or maybe someone had gotten smart and not cut them down in the first place. So even though the buildings looked ugly as flattened dog turds, everything was green around it. People planted flowers, too, lots of them. I had the feeling that if you just turned away for a second and quit building things, nature would just grow over it all and suck it back up. You could see that in places where there were old houses maybe 50 years ago, where someone had cut those trees down and flattened the land and built some little house, only now new trees had come in.

We drove past six big box stores, more strip malls than I could count, some ugly as sin huge churches, and one trailer park just waiting for a good earthquake, until we came to this little park. It was like those old campgrounds they used to have, before the RVers got all insistent on big camping pads and cable-TV hookups and turnarounds and stuff. That campground had places for tents, imagine that, or if you had a van or a little truck camper or a small pull-behind trailer, the space would work. Because the spaces weren't given over to big parking spaces, the campground had more trees and bushes and stuff, making it kinda private. We got us a space out in the back, up against this state park, so we had even more privacy.

I helped Lilly pop the top and get her place set up. She put Bobo on his line and got him supper. The camping space had some room on it, with a nice spot I could set up my tent. I opened up my ruck and started pulling out poles and stuff.

"Jimmo," Lilly said, "what are you doing?"

"Setting up my tent. That's cool, isn't it?"

"I only paid for a van. I think tents are extra."

"I can pay."

"Money's probably tight for you, Jimmo. You don't have to."

I shrugged. I hadn't told her about the Krugerrands I had tucked away in my money belt.

"Well, I've been economizing the whole trip. I can spring for one night."

"Gonna rain, Jimmo." She looked up at the sky, at some clouds looming over those mountains. I had to admit she might be right. "You can sleep in the van."

"Bobo won't mind?"

"I won't mind."

We were sitting side by side on a bench by a picnic table. When she said "mind," Lilly ran a finger up my arm, that thing women do when they want you to feel at ease, only, shit, it has the opposite effect on me.

I glanced over at her. She had this far-off look in her pale blue eyes, like she was remembering something, maybe an argument with Margo. I don't know. Women can be a mystery, ya know? Lilly arched her neck, exposing her throat to me, and I had to admit, it was a mighty fine looking piece of flesh. With her finger tips she tugged at her bangs.

Back in college, in psychology, we had covered that old Kinsey report, that one where these shrinks interviewed all these people, only it turned out about half of them were really cranked oddly, so the database was fucked, but never mind. That report said that sexual orientation wasn't a matter of on/off, like you were either gay or you weren't. What it said was that orientation was a spectrum, so someone who was mostly homo would be like a six and mostly hetero a zero. Or maybe it went the other way. Some people fell in the middle, and they could be hetero or homo, depending on what they ate for lunch and like if their momma had beat them with a hairbrush or a cat-o'-nine-tails. You know, all that shrink stuff.

I kinda got the impression Lilly might have been a three, not quite homo, not quite hetero.

Our bowls of half-eaten ramen were on the table before us, a couple of empty beer bottles showing our priorities in nutritional supplements. Lilly did that arched neck thing again, and then pointed with her head at the van. Then she yawned, a real long stretch, hands behind her back and shoving her breasts out, oldest trick in the book.

"I think I'll turn in," she said.

"Uh, sure. Need me to help you set up?"

"I'm set." She stood up, took my hand.

I was thinking maybe she would need help with sliding open the top bed. The VW had this bed on top that folded out, so you could sleep someone upstairs, like an upper bunk. Bobo glanced up as Lilly slid open the van door. She looked at him, and he put his head back down between his paws. She slid the door shut behind us and began pulling the curtains shut.

"I'll get on top," I said.

"No, I like to be on top." She winked at me.

I couldn't believe she said that. What did she do, learn all her moves from movies?

"Uh, yeah."

Lilly had to snap this curtain over the sliding door and she gave me another curtain to put across the front windshield. The curtains were made of brown material, a really ugly shade of brown, but they were dark. I finished snapping the last snap in place and turned around, moving toward her. She'd lit this cute candle lantern and while I stood there, trying to figure out what to do, Lilly took off those dorky retro black eyeglasses—which I discovered later were like totally fake—and slipped off her sweatshirt. Underneath she had a really fem camisole, white silk with little rose flowers. The hem came to just halfway up her crotch, her bush poking out underneath, the strands of her red hair glistening in the candle light. Red pubic hair: Lilly was a natural.

Falling back on the bed, Lilly opened her legs up, her ankles crossing over on each other as she grabbed me in a scissors lock. I stood, shins against the edge of the bed, and she shuffled forward. Old Man Jones had grown into the gargoyle position, spout aiming for the sky. Lilly reached up, loosened my belt and unsnapped my shorts, and pulled them down with my blue long johns. She reached up to yank down my jockey shorts.

"Uh, Lilly—" I didn't want to complicate her relationship. Well, screw that, I did want to complicate her relationship, but in any sexual encounter, there's a go/no go point where certain rational thoughts can be entertained.

"It's OK, Jimmo."

"What about Mar–"

"Shhh."

"I mean, you're a les–"

Lilly looked up at me, her hands shucking my shorts, my hard cock inches from those lips. "You think so?"

"Well, uh, not now."

"Then let's just take now as it comes." Lilly reached up with her tongue and ran the tip of it along the bottom of my presidential lollipop. As the saying goes, she had her knee-pads on and was ready to serve her country.

"I gotta get a raincoat."

"Taken care of, Jimmo." In her hand she already had an unwrapped condom. "My personal brand."

Lilly unrolled the rubber enough so that the end just covered Mr. Cyclops, and to steady it, she put her lips around it, dressing my penis as she began to suck on it. A faint whiff of strawberries came up from the condom.

"I like the taste. Sometimes I'll put one on a vibrator like a sucker." Lilly took a breath, slid my penis all the way into her mouth, tickled the reed a bit, then opened her mouth again. "But a man's penis is so much warmer."

She fell back onto the bed, taking me down with her. I kicked off my shorts and 'johns, trying not to fall on top of her. As I rolled to one side, she twisted me over and sat on top. Lilly put her hands palm down to either side of my head, raised her hips, and lowered herself down on me.

"Uh, I should tell you one thing," I said.

She paused as she came down, looked at me. "What?"

"It's these, uh, drugs I take. Makes it hard for me to come."

"Oh, that. I know all about that. It just makes it last longer, baby. Much longer."

Was she ever right.

*

Early the next morning, Lilly went back downtown to pick up Margo, having apparently found and used that space she needed. Oh yeah. We made kind of a deal: if I magically appeared on the Seward Highway south of the last exit between three and four that afternoon, the orange VW might magically be going by around then and Lilly might magically pick me up. Alaska had a lot of magic. It was that kind of place.

I had a half day to kill, so I had Lilly drop me off at the same bus stop she'd picked me up at the day before. Not knowing squat about Anchorage, and not really wanting to, I had this feeling that where there was one hospital there would maybe be another, and where there was a hospital or two, there would bound to be a public health shrink.

See, part of my deep cover act as being a member of the resistance is that I appear to be certifiably in need of mental health care. When you get sucked up into a Gray mother ship, just the ride up the glitter tube can screw up your brain chemistry. It's not like you're seriously fucked in the head; it's just that the Grays don't quite understand human anatomy and as a result have really messed up some people.

I'm perfectly sane, honest. I just need some meds, or rather, my cover requires that I take meds to counter the effects of things like that butt chip. It's a little confusing: my brain did get scrambled, but then the aliens put in the butt chip and other stuff to make it appear like I am perfectly normal, only so that no one suspects I am part of the resistance, I take these drugs the shrinks prescribe me. My body treats them like water, so it's not like it changes things. Well, OK: it changes a few things, like that little problem with Mr. Johnson.

Anyway, I needed to get my Outside scrips renewed by a state psychiatrist. I talked with some more Natives at that bus stop—didn't see Old Man Tom that day—and found out that the walk-in clinic was a few blocks away. It was in-and-out service, that's all you need to know. I'll explain the whole process later, when I get to Della, because, well, frankly, the Della MentalHeal place is a lot cooler and more interesting. You get a better class of crazy in Della, for a good reason, I found out.

When I explained my whole situation to the shrink—a guy named Dr. Compton who kept complaining about his gout—Dr. C. kinda zoned out as I got to the whole thing about the vast alien Gray conspiracy, the butt chips, the 87 abductions, and the black helicopters I'd seen at the border. Shrinks always do that. It's not like they haven't heard the story before, I understand. When I wound down a bit, Dr. C. put up his hand and said one word:

"Della."

"It's a town down south. That's where I'm going."

"Good choice," he said. He wrote down the name of the MentalHeal place there. "Check in when you get there. Della will suit you just fine—it's a damned comfortable place for the reality challenged."

That's the term he used: "reality challenged." It was so fucking peecee I wanted to lean over, drop my shorts, and make him feel my butt chip. Reality challenged, my ass. Cute. Wait'll Doctor C. reads this Goddamned book. He'll find out who's reality challenged.

Only, I understood the rules in the shrink-crazy relationship. Shrink prescribes meds, you want meds, you suck up to shrink. "Sounds like just my kind of town." I winked at him.

"Yeah, you'll like it. You got enough money and stuff to get you there?"

"I'm cool." I didn't tell him about the Krugerrands in my money belt, either.

"You can get a cannery job or something. Fish are in and they'll hire anybody who can stand the slime line. Check with job service. Camp on the Spit. You'll be fine."

The way he brushed me off, the way he got me in and out of there so quick, I figured it out. Right. Keep the problem moving. It was the classic burned-out b'cratic way. Worked for me. I was heading to Della anyway.

So, a few hours later, sampler packs of my meds in my ruck, I took a bus as far south as I could go, and walked down from this Old Seward Highway to a New Seward Highway, found a good place to put out my thumb, and waited. I had to give up two good rides until that orange VW came down the long grade heading south.

"Jimmo!" Lilly said after she'd pulled over and I'd climbed in the back. "Funny running into you again."

I winked at her. Margo gave me a foul look from the passenger seat. Bobo snuggled up against me as I buckled in.

"Quel coincidence," I said.

Later that evening, we arrived in Della.

Chapter 3

Just like every crappy sourdough has a damn coming into the country story, everyone who has ever visited Della has a damn Rising the Hill story. See, the road to Della goes along Cook Inlet for most of the way, and then it turns inland and goes through some forests and such—only it's a pretty lame forest, since it's mostly been cut down—and then goes up this big ass hill to Della. Supposedly, when you get to the top of that hill, or so the Rising the Hill story goes, you come to this open vista with like this view of K-Bay and the mountains beyond and, wow, you get punched in the gut by the glorious beauty of it all and your life is transformed forever. I'd like to say that was what happened, only it wasn't. Not that my life wasn't transformed forever.

First of all, Lilly and Margo took a left onto a side road about ten miles out of town before we ever got to that open vista, and second of all, it was dark. Twilight, I mean, since I came into Della in the summer. Dark enough. They'd been fighting or something—crap, those women fought like cats, it made me jumpy around lesbians the rest of my life—and all of sudden, Lilly took a hard left onto this side road, Something Ridge Road. Said she knew a shortcut or some damn thing.

I should know all these names, you know, having been in Della a while now, only the truth is, I can never remember street names. Fuck, I can't really remember names period, if you ask me. Roads, people, rocks, they're all the same. A lot of these names here probably aren't the actual names of the people I met, not because I didn't want to embarrass them, but because I forgot. I just made up some new ones. The only names I do remember are those of dogs. Anyway, if I go down a road once, I remember it, so it's not like I need a name. Besides, in Della most of the street signs have been ripped off or shot up, so learning street names is a futile exercise. I remember "the Ridge," though. Descriptive names make sense to me. We went along this ridge.

Thus I was deprived of the Rising the Hill Story, and it wasn't for a whole six months until I could figure out what that meant. So my first experience of Della was driving along this road at the back of a ridge. We passed a huge radio antenna. Right off I thought, aliens, and I was right. A sign out front of the radio station said KGNL, BEAUTIFUL GENTLE RADIO, only someone had stuck an I in between the T and the L. Christians—they're such kidders.

You know how when some evangelist comes up to your door with that glazed look in his eyes and you think, Alien? You'd be right. The only Christians who don't get abducted by the Grays are Mormons. I asked this Mormon in the Resistance why that was so, and he said, "Because we're too damn weird for the bigheads." Which is not to put down believers in Christ, which I am in my own twister way, it's just the organized ones that drive me all wonky.

Anyway, we passed another antenna, a microwave tower, only I recognized the design as the Gray's brain confusion beam emitter. That little butt chip I have? It also warms up when I pass a Gray brain confusion beam emitter. We passed those antennae and the country opened up to the northeast. A huge field covered with fireweed fell down away from the road toward a steep gully, then rose up to another ridge, then down to another gully with a creek in it, then up to another ridge and this big flat mountain.

"Holy shit," I said out loud, not even thinking.

"What?" Margo shouted.

"Stop the van, just for a second."

Margo shrugged, but stopped, leaving the VW's engine running. With old VWs, you try not to shut off the engine if you can avoid it. So with that engine thrumming, I slid back the door. Bobo got out with me to pee and there I saw it.

The mother of all alien bases. The big one, the megabase, the center of the Alien Occupation Government, the headquarters, the brain, the nerve center, the absolute pinpoint big base, right there, right in the hills above Della. Forget Roswell. Forget Machu Picchu. Forget Stonehenge and Tikal and all those alleged alien bases, abandoned every one of them. This was the big one, right now, the source of all my troubles, the world's troubles, the whole solar system's troubles. Right there.

Out there across the valley, shining across it like a beacon, was a big flat mountain. "Oly's Mountain" I later heard it called, or Table Top, some said. I could feel it, feel the humming and the disruption of the ether right down to my bones. I didn't even have to take out my little pocket detector that's disguised as a Swiss Army knife. I knew, I just knew. And my butt chip burned like an exploded capsule of sulfuric acid. God damn, right there in the mountain—not *on* it, *in* it.

"Nothing," I said to Lilly and Margo. Bobo and I got back in the van. "Just thought I saw a moose."

So that was my Rising the Hill story—just a different hill than everyone else. But what the hell. Not everyone who comes into Della turns out to be the liberator of mankind. Fuck, most of them are Goddamn Grays.

Not Jimmo, though. But I'm getting ahead of the story.

*

Now here we parted, my two lady friends and I. They had taken me as far as we could go together. We drove down a hill into Della, down a five-lane road that narrowed to a three-lane road and then a two-lane road, past quaint little bleached-wood buildings and big ugly industrial barns and all the usual crap that develops in Alaska small towns which can't decide their character. Tourist trap? Artsy-fartsy bourgeois destination? Junkyard? Give Alaska another century or two and they'll figure it out or fuck it up beyond repair. We drove off the mainland and onto the Spit, a finger of land sticking out into that glorious bay.

If you do the Rising the Hill thing, you see K-Bay from above, and the Spit as a sliver of land into it. Coming out of the forest and onto the Spit, though, you see the bay from eye level, sea level, and it's a little less dramatic. There are a couple of houses along the way, but no one really lives out there. Then you pass another one of those industrial junk yards, a big steel building that looked like it hadn't been painted since the invention of whitewash, then this muddy lagoon full of dead boats, then piles and piles of the trees that used to be attached to all those stumps I'd seen, and then a bunch of boardwalks. A harbor. Parked around the edges, in whatever available spot they could find, were those damn RVs which had passed me by in Tok, I was sure of it.

We drove to the end of the road, just to say we had, and then drove back out to a campground at the base of the Spit. Lilly and Margo picked a spot squeezed between an old Blue Bird school bus belching coal smoke and a 60-foot land yacht that had the Last Supper painted on the side, Michigan license plate GODSLUV. A papist, probably. I helped the twins pop their top and then went on my way. I knew the routine. It was as far as I wanted to go, though, something I realized as I walked away.

"Hey," I said, "thanks for the lift."

"You staying in Della for long, Jimmo?" Lilly asked.

"Whatever the Lord tells me," I said. They didn't like the Jesus crap I pulled on them, so I laid it on thicker than usual, just to fuck with their heads.

"Then we'll probably see you around," Margo said, putting her arm around Lilly. Lilly squirmed a little under Margo's embrace, then came over to me and gave me a hug. She leaned in close and put her lips to my ear.

"Thanks for the other night," she whispered. Her cute little tongue, with that little gold stud, flicked into my ear. "Take care, Jimmo."

"Yeah. Hey, thanks for all the rides." I looked at Margo, looked at Lilly, and somehow I knew I'd never see Margo again, which wouldn't rip me up much. Lilly I wasn't sure about, and if I did, now that would be a whole other story. I'd been in their hair enough, though. "I'll just camp down the beach," I told them, and walked off.

There were signs all around saying you had to pay and should check in *Night Or Day* at some campground shack, but I knew campgrounds. If you pulled in after midnight, like we had, no one gave a hoot. They'd nail you in the morning or whatever. I had plans not to be around. So I found a spot on some dry ground, up above the tide line—what? you think I'm stupid?—and as far away as I could get from all the RVs and their damn satellite dishes.

Della, Alaska. Truck Stop Earth. I'd finally found it, and I didn't even know I was looking for it.

*

Even though I had been traveling in the north for a solid month, I still couldn't get used to that damn sunlight. Looking back, I realize that's something that makes you a sourdough: when you can ease into longer daylight hours gradually. If you move into the long days quickly, like anyone who travels north, it's a big shock. That pegged me as a cheechako right away. Didn't care. You're always new somewhere if you were old somewhere else, so what the hell? I should stay in one place just because someone is gonna peg me a newbie? I could give a damn. Ol' Jimmo is a child of the universe, this solar system, buckos, and that's all the home I need.

Truth is, though, despite all that traveling, I knew I'd come someplace I'd be setting a spell. Something told me right then I'd be in Della a long time. If I'd only known . . . Oh, I'm not gonna spill the beans here in only the second chapter. My agent told me that. "Jimmo, this is a memoir about how you saved the universe," she said when we had to convince all these damn Gray-owned sleazy book publishers to print *The Truth* about their damned activities. "We have pages to fill and books to sell. Keep it moving but don't reveal the kicker until the second to the last chapter." God, I love that Martha. Between her and my coauthor, they taught me everything I know about writing, which Doc Word Weird (that's what I sometimes call the guy who helped me) says ain't diddly, but I have a good story.

So my first sunrise in Della, I knew I would stay. I'd barely fallen asleep when I felt the hot rays blasting into my tent. That woke me up. I've got this little photo cell like thing behind my eyes, courtesy of the AOG when they did the Mengele stuff on me up on the mother ship. About umpity-ump photons hit that cell, and bingo, I'm up. It simulates the effect of speed balling a double-espresso. My friend Connie, who got one of those photo cells when the AOG sent her to do Peace Corps work in Kenya, calls that her "Cuban coffee chip." I can adjust it to match a certain time and it works better than any damn alarm clock.

I was up, all right. I unzipped my tent, and since there wasn't anyone else up, took a whiz right there in the sand. Fuck 'em if those oldsters hadn't ever seen a penis. I was in Alaska, and one of the side benefits of the Last Frontier is that you can damn near take a piss anywhere you want to. Read that in a book somewhere. The tide had gone out so I walked down to the flat sands below all the rocks and stuff.

This gorgeous sun, the one you all probably see in your part of the world, too, rose up over this peak I later learned was called Poop Peak. I think. I might have gotten the name wrong. It sort of looked like a drop of poop, this little kiss of chocolate with a frosting of snow still at the peak. Now I knew the Alaska sun wasn't as reliable as a compass for determining direction, but I sort of memorized that peak as my east reference. Over there is East. Close enough for resistance work, I always said.

When I see the first rays of the morning sun, I let them fall on my face and repeat the mantra that I have dedicated my life to. I let that sun wash over my face, the only pure thing around in this solar system that hasn't been tainted by the alien motherfuckers; and I say to myself, "As free as the sun remains, so I swear I will remain free, and dedicate my life to freeing the universe of the lying alien scum who exploit the precious lives of free Terrans." I sort of do a riff on that last line. And I say this in tongues, because the aliens don't understand tongues, on account of it's not a language.

See, you think what you want to say, and that's the true thought, with the tongues only the verbal expression. It doesn't mean shit what you say, but what you think. Then I said a little prayer to Jesus, thank you Lord, but you don't need to know what I said to Jesus. We have this personal relationship, the Lord and I, and I'm not one of those Rolex preachers—who are all Grays anyway—who prays out loud, usually in the process of fleecing the citizens out of their hard-earned dollars. Jimmo 'n' Jesus: Don't ask, don't tell.

I'd lost my jo somewhere in Oregon—Goddamn kid took it, if you want to know the truth—and I'd have to carve me one or something. So after my morning prayer, I did my aikido exercises, a few thrusts and swirls and rolls and shit. My time chip said 3:43 a.m. exactly. I could see lights coming on in some of the RVs. Now why the hell would oldsters be getting up so soon? Go figure.

Rolling up my sleeping bag, pad, and tent, I got packed and out of there before the first RV had started its generators. God, I hate those damn generators. One of these days I'm going steal me an alien EMP gun, I am, and go around firing that little thing—it looks like a ball point pen—at those RVs, blowing every damn microchip in 'em.

As I passed Lilly and Margo's van, I could see they had the curtains drawn tight, even the front ones (which are a pain in the ass to put on, as I've told you), which meant they must have gotten the van rocking. Good for them. Thinking of those two made me think of Lilly and then Hannah, so that as I strolled up to the Spit road, I had a pleasant thought in my head. OK, I got a little woody, too. I can't quite explain this, but when I think of Jesus, I think of women, and then I get all horny, which is maybe why the Lord and I have such a good relationship, if you know what I mean.

Now that may sound all kinky and homosexual, getting a hard-on from Jesus. The way the aliens messed with my head, it's possible that somehow they scrambled the delicate neuron wiring of my brain so that it's their fault I get a hard-on when I think of Jesus. (Crap, even as I'm writing this I have a first-class boner that's already leaking.) What I think is the truth, though, has to do with theology and stuff like that.

Now, in the Bible it says that God created man in His own image. It says "man" and "His," which really pisses off the feminazis, but that's what it says. A rabbi, this really cool woman who used to do performance art on the side, explained this to me once. Rabbi Glasser said that "man" means "humanity," which is like men and women. So if God created humanity in His image, that means God is man and woman. He's this all powerful force that is human and then something else. Which means, when you get right down to it, that God is a Woman. Jesus is the Son of God, which Rabbi Glasser also explained to me as meaning that Jesus is the Child of God, sort of a little extension of God that walked the earth 2,000 years ago. So Jesus appeared to be a man, as in, penis, etc., but since he's an aspect of God, Jesus is a woman, too. My own personal take on this is that Mary Magdalene is Jesus' feminine side, and that the Apostles kind of fucked things up, but that's only an unauthorized human interpretation and shouldn't be taken as gospel, ha ha.

So if God is a woman and Jesus is a woman, it stands to reason that when you pray to Jesus, if you're a guy, you can think of Him as a Her, unless, of course, you like thinking of Him as a Him. Whatever lifts up your skirts, as they say. I used to think of Jesus as this guy with a little Van Dyke beard and neatly trimmed shoulder-length hair wearing a snappy blue silk robe, but now I think of Jesus as this sort of pan-African European Middle Eastern Asian woman with wavy light brown hair, one blue eye, one brown eye, olive skin, nice little breasts big enough to suck on, but nothing that will slap you in the face, maybe some hips with some motion to them, and great legs. Sweet Jesus, just thinking of that makes me want to come in my jeans.

On the other hand, like I said, maybe the aliens scrambled my brains.

Anyway, there I was at just past oh-light-hundred up on the Spit road, the sun rising above Poop Peak, and I saw her, the first, genuine, totally strange person in Della. Bicycle Lady would be one of many genuine, totally strange people I'd meet in Della, but right off, my first morning, there she was. I took it to be a good sign.

Bicycle Lady pedaled up the Spit Road toward town on an old pink mountain bike that looked like it had been ridden over the Chilkoot Pass and down the frozen Yukon River. Little reflectors had been stuck in the spokes, and she had six US flags flapping from the fenders on sticks, three in the front, three in the back. Her bike panniers had been packed to bulging with unknown junk, and strapped to the bike rack was a collection of really warped driftwood. She had purple tights, cut-off khaki shorts, some ratty old navy-blue sweatshirt, and a bright orange reflector vest. No helmet, though.

It was her face that convinced me she was genuinely, totally strange. Being GETS myself, I know the type. Her face had been weathered by long winters in the sun, so that it had a kind of pinched tight look, the sort of look vain women get after one too many face lifts. Only, Bicycle Lady had wrinkles that belied any surgery, fine wrinkles around the eyes and mouth. I'd guessed her to be about 50, maybe 55. Even in the dim morning light I could see her eyes, bright hazel eyes that had looked into true terror and hadn't come back. I bet she'd been abducted at least once. You get eyes like that after the Grays take you up to the mother craft one too many times.

She had dark brown hair streaked with silver, but not streaks scattered throughout like most people. One big chunk of silver, as if she'd painted it on, flared back from her forehead and to the back of her neck, where she'd braided her hair into a long rope down her back. One strand of the braid was that silver hair, the rest dark brown. As she rode past me, the braid swished back and forth with the motion of her legs.

Down the road she pedaled, determined, not looking to either side. I knew Bicycle Lady lived in her own world, the true and free world, not the world corrupted by alien occupiers. As she went by, she shot me a brief glance, nothing more than a second. We locked eyes, and in that moment I knew enough about her and she learned enough about me.

Ten yards or so down the road she stopped and looked back at me.

"About fucking time you got here," Bicycle Lady said.

I nodded, not sure what to say, and she turned away and went on.

Genuinely, truly strange. It gave me hope for the resistance, and for Della.

Chapter 4

As I walked down the Spit Road, RVs and rental cars began to pass me, even at that early hour. No matter where I went in Alaska, I could always spot a rental car: they had the same bland paint job, the same black wall tires, and unlike most any other car in Alaska, they were clean. I have a rule about hitchhiking, what I call the Unnecessary Withdrawal From the Karma Bank Rule: I don't hitch if I'm going somewhere less than five miles. If someone stops and gives me a ride, kismet, I'll take it. I just don't ask. I save hitching for serious distance.

So I didn't stick out my thumb, just kept trucking down that road. With all the walking I do, plus the fact that I am a superior physical specimen, praise the Lord, I can eat up the miles fast. One time I entered this serious wilderness race, just for shits and grins. I can't remember the name of the race, much less where it happened—someplace in the Cascades, I think. You had to get from start to finish, a distance of maybe 200 klicks, with nothing but the ruck on your back. All sorts of hyper-aerobic yuppie types stood around bouncing like bunched up bungee cords at the start. They had the latest gear, the slickest damn shoes, but not ol' Jimmo. I had my standard busted in Doc Martens, jeans, and this surplus ruck I carry around.

I beat their fucking asses but good.

The whole trick to walking is to keep up a good pace and stick to it. Those pathetic excuses for distance runners ran, thinking that if they pushed it, they'd blow away everyone else. That was rugged country, with tortured gullies and continuous up and down climbing, not to mention serious bushwhacking. I just kept walking. I kept my camp tight, only stopping to boil a quick meal and catch a few winks. One by one those jerks blew up. I'd pass them, dehydrated, fat starved wrecks, pale and gray-taupe like spawned-out fish. The only person who gave me any serious competition was this thin Asian woman. She actually had me beat solid until she twisted an ankle, and she still only lost by ten minutes.

I'm not bragging; this is just a statement of fact.

So I just walked down the lousy road in about a half hour. Maybe it was more, maybe less. I could have accessed my eye chip, but what did it matter that morning? Time be time, as that Willy Gibson fellow says.

At the end of the Spit I figured out where all those people in the RVs and rental cars had gone off to in such a goddamn hurry. Sort of tacked together and set on pilings were a bunch of shacks set on boardwalks. Every other shack seemed to be surrounded by tourists or old pharts standing around like flocks of seagulls waiting for a handout. I got this funny little feeling seeing them. My butt chip itched a bit, then I figured it out. They looked like a herd of abductees waiting in the vivisection hold on a mother ship, with that same look in their eyes, like they were going to be lead off somewhere they weren't quite sure of.

Only, well, it turned out OK. Reading the signs I understood that they were all going off fishing, halibut fishing, which explained why and how they all got up so early. Later I learned that in the late afternoon the day breeze kicked up and the bay got rough, so to make things better for the puk-ers—which is what you called the tourists who went out on charters—the boats went out at first light. Sure enough, one by one some grizzled old sourdough or sourdoughette would gather up the gang and take them out to a boat. Sometimes the boats went out on overnight trips, which was asking for an abduction, if you ask me. A mother ship could suck up one of those boats whole, do their little tricks, and buzz it back before they'd even be missed.

I watched the halibut captains gather up their victims, and after a while the rush of tourists waned. Then I noticed another waking up. Near one set of the ticky-tacky charter huts was a little terrace of beach, a bit higher than the sur-rounding area. Sea grass grew around the edges while years of campers had trampled the rocky beach into a solid sur-face softened only by a thin layer of sand. Set on the beach were dozens of small tents of all designs and colors, but to a one covered by a blue plastic tarp. Driftwood logs had been dragged into circles of crude benches. A few fires smoldered in the early morning stillness. I got a whiff of coal smoke coming from one fire. An American flag hung listlessly from a driftwood pole, an Alaskan flag under that.

Someone had tacked up one of those DETROIT: 6573 MILES clusters of signposts, with the idea being that you put up a sign saying where you were from and pointing in the general direction. People had come from all over, with no sense of either direction or distance. The most accurate sign said POLARIS: 782 LIGHT YEARS. You'd have to be pretty stupid to not know the angle and direction of that one: 59 degrees North.

In ones and twos people started coming out of those tents. I sat on a log watching the tent city come alive. There were more than a few couples, which led me to believe some of them had traveled well together—it was a trick to come all the way to Alaska and still be a couple—or had lucked out upon their arrival. Most of them came out alone. Almost all of them looked about my age, vaguely 30ish, even under 20, with a few old pharts above 40 there to play the bachelor uncle. It didn't take me long to figure out what was going on there. All over the world, whether at a Mt. Everest base camp or a French vineyard encampment, young people came together for adventure. In late adolescence they turned Roma, heading off on their own and when they got wherever they decided there should be an adventure, gathering together.

I'd spent a good five years drifting in and out of camps like those. They had their attractions: good drugs, great sex, cheap food, and lots of stories. There had been a time when the pseudo-Roma had been true wanderers, living that way out of necessity more than choice. Lately they had become rich college kids slumming for the summer. You could tell by their teeth.

Now, I have great teeth, thanks to one of the Gray's abductions—they smear this stuff on your enamel that's better than fluoride—but your average wandering bum will have rotten teeth. Either he's missing a tooth or two, or his teeth have become faded and yellow. Not the slummers. They have great teeth, gorgeous white pegs shiny and bright. They don't have scars, don't have lousy shoes, don't have surplus backpacks, don't have ragged clothes. OK, some of them have ragged clothes, but they're the best ragged clothes, state of the art outdoor gear.

The slummers also have good haircuts. Not good hair, but good haircuts. You think a white kid can grow dreadlocks out of the can? No, it takes some work. I've been ratting my dreads for years, enough so that I hardly have to do anything to keep them nice and coarse. Even then, should I not keep up with them, they'll grow out into straight hair. A rich kid, he can't put that much time into it. The thing about rich people—I figured this out long ago—is that they want everything *now*. They can't wait. Rich people have absolutely fucking no patience. If you know that, you can really screw up a rich person bad, cuz all you have to do to throw them off is make them wait. This is why guerillas always win wars: they have far more patience than rich people.

So a rich slummer, he has to have those dreads right now. Maybe he's going home for Christmas after his first semester at Oberlin. He wants to piss off his parents. Dreads will do that. It shows a certain effort, nothing easy like shaving your head into a Mohawk. Dreads on white people say that you've gone out of your way to piss off the 'rents. You can tell instant dreads from worked in dreads, you just can. The instant dreads are kinkier or something—I don't know, it takes a certain eye to spot these things.

Or, suppose you're some babe who wants that looks-like-it's-been-hacked-with-hedge-clippers, but-it-hasn't look. You could hack off your hair with hedge clippers in random hunks, but it would look that way. You want it to look like that, except the idea is that some artiste in Westwood charged you $500 for the privilege. You can tell that, too. I mean, these kids had great haircuts. The ones without tortured hair had those hot haircuts that looked about a week past being trimmed.

Anyway, that's who lived in those camps mostly. Slummers. Come the Revolution, those assholes are going to be the first to be shot, even before their parents.

Only, getting up at such an early hour meant that either they were going to catch the right wave—not likely on Della's beaches—or that they had some adventure kind of purpose that required them to be up so early. Otherwise, they'd sleep in. I couldn't quite see that they were going fishing, because I didn't see any rich kids with dreadlocks among those crowds of pukers.

Then they did something that surprised me. I followed a little bunch of them across the street, over to the harbor. Kind of hung back a bit, the way I might tail someone I suspected was an AOG, just to see where they'd go. A few wandered off over to the charter huts, but most of them kept going up the road and to a big huge blue steel building. I couldn't see a sign on the building until I got right up to the entrance.

Zapata Seafoods, the sign read.

A cannery! Sonofabitch if these slummers weren't working the slime line. No shit. Maybe this was part of some sort of Commie ideology. I'd seen that, where slummers pretend to be in sympathy with the masses so they take on shitass dirt jobs. I mean, Hillary Rodham did that one summer, and I think she lasted like two weeks. Then they discover how crummy manual labor is and how you're much better off working indoors, at a desk, with nothing more dangerous than a crazed boss, which is a danger in and of itself, mind you, but nothing that will cause you severe physical pain.

"We ain't hiring until noon," a guy said to me.

"What?" I looked up to see this guy with shoulders about as wide as he was tall, in orange bib rain pants, XtraTuf boots, and a red bandana around his head, do-rag style.

"I said we ain't hiring until noon. Appreciate you coming out so early, but if you want to work the line, go to Job Service and they'll give you an interview pass." He looked me up and down. "Although, based on what we've been hiring, you look like you'd work about twice as hard as any of these other shits."

"Thanks," I said. I hadn't really been looking for a job, but now that he mentioned it, it might be the thing to do.

"Here," he said. He handed me a little metal disk with a big Z on it and a number. "That'll get you into the Rat Hole. You can camp free on the company, and the city won't hassle you." He pointed toward the tents I'd seen. "Talk to Tom. He'll find you a spot. You don't get a job with the company in a week, you're on your own."

"Who's Tom?" I asked.

"Oh, you'll find Tom," he said.

I palmed the little disk, pinched it between my two fingers. I could feel a little humming inside of it, even though it looked like a cheap piece of stamped tin. It burned a bit, too, just like my butt chip. Made me wonder if I became a slummer and camped with them if that would mark me by the AOGs. Hell, they had me marked anyway. What did I care?

I flipped the disk up and watched it catch the morning sun as it rotated over and over. OK, I had a place to camp, free, for a week. Maybe even a job, if I wanted it. I watched some of the babes coming in alone, and thought, Hey, I might even be able to score some good dope. Or great sex.

All of a sudden, Della looked real good. Really good.

*

I'd been humping that ruck all morning, so that camp chit seemed like a good idea to use. I could get a spot, set up my tent again, maybe stash some stuff. By now more people seemed to have woken up on the Spit. People began to walk down to some of the fishing boats, or from the boats up to various cafes along the Spit Road. I noticed a steady stream of fishermen going into a real dive of a cafe—the Korner Kitchen—and marked this as a possible breakfast spot. Some of the generators began to hum in the RVs parked in another lot. By then the sun had risen well above the mountains, a solid sun, the dawn clear and bright but with that hint of dew that marked the morning.

Back at the Rat Hole, I could see that most of the camp had cleared out. A few young guys hung around the campfire, firing it up some and getting it going again. They might have come in the last day or so like me and were waiting for work. Lording over them stood a tall skinny guy wearing dark glasses.

The guy was really skinny, now that I looked at him, with long arms and long legs, only a short little torso. His arm seemed to bend where arms usually didn't bend, high up toward the shoulder, so his lower arms flopped around like eels. He had a pointed chin covered with a thick red beard, only the hair sticking out of his floppy black pile beret was coal black streaked with gray. Either the hair covered his ears or he didn't have ears. He had long narrow feet and wore purple tennis shoes. I walked lightly on the sand, my usual stealth walk that an old Indian had taught me, but even then, at five yards the guy swiveled his face around to look at me. The way he moved his head, and that he could turn his head 135 degrees, clinched it for me.

Yup, he was a Gray all right.

OK, plus my butt chip seared like a hot poker. I can spot aliens easily, or spot people who look like aliens easily. The thing is, after nearly 500 years of occupation, people look more and more like the aliens, or maybe the aliens look more and more like us. It's not that we interbreed or anything—that would be like a platypus breeding with a duck—but that over time the aliens have corrupted our body memes and we've corrupted theirs.

I knew this woman into fashion design who had figured out everything about the AOG—she'd been abducted twice—and she tracked fashions through the occupation. Showed that there had been regular influences throughout. Take pant suits: an alien influence, you bet. I couldn't think of any other way to explain modern fashion, unless you bought into the idea that it was a conspiracy by misogynist homosexuals to humiliate women. Right.

So when I saw this guy, I had to figure out not if he wasn't alien, but if he wasn't human. He shifted his body to me, cocked his head, and even from there I could hear the servos whir on his braces. A long Gray, I called them, not like those stumpy midgets I'd seen at the border, but the skinny type. Their leg bones were so fragile they had to wear exoskeletal braces. Don't even think a long Gray is weak, though. What they lacked in bone structure they made up for in muscles. They were like thousands of wind-up toys wrapped tight and ready to bounce.

"Rat Hole's closed to camping," he said to me as I came up to him.

"Got a chit," I said. I showed him the little piece of stamped metal.

"'Kay." He had that little click some of the aliens have, not quite a lisp, just a click. "I'm Tom. I run the Rat Hole."

"Jimmo," I said.

Tom pulled out an iPad or one of those tablet computers. The brand name didn't matter cuz I knew the Grays used their own equipment and just put their computers inside whatever handy shell they could pick up from the sale table at Comp City. His fingers zipped over the screen. Fucker didn't even care about putting on appearances; he was using Grayware, the alien handwriting system. Never mind what I'd seen up on the Ridge the night before. That alone convinced me the Grays had locked up Della for their own use. Anywhere else, an alien so open would be toast. The Resistance wasn't all powerful, but at least we could force the Grays to put on appearances out among the citizens.

"Name?" Tom asked me. I gave him my cover name, and that's all he cared about. No address or city or any of that shit. Maybe Tom knew I'd lie or maybe it didn't matter to him. He handed me a flimsy, a sheet of paper his tablet spat out. That was really bold: the flimsy was made of that petroplas that's like their universal material, the crap their forming machines use as raw products. The aliens think we're batfuck for burning up the stuff they use to make everything from clothes to starships.

I took the flimsy and saw that Tom even used the alien font they like so much, the funny one that makes all our Roman letters slanted backwards, and puts serifs on some letters and not on others. That really pissed me off. You'd think that an alien occupation government that had secretly controlled the world for half a millennium would at least be coy. *Assholes*.

"Read it," Tom said, "Them's the rules. Break any rule and you're out on your butt. Understand?"

I nodded. The only rule that really mattered was "Don't get caught."

"Say it."

I squinted at that. That meant he was recording and didn't want to waste the storage space on recording a nod. "I understand."

"Cool." He pointed his finger at me in that stupid little cocked gun gesture. Shit, I really hate that. Aliens are like pit bulls gnawing on a good bone: once they find something they like, they stick with it. Tom waved at the camping area, logs and stuff around it and maybe a few spots left. "Camp anywhere inside the logs and don't rip up any vegetation."

"Cool," I said, and pointed my finger back at him, same gesture. I even put a little click at the end. He turned his head at that, smiled that pointy-toothed grin the long Grays have, and walked away.

So, I thought. Already a day in Della and I'd found my first alien.

I couldn't wait to toast the fucker.

Chapter 5

Toast Tom? If he'd been standing two feet to his left, the Zapata plant would have saved me the trouble. Just as I had turned away from him to pick out a spot, I heard this sound like the bottom ten stories had dropped out of an eleven-story building. "Ka-whump" would describe the general sound, but not its intensity.

Naturally, I turned toward the noise. However, because of my rigid military training, I stopped the motion and did what anyone who has been ever in a firefight would do: I kissed the beach. No, not kissed. I made love to that fucking beach, got my face down in the sand where I could see the broken shells up close, could see cigarette butts fading into fibrous filters, could see little dead crabs and a piece of blue beach glass that looked like the iris of my dead uncle's glass eye.

Someone screamed. Then someone else called for his mother. Then these end-of-the-world sirens let loose, and the whole damn Spit turned into chaos. I didn't hear any shooting, didn't hear any more explosions, and so hazarded a glance up. Tom stood there, stiff as a robot, with a bleeding score in his shoulder. You think Gray blood isn't red? Nah, that's the one thing they have in common with us. Iron.

I looked beyond Tom to see what might have made that scratch, and in the sand I saw a chunk of steel like a circular saw blade buried half-way in a piece of driftwood.

I had been standing by that piece of driftwood.

"Move it, move it," Tom barked.

Streaming, running, tearing, evac-u-ating out of the Zapata plant came all those slummin' rich brats I had seen a moment ago. Some of them bled. Some of them had the 'dreads scorched off their precious heads. All of them had that stunned look on their face that they would of gotten sooner or later, the look that convinced them despite all their wealth and privilege, death didn't give a shit.

And the Zapata plant? It no longer had a roof. Rather, it still had a roof, but in about ten minutes, that roof would be chemically transformed into a looming dark cloud rising up from the plant. The sucker had blown up. Later, it would be revealed that the freon tanks used for freezing fish had blown, something to do with a defect in one of the valves. Uh-huh. I could smell a Gray conspiracy. They'd wasted that plant to try to kill me.

Out of that initial chaos, just as they always do, people began to assert order. It's our job. We're not very good at *averting* chaos, but 200,000 years as a species have made us good at asserting order out of chaos. Police cars sped down the Spit road, followed by fire trucks, ambulances, and—no shit—a big yellow school bus. Coast Guardsmen off of the cutter in the harbor in sharp blue work uniforms started walking purposely, deliberately, officially along the harbor road, onto the boat ramps.

"Evacuate," the word went out. No shit. Here's this 60,000-square-foot plant burning and burning, with an attic full of waxed cardboard fish totes, a shed full of freon, another shed full of propane, 500 yards away six four-story high fuel tanks, and you think it's a good idea to let all those people stick around and breathe noxious smoke?

I sighed, got up, and shouldered my ruck. Not even time to set up my tent and get settled in, and here I was, on the move again. Then I looked down at that Rat Hole chit, at the other Spit Rats wandering around dazed, and I smiled. Wasn't I a Spit Rat? So maybe they'd be loading up the cannery workers, the campers, and putting us up. . . Oh, I don't know. Someplace with free food, most likely.

Tom got us lined up then, those of us not wounded, and he wouldn't let anyone take down their tents, just let them pack a quick ruck and get ready to move out. The bleeders and the burners someone herded off into a triage park. I thought of maybe going over and helping, and then thought of how that piece of steel had almost taken off my head, and figgered, nah, now's the time to blend into the background. Besides, there wasn't a lot to do for most of the suckers in the triage park, because those that could walk, would soon start to bitch when they realized no one was gonna take care of their little scratches right away. No, the real bleeders would get all the attention, better attention that I could give them, even with my med degree from UVA.

Two more school buses came out onto the Spit, which still confused me until I looked around and realized, Hey, not all of us had wheels. Those that did have cars, like some RVers who had the sense to get their butts in gear, got dragooned into giving riffraff like me rides. I was gonna hold out for a bus when I saw this blue hair about my mom's age grinding the gears on a 26-foot cab-over Jamboree on a Ford chassis. She stalled out the engine and a guy in a diesel Dodge who had not been allowed to haul his third-wheel trailer leaned on his horn. I quickly tucked my dreads under my ball cap and banged on her door.

"Drive for you?" I shouted.

"Oh, oh," the lady said. She had that stunned look abductees always got right before the column of green light sucked them up into a shuttle craft. "My husband is on a charter, I don't know how—"

"Ma'am," I said, "I used to drive an M-1 tank. I think I can handle an RV."

"You military?" I saw her relax a little as she took in my clean-shaven sides, the ball cap, the old surplus ruck, the Doc Marten's.

"On leave," I said. "We'd better hurry."

"Get right in, son." She scooted over into the copilot's seat, her usual seat, I could tell. Why the fuck these old farts never let their wives drive made no sense to me.

"I think we had better give some people a lift," I said. "It's the evacuation policy." Not that I knew that, only it made sense.

"Oh—I don't know." She looked over at a group of scared Spit Rats, mostly women, but with one or two guys.

"We had better." I found the switch that opened the side door, and waved the gang on board. A little Gray cockapoo drop-kick of a dog almost bailed off of the RV, only one of the cannery workers grabbed it.

"Let's move it," I said in my best commander voice. The old lady wasn't gonna be in charge. The kids weren't gonna be in charge. As usual, it was up to ol' Jimmo. Three women got on the RV, but the two guys held back.

I saw another cluster of Rats rushing toward the RV, all big guys. Something told me they would be bad passengers, that perhaps they should wait for the bus, so I slammed the door shut, letting only the women on board. None of the refugees I had picked up had backpacks, and I had a hunch that maybe some of the babes would want to get Grandma to play Mom for them.

It took me a few changes to figure out the gears, not that it mattered since traffic had already slowed to an easy crawl. Things relaxed a bit, about how I'd imagine they relaxed if you were on a lifeboat pulling away from the Titanic. Sure, it was going to be rough, but you had a way out, they didn't, and it wasn't gonna be your face with the frozen eyelashes. Schaudenfreude, the krauts call it, which means, I live another day, asshole, and you don't.

"Name's Jimmo," I said to Grandma.

"Uh, Missus—oh, call me Louanne."

I nodded at her.

"I'm Sarah," one of the Rats said from behind me. The others had moved to the couches in the back. Behind the cockpit—the front two seats—there was like a third smaller seat, sort of a jump seat. I could imagine a little grandson watching the road with his grandparents in that seat. Sarah had great teeth and a lousy haircut, not even a good lousy haircut. It looked like a buzz cut growing out, actually, a buzz dyed that Goth black.

"You in the Force? My ex-boyfriend was in the Force." Sarah pointed at my ball cap.

I glared back at her for a moment, then turned back to the road. "Special forces. I ain't no flyboy." No sooner had I said that then I thought, Louanne was a career military wife, I could feel it; so what if she was Air Force?

Louanne smiled. "Ralph is ex-Army." She turned to Sarah. "The Army wins wars, you know, dear. They don't just support them."

Sarah slunk back in her seat. I smiled at Louanne and she smiled at me, and I could see we were gonna get along just fine, just fine.

*

We got e'vac'ed off the Spit in about fifteen minutes, not bad considering the chaos going on behind us. Maybe we got lucky. Maybe Louanne had the presence to get that RV in gear right before the cars and buses got bogged down in a mad rush to get away. Anyway, once we had the smoke behind us and had moved close to the base of the Spit, where I had camped the night before, I relaxed. I glanced over at the park to see if I could see Lilly and Margo's Orange van, but they'd already vamoosed, I guess. As we moved back into town, more cops and some firefighters directed us toward the high school. Not directed us really, because by then we had become part of this long train of cars, a mass of machines following the car ahead and assuming that you knew what they were doing, which was a bunch of crap.

Once in the special forces we had done this little exercise. The regular grunts were doing some war games, part of which involved moving long convoys of trucks and Hummers. A couple of us had stolen a Hummer and cut into the line. When we came to a cutoff, we went right while the rest of the convoy went left. The guy behind us balked until my CO yelled that it was orders, we had to go right. That was all it took. You lead a line of cars, and if you can get the car behind you to follow, pretty soon the whole convoy is yours to appropriate. What we did was lead them all into this big stadium, and when the last truck in the convoy drove onto the ball field, we had him park nice and neat behind the fifty other trucks and cars. As they parked, one of us would pop the hood on the Hummer, yank the spark plug wires, and take them captive.

I thought of that as I followed a guy in a Blazer in front of me, but pretty soon we did come to a big parking lot, it looked like a high school, and I figured, no, this wasn't some Gray conspiracy to off me, we were part of a refugee tide. I parked the RV nice and tidy for Louanne, nose out, and killed the big kicker diesel.

"Home sweet home," I said. "Thanks for the lift." I handed her the keys. I realized then that I was in an RV that could sleep six with four women, all of them pretty damn good looking, even Louanne, if your taste ran to oldsters. Sometimes my taste did. Hey, they'll surprise ya with their passion and their sexual technique.

"I suppose we're stuck here for at least the night," Louanne said. "Girls, I could use some company, and Jimmo, it's always nice to have a man around the house, particularly a nice young man like you. What say we rustle up some lunch?"

She really said that: "rustle up some lunch."

The other two Spit Rats came out from the back of Louanne's RV. One of 'em had the dropkick dog in her arms, which Louanne promptly took. She cooed over the damn thing like it was her long lost little boy, which I guess it was. Dogs could be a damn sight more loyal to oldsters than their own children, that I had to admit. The other two women turned out to be friends of Sarah's, Elaine and Trish, just settling down off of the night shift when the Zapata plant had blown.

"Well, this is quite an adventure," Louanne said.

She'd herded us back to a table in the RV's gallery and began to make sandwiches, tuna fish salad with pickles and celery, actually. I could see those wymmin turn up their noses at such classic white bread cuisine, only hunger and a middle-class upbringing won out.

Trish and Elaine had the same hip Buchenwalden hairdo, a two-month-old buzz, and I could see it then: college is out, let's hitch up to Alaska and get a job in a cannery, it's such a drag taking care of our hair, so we'll buzz it all off, which is when they discover that not everyone has the skull shape to carry off the lack of hair. I thought they all looked kind of cute, but only Sarah had the skull, you know?

Louanne put the sandwiches down, neatly sliced in triangles on blue paper plates, with a half pickle, chips, and Co-Cola in clear plastic glasses. These RVers traveled in style. Sarah reached for a sandwich, only Louanne shot her a Look.

"Let us pray," she said.

"Uh, I'm Jewish," Elaine said.

"That's OK," Louanne said, "so was Jesus. Jimmo?"

I caught that look and knew I was being tested. If I passed, well, military take care of military, I could see that coming.

"I'd be honored," I said. I watched Louanne out of the corner of my eye. Would she go for the deep reverence or the arms raised to heaven Pentecostal style? She bowed her head. Good, I thought—I hate that Jesus freak crap.

"Dear Lord God and Savior—" when in doubt, lay it on thick—"we thank you for delivering us from danger and tragedy. Bless this food and this house and this good woman and your humble servant who have helped us, and pray that our loved ones will be well and safe, and catch big fish."

"Amen," Louanne said. She smiled at me, and I knew I was in like Mickey Finn.

"Amen," Elaine and Trish mumbled.

"Amen," Sarah said a little louder. She'd figured out the rules, all right.

*

After lunch and getting the place cleaned up and stuff, Louanne took "the girls," as she called them, into that high school to maybe find them a shower and to see if Louanne could connect with that charter boat where her husband was—probably out on the water, totally oblivious to the fact that the Spit burned and he might be spending the night in some hither-yon port. I could see that the whole evac scene might turn into organized madness soon enough, if not already, but that was OK, cuz soon it would turn into giddy madness, always did. I decided to take a walk.

You survive a big tragedy that damn near kills you, only it didn't, and now you have someplace warm with food in your stomach, thing is, you party. Once't all those charter widows got connected with their hubbies, once all the old farts got their meds refilled, once all the Spit Rats got showers, they'd party. Glad as I would normally be to party, especially with those hot buzzed babes, I could see that what old Jimmo had to do was fade away into the ductwork, you know?

The Grays had laid down the law to me, had drawn the line in the sand with that Zapata blast. Maybe they had intended to kill me, or maybe they had just wanted to frighten me, I dunno. I got the message, though. Tom didn't die. Tom didn't have to jump out of the way of the whirling piece of metal, since it had been aimed at me. The Grays, when they aim at things, they don't miss. And they wouldn't of, except that honey, I ducked.

OK. Time to fade away.

Only, thing was, I liked Della. Been there one day, and I liked it. I could feel the cosmic energy of the place, feel that Della would be a place to make a stand. You ever come to one of those points in your life, one of those passages, where what you gotta do is, you gotta leap off the ledge and just fucking go for it? That was Della. I wasn't going back to the Lower 49, not back Outside, not going to get my butt chased back and forth until the Grays harried me like a wet fox. Shit no. Citizens, the Alien Occupation Guvmint might have pushed me against the wall and 'pected me to squeeze. Not this time.

Walking down this main street, I thought to myself, Not this time. "Time to lock and load," I said aloud.

An old blue-hair phart, some kinda confused geezer twice as ancient as sweet ol' Louanne, looked up at me with That Look, which I'd learned to live with my whole ding-dong damn life. Yeah, crazymutha, aren't I? I thought. Then no sooner had I thought that, I came by this storefront window, a big gabled-roofed building with plastic siding half-way being installed, the rest white chintzy sheeting that said BARRICADE and had this bear on it. It was the sign that caught my eye.

COMMUNITY MENTAL HEALTH, the sign said, and above that in a font called Funstuff, MENTALHEAL.

I walked in.

*

Let's suppose you're in a little hick town, with no job, no place to stay, not much money, and you have this like attitude to start with that makes it sometimes hard to get a job, a place to live, some money, not to mention salvation, a good lay, or even a shower. What're you gonna do? I'd gotten this ride in with some lezzie chicks, only that hadn't lasted, despite the possibility that one of 'em wasn't quite batting six on the Kinsey scale, you know? Then I thought I had this deal lined up slinging fish and camping with some bourgeois brats slumming it, only that hadn't worked out. I could have lived in a cramped RV with some blue hairs, only that wouldn't of worked out after a day or two. Now if you're crazy, certified mentally ill, with a scrip for some serious anti-depressants, serious anti-anxieters, serious anti-psychotics, the whole shit short of Librium . . . OK, if you're a liberator of humanity disguised as an ex-special forces cosmic guerrilla out looking to put the nasty to the AOGs, you can find help.

I walked in that door, right past this guy rocking back and forth in a steel-gray chair, past a woman with bad teeth and an even worse perm, past a short brunette with big hair babbling on and on to a serious looking gray-haired woman with a turtleneck unrolled all the way up to her chin, right up to the counter that said SIGN IN HERE, and smiled. Pulled off my ball cap, let my dreadlocks fall down over my face, and smiled.

"I'm out of my meds," I said.

The receptionist looked up from the counter, over the top of her half-moon reading glasses on this beaded chain, and stared at me. She had one of this cute little blue-black bob haircuts with short bangs. She pointed at the clipboard. I picked up the cheap bank pen on a long bungee cord, signed in, and let the pen snap back.

"And I don't have a job," I added. "Or a place to stay."

"You a cannery worker?" she asked.

"Never got that far."

"If you are, disaster relief at the high school can help you there."

"Did I mention I'm out of meds?" I said.

"We'll call your name."

"You don't know my name."

She picked up the clipboard, looked at the last line, read it. "Xavier Zyphius Berjohnson."

"Not my name. An alias. Long story."

"We'll call that name, Xavier, and then you can talk to a counselor, OK?"

"Works for me."

I sat down. I liked to rattle them like that, only with that woman, I could see I was probably outclassed.

The guy in the gray chair kept rocking. The babbling lady looked over at me, and the woman with the turtleneck seized the chance to get up and move four chairs down. I glared at the babbling lady, she smiled at me, and then sat down right to my left. GETS, all right.

"Did you hear about the Spit?" she asked. "I was there, you know, right in the middle of it, see how my bangs got torched." She touched her head and I could see that the hair above her forehead had, in fact, been burnt into frizzies. "I had to walk all the way off the Spit cuz no one would give me a ride, can you believe that? No one. I kept pounding on doors, the cars were moving so slow I could do that, and no one would give me a ride. Then I figured I could walk as fast anyway and what did I need those people for, you know?"

"The joy of human companionship," I said.

"Huh?"

"You need people for the joy of human companionship, that's what you need people for. We're social animals."

"Oh." She thought about that for about six nanoseconds, shifted gears, then laughed. "Did you hear about the Spit fire?"

"I was there," I said. "Right in the middle of it. It torched my hair off, right here on the sides. Had to buzz it." I rubbed the short hairs on the side of my head.

"You too?"

"Cally?" the receptionist asked.

The brunette got up. "Well, it looks good that way," she said, pointing at the whitewalls around my ear. "Kind of butch. Maybe I should get my hair fixed that way. Put a gimme cap on, hike those dreads up inside, and you could pass for a Coastie."

"That's sort of the idea."

"Nice talking to you—"

"Harvey," I said. "Harvey."

Sally went away, back into the back with the woman with the half-moon glasses, and I waited my turn. Up in Anchorage after I'd gotten busted for camping out in that park, after they'd referred me to the local head clinic—no wait, that's not what happened, Lilly picked me up—anyway, the shrinks up there did a whole work up on me, reaffirmed my cover. Said I was delusional borderline schizophrenic with clinical depression suffering from acute anxiety. Wrote it all down. Gave me meds for two days. Gave me a scrip. They said that I really didn't want to be in Anchorage, said Della was the place for me, "because down there, well, people with mental illness don't have such reality problems." That was how they put it: reality problems. Oh, I have problems with reality. That *is* my problem.

So while I waited for Cecilia or Marie or Boots or whatever the receptionist's name was—they always had weird names—I rustled in my ruck for that file, the documents the Anchorage shrinks had given me. "Give this to MentalHeal in Della," they had said, "and they'll take care of you."

"Xavier?" the receptionist said.

I stared at her, she blinked, I blinked, and then I remembered that was my cover. "Oh yeah."

"You can use your real name here," she said to me as she stood up. She wore kick-butt purple Doc Martens and a short leather skirt with striped tights. Boots, uh-huh. "We respect your confidentiality." I handed her my file. She put on those half-moon glasses again, read the name aloud. "James Ignatius Malachi Obadiah Osborne?"

"Call me Jimmo," I said.

*

This is one of the miracles of the modern American social services industry: if you're only partially needful, walk in, and explain your problems, within an hour you've got all the meds you need, a lead on six jobs, and a check for a week's lodging or rent. If you're truly a basket case, you're fucked, of course, and if you're not truly needful, you don't need help. Fall somewhere in the middle, and there isn't a social worker in the world who won't help you. They *want* to help you. If you've got an MSW and your ticket punched, the whole idea is that now and then you can help someone manage his life. The way I figure it, I exist in this world to make social workers happy. It's my special calling, that and liberating the world from the clutches of the Alien Occupation Government.

'Course, there's an inherent contradiction in the fact that some social workers are aliens and they know me and the threat I represent to them. Only, they've been so corrupted by the culture of social work that even then they will help you. I don't think this guy Dean was an alien anyway. Boots led me back to his office.

He looked about 55, graying with a short beard, short hair, and these big Buddy Holly black glasses, the sort of frames you get in the Army if you don't have any pull with the quartermaster, "dick" frames we called them. Dean had gotten pumped though, mongo biceps stretching out his T-shirt and a V-6 set of abs that babes would lick sweat off. When he wheeled out from behind his fakey-wood desk, I realized why he had such a bod. I tensed when I saw his wheelchair. Grays did that some time, the ones who couldn't handle the servos on stilts, just got around in a chair. Dean's legs dangled to the floor, though, and he could push around with his left foot.

"MS," he said, noticing my glance.

I nodded. "I thought you might have walked into a Bouncing Betty in the Nam."

He smiled. "Hard to do that in Toronto. I went over the border and came back after Carter's amnesty."

"Hey—fucked war, it's cool. Lots of dudes your age would have claimed the combat, brass bracelets and all that."

Dean smiled. "About every guy that comes in here born between '46 and '56 claims to be a whacked out 'Nam vet. We're starting to get Gulf War vets, too. I know the real thing." He stared at me. "You did the Gulf, right?"

I could see this was a test, uh-huh. Now I didn't want to lie to Dean, not when he'd set me up like that, and not like I would have to anyway. When you've got a head doctor who vets you as certifiable, the back story isn't all that important. Only my cover was that I did the Gulf. I gave him the truth as best I could.

"It's a bit complicated, but yeah, I did serve in the Armed Forces during the Desert Storm conflict." Which was true, but how was I gonna tell this guy that I never got near Iraqi soldiers, that while everyone else was rolling over the poor bastards, I was out there in the desert with the free forces tracking Gray battle cruisers and keeping them from choosing sides? Like I could have told him that, only the thing is, sometimes when you tell a shrink the truth, they actually believe it. You can't be too careful.

"Special forces?" he asked. He'd at least looked at my records that far.

"I'm not at liberty to say."

"Uh-huh." He glared at me, and right then I knew I'd tripped his bullshit meter. Good. It was safer for everyone that way.

Dean read further down my file, looked up at me now and then, nodded a lot, then put the file down and passed it back to me. "Martha will need to photocopy that," he said, and I thought, Martha? Oh yeah: Boots. He went on. "She can get you a three-day supply of your meds, then the pharmacy can refill another month's supply. You'll need another evaluation to see how the dose is doing, but you should be fine by then."

He punched something on his computer, looked at the screen, back at my file. "That Spit fire really screwed up the job situation. You mind grunt jobs?" I shook my head. "Got a couple here. How you feel about logging?"

"People got to wipe their butts with something. I've tried pine cones. It's not fun."

"Yeah, that's what Circle-E says. You'll do just fine if you keep muttering that crap. There's a logging operation out East Road. You'd be humping brush, filling chainsaws, stuff like that. Eight bucks an hour. You got an Alaska Driver's License?"

"Just my old military one."

"Get a local license. Here's a list of motels that can take our chits. Spit fire has screwed that up, too. You got a tent?"

Dean glanced at my ruck. I nodded. "If nothing else doesn't work out, you can pitch it up at the city campground, maybe back out at the Spit when they get that crap taken care of."

"I got a pass to the cannery campground," I said. "Right before it burned."

Dean raised an eyebrow. "OK, that might get you in wherever they're relocating. You want to stay in Della?"

"Seems like a good place for now."

"Good. Guess if you got one of those cannery passes, then you could probably get relocated to the cannery at Seward. Then you'd be someone else's problem, not mine."

I could see the question in his eyes. He was putting his butt over the edge and taking me on, but if he was going to do that, he wanted to succeed. He wanted a check in the plus column, something to write up for his quarterly reports, something to show the agency that they were doing their job. If I was going to fuck up, his look said, then maybe I should go to Seward.

"I like Della," I said. "I've been running from things for too long and now I think it's time to take a stand." Dean couldn't possibly know what that meant, but he took it the regular way.

"OK then. I think things might work out," Dean said. He leaned across that ugly-ass desk, rising up a little out of his chair. The way his muscles trembled, I could see the effort it took. Brave bastard. He held out his hand and I shook it. Guy had a heart to go with those muscles; he didn't crush my fingers like other pumped-up bastards might do. He just took my hand lightly, once up and down, the way this Native guy out in Tok had done.

"Job service opens at eight tomorrow morning," Dean added as I went out. "There will be a line. Get there early."

"Bingo."

I was set up all right.

Chapter 6

Dean said to go to the Job Service the next day, but when I walked by there, it was still open, so I figured I'd get a jump on things and start on the paperwork. I could go on about how I filled out some more damn forms, and how there were other babbling people at the job service office, and stuff like that, only the thing is, except for the actual physical location, it wasn't much different from the mental health clinic across the street. Truth is, you've seen one social service agency, you've seen +em all: same crummy low-rent buildings, same cheap furniture, same burnt out social workers, same paperwork. My old buddy Chris used to joke that if you ever wanted a revolution, all you had to do was make sure everyone in the country had to walk into one of those places at least once.

The bullshit of it was that nearly everyone *did* have to walk into one of those places at least once. You think that caused a revolution? No, as long as the co-conspirators in the Alien Occupation Government didn't have to go into some dingy office and fill out some crap paperwork and deal with some suck-ass guvmint worker, there never would be a revolution. That's sort of the way the AOG worked it.

But never mind that. Suffice to say that soon enough ol' Jimmo got him a job and a place to sleep and the very next day, he was banging around in the back of a Ford crew cab four-by on his way out East End Road to hump brush on what Circle E said was a big logging operation, but which I knew was gonna be a Gray landing site. Only, afore I can tell about how I did that and the little accident with the Stihl chainsaw and how those things just cut nicely through prosthetic leg servos, I gotta tie up that loose end about Louanne and the RV, the Spit Fire, and Sarah. I've got this little yellow sticky noted attached to the manuscript here from my editor and coauthor saying, "What about the Spit Fire?" Mighty Mike didn't mention Sarah, but that reminds me.

Ah, Sarah.

I got all the paperwork done and lined up with that job, or the interview at ten aye-em for the next day where I'd for sure cinch the job, I figured I'd go back over to the high school and see how Louanne and the wymmin were doing. I'd seen a line on a job that maybe Sarah and her lady friends might want to pick up on, pulling lattes at this really hip cafe out there by the beach. Figured the wymmin would like that. Or maybe they'd want to do the logging thing, since it's not right to be all sexist and imply that wymmin can't hump a chainsaw.

About late afternoon things had settled down there at Refugee Central. The whole damn parking lot had filled up with RVs and campers and trucks and shit. A storm front in the morning had blown off, and damned if the day didn't turn out kinda nice. A big sloppy sun shone down on Della, the wind kept blowing steady to the southeast, shoving that fire smoke away from town, and it actually warmed up to the good side of 60 degrees. People had their fold-up picnic tables set up outside their campers, had their chairs and their little pads of Astroturf, even had the awnings stretched out in case it like rained all of a sudden.

I found Louanne grilling halibut on a hibachi she'd hauled out from the RV's basement. Sarah and her friends were lounging in fold-out chaise chairs, stripped to T-shirts and shorts, buffing up their tans a bit. Sarah waved a glass at me, and the way it tinkled and the way she grinned, I kinda got the impression she was working on maybe her third or fourth gin-and-tonic.

"Jimmo!" Louanne said. "We thought we'd lost you."

"Walked into town. Got a line on a job."

"I thought you were on leave?"

Oh yeah, I thought. "Uh, yeah, I am. But a guy like me can't stay idle for long. There's some, uh, forestry work going on out East End." I realized I couldn't say "logging" on the chance Sarah was one of those greenie earth mothers or something.

"Well that's great, great," Louanne said. "Sarah, hun, you want to make Jimmo a gin-and-tonic?"

I had to think if that would mess with my drugs, then thought, wait, gotta do the sensitive new age guy thing. "No, no, just show me the mixin's, Louanne. I can take care of myself." I winked at Sarah, and she winked back, settling into that chair.

"They're letting Spit Rats set up tents tonight on the ball field," Sarah said.

"Oh, I told you, you can spend the night here, Sarah, all of you girls." Louanne glanced at me. "You two, Jimmo, if you don't mind the front. Those chairs fold down, you know."

"That's fine. I've got my tent, I can take care of myself."

Louanne handed the barbecue tongs to Trish, then took me inside to show me the cocktail bar. "We have to be discreet," she whispered inside. "This is, after all, a public high school." She winked.

"You, uh, hear from your husband?" I asked. I didn't want to worry her, but then I figured I should check.

"Oh, he's fine. We got through to his charter boat—the captain has a cell phone. They're going to hole up across the bay. Probably having one fine party now, if I know that rascal."

"That's good, that's great." I poured a short jigger of gin into a glass, some tonic and lime on top. "Cheers."

Sarah and Trish were giggling about something when I came back out. I didn't see Elaine, but Sarah explained that she'd connected with some guy and was hanging out in the high school. I took my drink and sat down between them on a beat up old cooler.

"Got a line on some other jobs if you need something to do in town," I said. "Guy at the job service said the cannery would also give rides to Seward if you wanted to go there."

"I might stay here," Sarah said. "What kind of job?"

"Barista. Waitroid, stuff like that."

Sarah made a face, as if she'd done that before. "It could be cool, some little cafe by the beach, Twisted Sisters or something like that it's called." I thought of something then: I'd been in Della two days now, and hadn't really gotten a good beach walk in. If there's one thing I learned after too many damn years in the middle of a fucking continent, it's that I like beaches. "Maybe we could go check it out and watch a good sunset."

"The cafe is open until midnight?" she asked.

"Oh yeah." I was still having trouble figuring out day-light hours and crap like that. "No, it probably closes at six or something like that. You notice how everything closes early here?"

"It's a small town, Jimmo," Sarah said. "Of course everything closes early."

"Yeah, but it's so light so damned late." As if that cinched it.

Sarah and I were chatting over in this corner while Trish helped Louanne cook that halibut. You know how sometimes you kinda create this private space in the middle of people, like that old TV show with the goofy secret agent where the plastic cone comes down over him when he's telling his boss something important?

Sometimes I swear you create that cone, people could be two feet away and just listen in, only they're talking themselves and don't hear you over their own mindless chatter. We made this zone of silence with our own mindless chatter.

She went on about something and I kind of tuned out. An old shrink I saw once said that I had this sort of mental defect, not really a defect really, more like an attribute, that I would zone people out sometimes. Well, fuck, I zoned him out all the time because he kept blabbering away when the whole point was that he was supposed to listen to me. No wonder he got pissed. Only I listened to Sarah, like I heard the words and could nod at the right moment, but what I was doing then was looking at her, not just looking, but *looking*.

I noticed then that she had red roots to that buzz cut, that she'd dyed the buzz black and now that it had grown out about an inch-and-a-half, the top was black and the roots were red. How I hadn't seen that before, I don't know. Redheads just make me cream at the sight of them, as you probably have already figgered out. I could see then that she had the redhead coloring, blue eyes and pale skin, with slight freckles, not too many, though. I thought about those freckles and realized that she musta slathered the sunblock on, or lived in the north, or just didn't get out in the sun much. One of my uncles said people used to never use sunblock, which I believed looking at him, cuz he had craters all over his face from skin cancers.

I looked closer at her face and noticed Sarah had this real nose. You know those noses on women that have no bridge, no shape or dimension, they're just blobs of flesh pasted on with maybe nostrils stuck in as an afterthought? I hate those kinda noses. Sarah had a Scots nose, a nose that said like my ancestors got boffed by Romans and Normans, which might have been the same thing if you went back far enough. Got boffed by the Norse for all you know. The truly civilized cultures in the world have great noses. It's another thing that pisses me off about the Grays. They have lousy noses.

Sarah's nose had dimension. The nostrils flared out a little bit to either side, maybe a bit too much, like she was a daughter of a Jefferson on the Hemmings side, hee hee. The bridge rose straight and true, a solid hunk of cartilage with just this tiny little bump right below the brow. I wanted to caress that bump, run my tongue over it and down her nose, up one side, along the edges, maybe tickle the inside of her nostrils with my moist lingual member. Babes got hot for that, it's like they've got a clitoral bud up there. Really.

And she had cute ears. I looked at her ears then. She had solid ears, with definite earlobes and intricate folds, a real nice shape. Some babes shouldn't cut their hair close around their ears, on the same theory that some elephants should wear wigs, only not Sarah. Her skull had the right shape, flat up from those ears, and the ears didn't stick out. She could buzz her hair tight around the ears and it would make them look that much more striking.

Sarah turned her head, and I followed the line of her mastoids down to her neck. Her hair went down to this sort of series of V's back there, a triple-V, I guess, one big V in the middle and then two V's on the side. Right then she did that sort of thing that women do where they run their hands up the back of their neck. I figured it had been like a reflex, like she was pushing hair up off of her shoulders, only of course she'd buzzed it all off and so there wasn't much hair to push up. Or maybe she still couldn't get used to that bare neck and so was like feeling it, the way people do when they get a new haircut, because for a while there it feels like someone else's head.

That damn near drove me crazy, let me tell you.

Well, it was all I could do to get through dinner. Even though Louanne had barbecued that halibut and put some sauce on it that tasted like an intimate kiss, the fish melting away in slippery little flakes, I hardly tasted it. I looked at Sarah the whole time. Maybe she reminded me of Lilly. Maybe I hadn't been laid in like two days and I was getting blue balls. All I knew was I had to have her like then, right then.

As we cleaned up and I washed the dishes next to Sarah doing that SNAG thing, I could tell she had similar ideas. I washed, she dried, and Louanne's RV was a bit on the small side in the galley. If you washed and dried, you get in each other's face all the time, and if you were like a guy and a babe and you wanted to be in each other's face, you did. So we did that hip bumping stuff and the touching of hands thing in the sink and sometimes I'd lean over and rub my cheek close to hers or she'd do the same.

"Need a shave, Jimmo," she said once when I did that.

I ran my hand along my chin. "You're right. It's been so crazy today, I just haven't had time." Not that I worried about it: I was one of those guys who got a 36-hour shadow.

"Unless you're doing the sourdough thing." Sarah looked at me, imagining the beard growing out. "Only, I don't know. It wouldn't suit you."

"You think so?" Truth was, even if I wanted a beard, I wouldn't do it. Grays had beards all the time, partly to discuss their thin lips. "Could use a shave."

Sarah finished drying and putting away the last of the dishes. "Hate to let this warm water go to waste." Louanne's RV was low on propane, so she hadn't run the hot water heater, just boiled some dish water on the stove in a kettle. "Come on."

She glanced back toward the outside of the RV. Louanne and Elaine had gone up to the high school to check out the party and look for Trish. We had the RV to ourselves for a bit. Sarah took that kettle of water and then took my hand and led me to the little bathroom there, more a closet than anything else. It had a tiny sink and a sit-down toilet and as small a shower.

Sarah told me to sit down on that toilet, the lid on. We could barely fit in there together, so she had to sort of stand above me, her legs straddling my legs. There was this cabinet with a mirror on it and inside Sarah found a fresh disposable razor still in its package, one of the hubby's, I guess. She found a towel there, too, and put that around my neck. Sarah poured that warm water in the sink and then lathered me up with some of the old man's shaving soap. The old guy used shaving soap, for God's sake.

"Let's take off this gimme hat," she said, and let my dreads down. Sarah brushed the short kinky rods off of my face, let her fingers fondle them. You can't really run your fingers through dreads, though. "I sort of like this. You should do it more often."

"Scares the citizens sometimes," I said. "I don't let my dreads down for just anyone."

She ran her fingers along the buzzed sides of my head, her fingertips rustling them just so, like the wind had kissed me. "Oh, I like this," she said. I could see then that this thing with her running her hands up the back of her neck was what it was: she liked the feel of that short hair. Some women did, on men, on themselves.

Sarah snapped off the top of the plastic razor then. In smooth, sharp strokes she shaved my face. I had to think maybe she had done this before, maybe done it professionally. She had the touch. Most women don't understand how to shave a man's face. They pull too hard or too fast. She pushed down with the right pressure, kept the strokes long but not too long. Down the cheeks, over the jaw line, she worked her way from ear to ear. After each stroke she'd swish the razor around in the sink, then start clean.

When it came to shaving around my lips, she gently grabbed the upper lip, holding the skin tight. I wanted to bite those fingers when she did that. Sarah finished up on the neck, tilting my chin up, moving in swift strokes down to below my Adam's Apple. When she shaved and washed away the last bit of lather and stubble, Sarah ran her tongue up my neck, over my chin, and across my lips.

"How's that?" she whispered.

"Smooth," I said.

Sarah sat down on my lap, her legs outside of mine, and peeled off that tank top, one swift motion. I hadn't even noticed her breasts up until then, honest; they were firm, big enough to grab onto, not big enough to slap in your face. I like those kind of breasts. "You haven't seen smooth yet."

Still on my lap, she reached down and undid my shorts, and with her hips, peeled down my long johns underneath them, not too surprised I didn't wear underwear. Sarah slid her legs down my legs, so that she sat on the floor, back to the door. Did I mention she had shut the door behind her?

I'd had a woody since that first bite of halibut hours ago, only I swore the governor got even bigger. With those wide lips, those thick lips, those lips that had the same character as her nose, she took my johnson in hand and kissed the big eye. With that tongue, that long and nimble tongue, she explored the folds and bumps and ridges of my penis. I shuddered a bit then—I shuddered a lot. Sarah grabbed the base of my big creep and squeezed, slowin' me down.

Standing up, she dropped her pants, then shuffled forward and let me examine her bush. Well, not examine, like we were doing gynecology; I got the hint. I put my hands on her hips, hips wide enough to have some feel and promise, narrow enough not to block the door. Returning favor for favor, I lifted up my tongue and found her little Paula Jones, tickled that, then pulled her down to my face and lips and showed her how close she'd shaved me.

"Oh, stick it in now, Jimmo. Now." She looked at me, a moment's pause in our passion. "You got raincoats? Protection?"

I nodded. How could I tell her that when the Grays put in my butt chip, they'd nicked the vas deferens and made me sterile? Or that on the third time up to the mother ship they had tested a new vaccine that would scare away even the worst mutations of HIV? I knew what she meant, what she needed to hear, and pulled out from my hip pocket an ultrasensitive Gray's, the glow-in-the-dark condoms with the big-eye alien face printed on the head.

She shucked that on, unrolling the rubber slowly, pulling it down so only the tip stuck up, and snugging it tight. Grasping the latex with her lips, she sucked on it, pulling it up, pulling me up, so I sat erect on the stool again. Sarah let go, rose up, and lowered herself down on me. I grabbed her hips and she grabbed the bottom of the seat, so we squeezed each other together. Damn! She squeezed me dry, I swear. That toilet had a little window about head high above the toilet, and the western sun shone down through it, onto her face and her hair. The red roots glowed pink in the low evening light, making her face glow pink, the dark hair like a corona around her head. Her face fell down into shadow, then up into light, higher and higher into the sun, so that she leaned back and the light fell on her neck, and the little scar there, and we came.

Chapter 7

Now, I'd of really liked to spend the night with Sarah, you know? Only, in my considerable romantic experience, I've discovered that the best thing to do with a wymmin after you've first had screaming sex is not sleep with her. There's the tendency to snuggle, yeah, and that's nice. It can feel pretty damn good to wake up next to an interesting person, and real good to have breakfast with 'em—don't get me wrong. That will come, though. Too many people confuse sex with love and that can lead to all sorts of trouble. Keep +em separate to start and then ease into all that romantic stuff. Besides, that way wymmin don't get ideas. What if you have great sex but don't want to fall in love?

Anyway, Sarah didn't have a sleeping bag and that tent of mine can get damn cramped, particularly if you want a good night's sleep, which I did. I figured she'd be better in the RV with the girlz. I didn't have to be at the job service until 10 a.m., when the logging company guy would come by and pick us up for interviews and maybe work.

When I woke up at exactly 8:30 a.m., like I do every morning, Lorraine and the ladies were already up and making a big breakfast. I swung by just to pay my respects, and of course they invited me in for eggs, sourdough pancakes, sausage, home fries, and mighty fine coffee. It would have been impolite to refuse their hospitality.

"Sleep well?" Lorraine asked.

"Mmm," I said, being like mysterious. She looked at me and gave me this look, then over at Elaine and Trish, then Sarah. Sarah looked at me, I looked at her, Lorraine looked at both of us and sort of shook her head. Heck. Some of those oldsters you can't fool for shit.

"So," Lorraine went on, "What's on the itinerary today?"

Itinerary? My mom always said that, too. "Got that interview at ten. If it works out, I might be working out in the, uh, forest all day."

The radio was on, some hippie public radio station playing that sappy Jewel music. I hate that crap. Lorraine jabbed a thumb at it.

"Radio says the Spit might open soon. The harbor maybe later."

"Hey—hey, that's cool. Already?"

"Fire kind of burned itself out," Sarah said.

All day yesterday you could see that plume of smoke, but when I looked toward the Spit from the high school parking lot, it had died down to a wisp.

"I thought I'd drive the girls out to the Spit, see maybe if they could recover their gear."

"You going to move on to Seward?" I asked.

"Zapata is setting up a table here this morning," Trish said. "We'll find out then. I think Elaine and I might go, maybe Sarah." She looked at Sarah then, one of those girl looks, like they'd had a big discussion and nobody had resolved things.

"Jimmo," Sarah said, "I thought I might check out some of those jobs you told me about."

"Go on," Trish said. She sighed. "We'll pick up your gear and meet you back at the high school this afternoon."

"Thanks, Trish." She glanced down at her watch. "We'd better get going, Jimmo."

Hell, I knew from my eye clock that we had 45 minutes to kill, and it was only a five minute walk to the job service office. Only, I was done with breakfast, and it looked like Sarah wanted to get out of there. Cool with me.

"Jimmo," Sarah said as we walked down the road from the high school to Della's main drag, "what's this job you told me about?"

"Twee Sisters," I said. "It's some hipwazee cafe by the beach. I haven't been there myself. You'd be pulling lattes, working in the bakery, stuff like that. Basic grunt crap, but hey, what isn't?"

Sarah nodded. "Yeah, I know the place. Kind of funky. Bunch of radical chicks run it." She tugged at the third earring in her right ear when she said that, then ran her hand up the side of her head. "I could do the job."

"Sure you could. It's all attitude, right?"

"And I've got the 'tude, babe," she said. "Or will."

We'd come to the intersection of Lake and Pioneer. Lake went to the Spit, Pioneer north to the highway out of town. Sarah looked over at a purple building, one of those old '50s era homes that counts for historic in Della. The purple house was squeezed between a '60s-modern concrete building that housed the electric co-op offices and the co-op's cable supply yard.

Sarah turned down Lake toward the purple building. "What's the time look like, Jimmo?"

"We've got forty minutes until the job office opens for interviews. You want to get there a few minutes early to fill out some forms."

"Then I've got time to adjust my attitude. Let's go."

She took my hand—I liked that—and pulled me toward the purple building. As we got close I could see it had silhouettes of people's heads on it, with the hair like all exaggerated and stuff. "4-D Stylz," it said, with a "z." I realized the joke then: the silhouettes showed men and women with boring hair being made over with some really strange 'dos, like big cosmic flips and straight-edge flat tops, stuff like that. No dreads, though.

We walked in and there were these two operators behind chairs, a ma and pop shop it looked like. The guy had a neat little goatee and both of them had buzzed gray haircuts, except the guy's was a bit longer.

"—like that," a woman in the chair said, pointing at me.

I looked up, and with a start realized the woman sitting there with the cape around her was Cally, the babbling lady I'd seen at mental health. She kept pointing at me.

"Just like that, Gayle," Cally explained to the stylist.

"Honey, you want it totally buzzed?"

"No, no. Guy, take off your cap."

I shrugged, then removed my ball cap and let my dreads spill out.

"Like that," Cally said. "Just buzzed on the sides, and with those snake things on top."

"You're a white girl," Gayle said.

"Am not. Half Aleut."

"Well, you sure aren't black. Dreads in your hair . . ." Gayle shook her head. "It'll take some work."

"So how'd he do it?" Gayle asked.

Gayle looked at me, sighed. "I think the process involves, uh, well, a permanent and. . ."

"A lack of maintenance," I added. She was trying to be polite. I could understand that.

"Just do it," Gayle said. "I think it's like a major cool look and it will really piss off my old lady."

"You're the boss." Cally spun her around, away from the mirror. Wise move. People tended to freak when you ran clippers up the side of a head and sheared away two feet of hair at a whack.

"What can I do for you two?" the guy asked. He had his name embroidered on his tie-dyed smock: Gregg, with two g's.

I looked at Sarah. "A trim for me today," she said. She did that thing with her hands again, running them up the side and back. "Short on the sides, longer on the top, kind of a long flat top."

Gregg waved at the chair, and she got up in it. He snapped a glossy black cape around her neck, one with pink poodles on it, and then did that thing old time barber shops do, fastening tissue above the cape nice and tight so the little tiny hairs didn't fall down her shirt, except they always did.

"This'll look hot," Gregg said. "You've got the head for a short cut."

See? I knew that. I went over and sat down. Gregg pulled out some vicious looking clippers, put on a short guard comb. The way he handled it I figured he had to have started out as a military barber. He held Sarah's head steady, starting at the back of the neck. He'd turned her halfway to the mirror, so he could get the northern light shining in. The guy was an artist, let me tell you.

The clippers came on with that vibrator hum, the teeth making that clicking sound. He didn't cut the hair close, just enough to shear away that ugly black dye job. As he made each pass, a row of crisp red hairs emerged, her skin pale underneath, making the red stand out more. Gregg didn't follow the skin all the way, but pulled up as he came about halfway up, so the hair at the top was a bit longer. He worked his way from the back to Sarah's right side, around her ears.

"How's it looking, Jimmo?" Sarah asked.

"Looking good."

She smiled, and leaned over to her left as Gregg gently pushed the clippers up the right. He carved out a sharp V at her sideburn, then moved to the other side. The half-black, half-red longer hair stood out on top, kind of flopping over. Gregg changed combs on the clippers, using a longer one, and then began moving the clippers across the top, from back to front. He pulled up a bit as he came to the bangs, or the longer hair on front that would have to pass for bangs. With a brush the barber pushed the side hair up, and then cut that even with the hair on the top. He got the rough shape in and then put down the clippers.

Gregg took up another pair of clippers, electric scissors, really, and then looked at Sarah. He turned her slightly away from me, more toward the light, I suppose. With a big flat comb he held up her hair and trimmed the tiny hairs sticking up above that. He kept buzzing across and back that comb, futzing with it until he finally seemed satisfied. Gregg smeared some gel into Sarah's hair. The short hair on the side shone nice and glossy, and he got the hair on top flat and stiff. He undid the tissue and then spun her chair around, letting Sarah look at herself in the big mirror. All I could see was that nice clean nape with the three-valley hairline.

"Oh, hot," Sarah said. "That's sharp."

Gregg spun the chair around so I could see—well, so he could razor the back of her neck and around her ears. He'd left a few strands longer over her forehead, and they kind of flopped down in curly spikes. It had this subtle, fem-butch look to it. If she ever ran into Margo or Lilly, they'd jump her in a hummingbird's heartbeat. The longer hair on top and the sides had a brief touch of black still left, a kind of neat effect, I thought. Gregg finished cleaning up the neck and then wiped off the shaving foam, whipped off the cape.

Sarah rubbed that clean neck and the even shorter hairs as she got down out of the chair. I couldn't resist, and felt it myself. The gel made it nice and stiff, but soft, too. Mr. Woody was announcing his presence, but a quick glance at my time chip told me we wouldn't have time for any of that. Later. Oh yeah, later.

"Trim for you, dude?" Gregg said.

I nervously ran my hand along the buzzed sides. I could use a trim, only. . . "Don't have time today. Maybe later." I pushed my dreads up and back under my ball cap. Sarah paid Gregg, and tipped him a few bucks. She looked really sharp. As we were leaving, Gayle put down her clippers. Then she let down the uncut long hair on top of Cally's head and spun her around to look at the mirror.

"But you didn't do anything!" Cally said.

Gayle glanced at us, winked, then lifted up that hair on top. We couldn't see Cally's expression, just the back of her head and the hair buzzed barely an eighth of an inch from a line halfway up the side of her head and all the way down. Cally didn't say anything, just sat stunned in silence, but as we walked out the door, her shriek pierced the morning like a manic fire alarm.

*

Up at the job service, I showed Sarah how to navigate their peculiar bureaucratic process. You had to examine the daily computerized list of job openings, then fill out a card for each job. While doing that, you kind of jostled around the door waiting for the inner office to open, and then you rushed in with all the other job seekers and put your slip in a box on the front counter. Then you waited, as usual. What with the chaos out at the Spit, the job office was less crowded, probably because all the Zapata workers hadn't decided if they were leaving town or not. Sarah had beat the rush. She got called within ten minutes of opening, right when my truck pulled up. We agreed to meet at the high school later that night.

"Mister Osborne?" this guy with a clipboard asked. He had Carhartts cut off above his boots, orange suspenders that read STIHL, and a long-sleeve blue chambray shirt. His hair was buzzed even closer than mine, like he'd just walked out of boot camp, but for all I knew, he could be hiding dreads under his ball cap, too. He called out a few more names, two guys and a woman. The woman looked like she could out bench-press any of us.

The guy introduced himself as "Samm, two m's"—I began to wonder if everybody in Della use double consonants when one would do—and took us out to a mud-splattered Ford F-350 4x4 with a crew cab. I think it was a dark green Ford, but it was kinda hard to tell. Samm lowered the tailgate and pointed at a chainsaw with a blade longer than my leg in the back.

"You! " He pointed to a short blond guy to my left. "Go get that chainsaw and bring it over here." The blond guy nodded, reached up and with an easy one-handed lift, took the chainsaw out, grabbing it by the handle so that the blade hung horizontally in front of him, and walked over with it to Samm, then put it down. Samm made a note, then said, "OK, put it back."

He pointed at the second guy, told him to do the same thing. The second guy walked to the truck, lifted the chainsaw with both hands, and then held it in front of him, blade vertical. Samm stopped him as he started to walk toward him, then waved him to put it back.

"OK, honey, same thing," he said to the woman.

She glared at him, but nodded. The second guy had shoved the chainsaw far back in the truck. She walked around the side, reached over, and lifted it slightly so that she could drag it back to the tailgate. Then she walked back around, bent her legs, got a grip with both hands, and gently took it out of the back of the truck. She carried it in her right hand, the blade pointed away from her. As she came up to Samm, her toe stubbed on a freeze-bump in the unpatched asphalt. With one smooth gesture she tossed the saw to her right. It hit blade first, then rolled onto the hard metal casing. The two guys laughed at her.

"Good," Samm said. He made a note next to her name. "You"—he pointed at me—"pick it up."

I could see the test. Pretty clever, I thought. I went to the back of the track, rummaged around until I found a hard-plastic blade scabbard. Then I noticed a package of fuel wipes, and grabbed one. I knelt down next to the chainsaw, righted it, and put that pad in a little puddle of spilled fuel. After pulling the spark plug wire loose, I put the scabbard on the blade and walked it back over to the truck.

"If you've got a hazmat bag and some gloves, I'll clean up that little spill," I said.

Samm squinted at me. "You got hazmat training?"

"My card's not current, but I had one in the Army."

"We can get you updated if you work out." Samm pointed at me and the woman. "You, Osborne, and, uh, how do you say your last name?"

"Just call me 'Fredricka.' Freddy is OK."

"Freddy, then. You and—James is it?"

"Jimmo."

"Jimmo. You're hired. Gentlemen—" He glanced over at the two guys. They stared at Freddy with hard glares. "You're not. Better luck next time."

"But she's a babe."

"Aren't I?" Freddy said. She brushed out of her eyes a strand of light-brown hair, curls as tight as corkscrews.

"She's a 'babe' who can handle a chainsaw."

"But she dropped the chainsaw," the blond guy said.

"Yup. Exactly what she should do. Chainsaws I can replace easily. Legs are a bit harder, but they're working on that. Come with me, you two. You can do the paperwork out at the operation."

Chapter 8

Samm had a bunch of crap up in the front of the truck, so Freddy and I sat in the back. Now, I know what you're thinking, that because Freddy had one of those big solid Amazon bodies, she had to be butch, right? Uh-uh. Jimmo knows these things, and besides, I've already explained about the Kinsey scale and that crap. Sitting down next to her, I noticed right off that, buff body or not, those blond assholes were right about one thing: she was a babe. Freddy took off her faded Carhartt jacket and had on a French-cut T-shirt underneath, the sleeves short enough to show some toned biceps, the neck low enough to show a respectable, but not too huge, cleavage. If she had been about 20 years younger and as many inches shorter, she could have been an Olympic gymnast. She had the upper body for it.

As Samm drove out us to the logging site, Freddy undid her hair from a ponytail and let it fall loose. It came to her shoulders, but with the tightness of those curls, for all I know you could stretch it out and it would go to her butt. With these long, graceful fingers that seemed out of place with her body she began combing her hair. It looked as wild and thick as my dreads, only not as matted. I mean, she could comb her hair, and short of a comb with razor teeth, nothing would cut through my hair.

I tried to be cool and watch the road, only, well, I get turned on watching women fuss with their hair. It's just one of those little kinks I have, OK—it's no big deal. Freddy braided her hair into a French braid above her right ear, that braid where you pick up strands from the scalp and work the other strands into it. I could never figure it out, but Freddy did it without a mirror and just by feeling. She braided the right side, then the left, then merged the two braids into one braid at the back of her head and down to the nape, which she then braided loose and tied up. Then she took that braid and doubled it up, so that her hair was tight to her head and only maybe a few inches poking down at the back. Cool, clean, and safe.

"So Jimmo, is it?" she asked me.

"Yeah. Fredricka or Freddy?"

"Freddy works fine. When I get all dolled up, you can call me Fredricka."

I noticed then that she had a little make-up on, some eyeliner and shadow, and a pale glossy lipstick. Between all the grease and sweat and trash in the truck, I smelled a faint whiff of perfume, too. White Shoulders, I realized. I thought she might be a patchouli kind of babe, but there it was, the sort of perfume girls tried in their teens and only a few could wear beyond adolescence. I'd like to see her dolled up, I thought to myself, and then I thought of Sarah and Liz and realized I was letting my hormones get ahead of me there.

A lot of men think with their dicks, but a rough course in anatomy reveals that the cerebrum has a hell of a lot more brain cells than a dick. It's a fact of life. Like Max says, the brain is the biggest sex organ around.

"You're new in town, aren't you, Jimmo?"

"Yeah." I glanced at her, tried to figure out how she could know that, and realized the obvious. "You live here, in Della."

"All my life. Second-generation K-Bay, third generation Alaskan. My grandmother is from Kodiak."

She looked out the window at the forest we drove through. In town it had been thin, a few big trees here and there, and as we drove out of town, the forest became thicker, great trees right up to the road. Most of them had reddish brown needles, or no needles at all, and the few big trees left were totally covered with cones.

"I got into Della two days ago," I said.

"You're staying." She said it that way, period, no question mark. Huh. I hadn't realized it yet, but she might be right.

"I guess I am." I shrugged. "If this job works out. If—" If I could defeat the Grays and keep them off my ass. Freddy didn't need to know about that yet.

"Always an if. You have a girlfriend, Jimmo?"

"If." I smiled.

"Hey—I'm not asking for me," she said.

As if, I thought.

"In Della, well, I know a lot of single women," Freddy went on. "Lot of single men, too, but they tend to use each other up, so we have to check out the new imports for each other."

"And then we use each other up?"

Freddy laughed. "Yeah, I guess we do. Always new blood. Only, well, sometimes it happens that two people who have lived here for years and gotten used up by other people discover each other, discover that they haven't used each other up and are just perfect. Well, it's only happened twice that I know of, but damn, those were some kick ass weddings."

Samm drove us out further, and as he drove, I noticed that it got lighter in the cab, hotter, even. It took me a moment to realize why. We drove higher up, into less treed country, but also through meadows and then into a forest again, only the forest seemed different, greener somehow. I looked out at the trees zipping by and realized that where there had been thick spruce forest, now we drove through sparse birch forest, the trunks a mottled white, shrubs of alder or willow in the clearing between the birch.

"We logged this two years ago," Samm said. "An old homestead, 500 acres, over 10,000 trees."

"Good God," Freddy said, whispering, almost reverently.

"Every tree over eight inches around was beetle killed," Samm said. "A lot of them were rotten in the middle. It would have taken forever to burn the slash, so some of the big trees we just cut up and scattered. They'll make nursery trees."

Driving up a long hill, I noticed that the forest had been cleared back. Some of the houses fronting the road had their lots cleared either totally, or a good distance back from the house. I saw a stand of black-scorched trees that had the telltale marks you get when a bighead blows the high-gee jets on a Zod-class scout ship too low in the atmosphere.

"Fire," Samm pointed out. "We had us a little flare-up in the spring, before green up. Some asshole let his slash burn smolder too long, hoped the spring break-up would put it out. It didn't. We got lucky. The whole East Road could have gone. That's what we're doing." He waved at the sides of the roads, stumps cleared back twenty feet on either side.

"Road clearing?" I asked.

Samm shook his head. "Logging. Easiest damn logging you could ask for. In two years the state will widen and re-pave this whole road, from six mile out to twenty-seven mile, all the way to the bus turnaround by the Russian villages' trailhead. We got the contract to clear the road right of way. On some state or Native land we're logging for firebreaks, and we picked us up some private contracts, too."

Samm turned off the main road and down into a clearing, the stumps ripped out and piled up and the ground bulldozed flat. The clearing must have been 200 yards wide, 500 yards long, like an airstrip. I saw a Cessna 185 at the far end and realized it *was* an airstrip. We parked among a neat row of trucks, D-9 Caterpillar bulldozers, logging trucks, and some weird tracked vehicle that looked like a tiny drill rig. I got out of the truck and walked over to it.

"Feller-buncher," Samm said as he came up to me. "It's a neat way to take down trees without tromping the little ones. The rig drives up to the tree, raises that derrick, grabs the tree, strips the branches, and cuts it clean off at the base. Then it hauls it over and sets the log down, nice and clean."

Now, I'd never seen a feller-buncher before, but I had seen a mobile missile launcher, and that machine looked suspiciously like the sort of the thing the Resistance used to take down Zod scouts. A Zod can evade just about anything—and it's not like the military-industrial complex of the Alien Occupation Government has gone out of its way to develop anti-Zod missiles anyway—anything but a Freon burst from a Resistance flak missile. Chlorofluorocarbons really fuck up the atmospheric jets of Zod scouts. You think those ozone holes have been caused by CFCs from spray cans? No way. It's all those Zods the Resistance has tried to shoot down. You gotta crack some jokes to make an omelet, as my Uncle Phil usta say.

Hey, Bigheads in general hate CFCs. It's why they never go to football games, don't hang out at truck stops, and avoid beauty parlors. This whole ban on CFCs is a big AOG conspiracy anyway, which is why back in the late '80s the Resistance bought up case after case of hair spray. If you ever see a real retro-looking wymmin with a frosted-blonde bouffant hairdo whip out a can of hair spray in a crowded store, she's not being tacky: she's trolling for bigheads.

OK, maybe she is being tacky. But she could be trolling for bigheads, still.

Looking a bit closer at the feller-buncher, I noticed it had all the dials and shit a mobile missile launcher might have. I looked around that logging camp, at those stacks of logs, and at Samm, and it dawned on me: I was in the middle of a Resistance missile site. I gave Samm a long look and then looked even closer at Freddy. Were they part of the Resistance, too? And had Samm hired me because he somehow figured I was with the Resistance? What the hell had I stumbled into?

A guy limped over to us then, the camp boss, I realized, because he had clean Carhartts and wore a cell phone strapped to his hip. Funniest damn cell phone I'd ever seen, not a brand I recognized, not even one of those Finnish brands you always see in action adventure movies. The camp boss came closer and my butt chip began to itch. He looked sort of funny and it took me a while to figure it out. The boss looked pregnant, with an otherwise skinny body and an incredible pot belly.

"These the two new workers, Samm?" the boss asked.

"Yessir, Mr. Sand—"

"Now Samm, I need you to call me by my first name. How many damn times do I have to tell you that? It's Kyle, Kyle."

"Er, Kyle. Yessir, this is Freddy and this is Jimmo. Good heads on their shoulders, sir."

Kyle looked at Freddy first—bosses always look at the wymmin first—and while he did that, I looked at him. He had a hard hat on, real clean and shiny, with these fold down ear protectors over his ears. How he could hold a conversation in a normal tone of voice I didn't understand. Well, I heard of these high-tech protectors that would muffle high-decibel sounds—maybe they were those. The boss had a real flat nose and a tiny mouth. He turned to me after making one of those macho-guy comments to Freddy that caught him an asshole glare from her. She had a real good glare, but as with most assholes, it only worked on people who didn't deserve it.

"And you're Jimmo?" he asked. "You look like a big strong boy." He winked, and I thought, Oh, great, we got us a Kinsey 4 here: he was gonna hit on me, too.

"Strong enough, sir."

"Cut the 'sir,' crap, Jimmo. You ex-military like Samm?"

"Yessir—er, uh-huh."

Samm looked at me, at Kyle, then back. If he was Resistance, it wasn't the time to make the contact, but I could see him start to mouth the right password. I shook my head slightly.

"Good, good," Kyle said. "Well, Samm here will show you what to do, get you all set up. I need you to listen closely to him, OK. Work your butt off, kids, and we'll get along just fine. Just fine." He stomped away, and as he got beyond the clearing, I felt my butt chip quit itching.

"Fucking Grays," I thought I heard Samm mumble. I looked over at him and saw him scratch his butt, right there at the middle of his cheeks, where the Grays like to put the chip in.

Yeah, I had figured it out, too. Our boss was a bighead. Only, if he was a bighead, then this had to be an alien enterprise. A Resistance missile site in the middle of some AOG project? This was damn strange. Damn strange.

*

I put all thoughts of the Resistance out of my head for the moment. We had work to do. Samm took us over to an Atco trailer which looked like it had been hauled up and down the Slope twenty times. Inside damned if there wasn't a real retro-looking wymmin with a frosted-blonde bouffant hairdo. Grace had tanned skin, cat's eye glasses with rhinestones, and an asymmetrical hairstyle that looked like a sheer cliff of shellacked streaked rock on one side and electrified surf on the other side. I'd of expected her to be about fifty with a hairstyle like that, but no, she was no older than thirty, and she had the tattoos and body piercings to prove it: eight earrings, one nose stud, and a tattooed rose on her cleavage.

"Nice hair," Freddy said to her.

"Just got it done yesterday," Grace said, pouffing her hair with her right hand. "I was thinking I should go totally blonde, but I don't know, the frosting makes me look mature, don'cha think?"

"Definitely." Freddy winked at me.

Grace got us all signed up and everything: workman's comp, W-2s, the whole crap. I had to show her my little red passport to prove I wasn't an alien, which always made me laugh when I had to do that. Here the bigheads had taken over the US government, and we had to worry about illegal immigrants?

*

The thing about starting any new job is the starting. You can't just leap right in; you hafta do all this paperwork and then get oriented and more or less stumble around a few days until you know what it is you need to know to do what you need to do, and then just when you think you have the job figured out, your goddamned supervisor springs some shit on you he forgot to tell you about but swears he did.

So the first day meant getting oriented, which meant getting to know Freddy, Samm, and Kyle. Mostly Freddy and Samm. Samm seemed to have a crush on Freddy, only I could see that Freddy was in what guys call Not Available Mode, and sure as shit sending off the appropriate signals. Only maybe she sent them off just to Samm, or meant to, because sometimes I swore she was sending me a little invitation to play carnival with her, as in, sit on my face and I'll guess your weight. *Respondez sil vous plait* you betcha.

Wymmin play this little game with guys sometimes, the Not Available Except I Really Am game, a.k.a. as Playing Hard to Get. It's a bunch of crap, if you ask me. I guess maybe that's the problem with men-wymmin relationships, that we're not always honest with each other. Ya think?

I could see that getting to know a genuine local might be a good idea. Freddy had pegged me right off—if I can flatter myself—as one of her kind. In any big town or social group or whatsoever there are groups of people who look at someone new and say, "My kind" or "not my kind." It's not universal cuz you sometimes have to see people as "human kind," like when some big disaster comes along like 9-11 and it's piss comes to shove, we're all in this shit together. In that town Freddy had accepted me, one of us, which had its benefits.

I mean, if nothing else, I soon knew where to get a good hamburger in Della.

Chapter 9

See, iffen you're new to town you can talk all you want about getting accepted by the locals or all of that butt-sniffing, ground-scratching bullshit tribes go through, but what really counts is if you know how to find a good hamburger. Thanks to Freddy, I learned that right off my first week in Della. That town grew on me right quick, let me tell ya. Thinking back, I'm kind of amazed how fast it all happened, as iffen it was my grand destiny to arrive in Della.

So what with humping logs and getting oriented and stuff like that, by about 1 p.m. Freddy and I had worked up a fucking damn appetite. Samm said he was so dang impressed—uh-huh, he said "dang," as if all of Della was this cornpone cute little town where they learned Dialect 101 from old Andy Griffith shows—so *dang* impressed with how hard we worked that he'd treat us to lunch.

He loaded us up in the company truck and then Kyle hobbled over to join us and then Grace, too, the five of us in the truck, Kyle riding shotgun and me stuck between those babe wymmin. Make-up, hair spray, body piercings et cetera, Grace had a certain charm that increased the pressure in my penile hydraulics, oh yeah. Or maybe it was Freddy. Maybe it was riding between those wymmin, their hips touching me on either side and the strange combination of the smell of hairspray, White Shoulders, and sweat triggering all kinds of fun memories.

Was it the hairspray? I thought. Grace wore Final Net, I swore, you just don't see that anymore, at least not in your higher class beauty salons—excuse me, it's finishing mist, thank you—but the smell was just like what my momma wore. It made me think of when Mom would drop me off at the barber shop for my monthly trim—Wahl clippers with a #4 guard one length all over—while she would get her hair done. It took a lot longer for Mom to "get the works," as she called it, so after I'd gotten my buzz cut I'd stroll down the mall to her salon and sit and wait. Beauty salons back when I was a kid had this sort of rarefied atmosphere based on hair spray, heavily perfumed hair spray. No matter if a woman got a pixie cut or a six-foot beehive, she always got a solid dose of Final Net to set the 'do.

Or maybe it was the White Shoulders. The first time I ever slow danced with a girl was at church camp, about the time I first got abducted, although I wouldn't remember it at the time. I found out later a lot of abductees got snatched at church camps. Eighth grade. No, seventh grade. Paula McLaughlin and I had fallen into this shuffling grope that passed for slow dancing at church camp, where you clung to each other and tried to avoid building up a woody just as she avoided trying to keep her sponge dry. Hah! Like we could. We were adolescents. Anyway, Paula McL wore White Shoulders, the Official Perfume of Teenage Girls Looking to Get Laid Or At Least Heavily Petted, and so the scent-memory connection got cemented: White Shoulders = lust.

Or could it be the sweat? My senior year in high school I fell in love with my first granola girl, my first Earth Momma, my first wymmin with fur, Katie Riggs. She had wild light brown hair—kinda like Freddy's, now that I thunk it—and blue eyes like the color of bleach bottles, so bleached out the blue almost vanished. Katie R. sweated, a gentle sweat, though, nothing harsh or bitter, just enough to make you realize she was human and real and honest.

Hairspray, White Shoulders, sweat. I was in lust, all right.

Anyways, we drove back down that East Road toward Della, and maybe a third of the way turned off on this side road that hung along the coast. I mean, when Samm turned the truck left and around the corner, you could see the bay right there and everything. We looked on the back side of the Spit, the harbor side, and I could still see the Zapata plant smoldering there at the end. I thought of Sarah out there packing her gear and stuff and getting ready to leave Della, unless she got that job.

Some big changes could be coming for Jimmo that night, I thought, only my years in the Resistance have taught me not just to take it one day at a time, but one hour at a time. "Be here immediately," as my old cell commander used to say. It was the sort of epitaph you could put on a bumper sticker. Fuck, for all I knew, Commander Q had seen it on a bumper sticker.

So down this other gravel road we went, round the corner, along the coast, and to the boatyard. No, *The* Boatyard. In Della, everything had a singular title. If there was a bookstore, it was The Bookstore; if a natural food store, The Natural Food Store; the mattress shop, The Mattress Shop. Now suppose another store came along, like some idiot had the idea that maybe, hey, the town could support two mattress stores. It would be The Mattress Store and The Other Mattress Store, like the two papers: The Della News and The Other Della News. No shit. You think I'm making all this crap up? I couldn't possibly make up shit like this.

The Boatyard was where all the boats went in the winter, what you call a dry land dock. We passed by a big-humping crane carrying a purse seiner—that's a kind of fishing boat—out of the water and over into the yard, to be set along a bunch of rotten old boats in various stages of hopeful repair. If a boat wasn't in the water in Della in the summer, it was because either the owner couldn't afford to run it anymore, it was in lousy shape, or both. Now and then the Boatyard—Freddy told me this—would auction off the old boats. Freddy said she had an old boyfriend everyone called Boatguy Bob, because he would buy old boats, haul 'em to his land, fix them up as cabins, and live in them. She said he'd chop off the rotten parts with a chainsaw and connect them to the other boats, so his house was like all these boats which had rammed into each other, with maybe pilot houses stuck on at the bow end.

In the boatyard was the best damn hamburger joint in Della. Two middle-aged lesbians ran it. I know, I know, you're thinking, what is it with these lesbians, Jimmo? Dog's truth, Della had a lot of lesbians. Not many studly gay dudes, though. My theory is that these wymmin moved there with their husbands, or maybe between husbands, or after they'd used up their last husband, and they wound up in a place where, frankly, a wymmin really didn't need a man. These babes not only looked hot, they could do just about anything a guy could do, including give good tongue. I think some of them who might have been tipping the Kinsey scale toward the middle thought to themselves, OK, it turns out I don't really need men after all, I like wymmin, so, oh, why not?

Kyle had called our orders ahead, not that it meant the burgers were steaming and ready when we got there, but it did mean we only had to wait ten minutes. The Best Damn Hamburger Joint in Della (except for the Best Damn

Hamburger Joint on the Spit) was this gray-planked shed roofed building at the entrance to the boatyard. Across the way was this place where they sold gear, called The Gear Shed, naturally, and next to it a tower made of an old section of the Alaskan pipeline with a shack on top and a big bright spotlight. Security, Samm said.

You could tell The Best Damn Hamburger Joint in Della had good burgers because it didn't just have guys in Carhartts hanging out there, although it did. It didn't just have boat people, it didn't just have old hippies, it didn't just have tourists—but only a few—or cab drivers or lineman or real estate sales ladies. It had *all* these people, which sort of defines a good burger joint. Outside of The Best Damn, Etc., some of these people might not give each other the time of day, so you knew something had to draw them together, i.e., quid pro quo, The Best Damn Burgers, Etc.

Ya notice I haven't actually named the place, have I? You think I'm gonna tell and make it easy for you to fit right into Della, if you've figured out by now where Della is? I might have even lied about the location, too. Or maybe not. You're just gonna have to hump your butt to Della on your own and find your own cosmic local guide. Mebbe my friend Max can help you out on sort of a consultin' basis like: $50 an hour.

I'd like to say we sat down in that burger joint, right there on one of the sunny tables that looks out over the bay, and that sort of a grand epiphany came over me, Gee, maybe I'd stay in Della after all, u.s.w., but it didn't happen. What happened was that no sooner had Samm paid for the burgers, no sooner had we sat down, when Samm's pager went off. He glanced down at it and his face took on this color like curdled milk. Some other guy's pager went off, too, and then two more guys and a wymmin—volunteer firefighters, I think—and someone said, "Oh, shit."

"Let's go," Samm said and he was out the door.

I looked at Freddy and she looked at me and then at the other people also rushing for their trucks. The phone rang in the back and one of the proprietors answered it and then she slammed the door over the counter shut, tossed down her apron, and she hustled out the door.

"Samm, Samm!" Freddy shouted. "What the hell—?" She stopped, cocked her ears, and then looked up.

I saw it, too. At first I thought, OK, this is it, the big moment, the Revolution, because these choppers went ka-whunk-thunk-whunk, ka-whunk-thunk-whunk over the sky, two of 'em. Only they didn't have weapons pods or any of that black helicopter paranoia; they had big bags slung underneath, streaming behind on ropes and water dripping out of the bags.

Freddy sniffed the air, so I did too, moving my nose toward the logging camp, up east. I got a faint whiff of smoke, only since the Zapata fire the day before, that was another spot on a leopard. As we got into the truck, Kyle gimping along after us, Freddy asked, "You don't happen to have a red card, do you?"

I had to think about that for a second, since I'm certified in so many damn things, the Army getting it into its head to train me eighty-two ways from midnight, I think just to justify all these poor-ass college professors doing summer teaching in the Reserves.

"No," I finally said. "What the hell's a red card?"

"Wildfire fighting." We got in, Grace sorta shoving Kyle before her. Samm punched the gas even before the doors slammed shut. "Fuck it, doesn't matter. You can handle a chainsaw."

As Samm sped out Bay Drive and onto East Road, Freddy dug around in the cargo space behind the back seat.

She pulled out a bunch of piss-yellow shirts and handed them up to Kyle and Grace in the front seat, then one to me. Grace had stripped off all her jewelry and wrapped her big hair in a bandana and then shucked off her dress to her panties. She put on that ugly shirt and then got into some pants Freddy tossed her. Freddy had taken off her own work shirt and put on the yellow shirt and told me to do the same.

"We marching in some sort of band?" I asked, being a smart ass. Sometimes I couldn't keep my mouth shut.

"Fighting wildfires," Freddy said. "Two helos. It's a big un."

"And spreading right to our camp," Samm said from up front. He'd gotten on his cell phone and called ahead. "One of the contract loggers had a little accident with a chainsaw and a gas can."

I thought of the missile crawlers and the secret code I'd almost given Samm and realized, fuck it, no code needed. The Grays had already figured things out. Fires seemed to follow me, I thought. "Out of the frying pan," I mumbled.

"What's that?" Freddy asked.

"Yesterday I tried to get a job with Zapata."

"Oh. Well, you might have more of a job than you bargained for on this one."

*

We hauled butt up East Road and might have had to pass a few trucks at the speed Samm put the crew-cab to, except that everyone else was hauling butt, too: cops, fire trucks, volunteer firefighters. It was as if that fire were a big drain hole and we were rubber duckies getting sucked down into the tub, that's how it pulled all of us to the fire. The smoke got thicker the closer we got, a nice stiff breeze out of the north whupping upon us, the day breeze. As we got closer, I began to think that maybe I should be going the other direction. Had no choice, though. I was in that damn truck.

We scarfed down our burgers as we trucked out there, Samm eating one-handed and driving with the other hand, a sort of frightening sight. I understood, though. It might be a while until we ate again. Soon enough we got to the logging camp. Samm didn't even close his door or yank out the keys to the truck—in fact, he left it running. The only thing he did was turn it around so it faced out, toward the road. I understood. That was our lifeboat.

"Grace, you take Freddy and Jimmo," Samm shouted. "Work on keeping the fire from jumping the road."

"And if it jumps the road?" she asked.

"That won't happen. Hold the line," Samm said.

"Hold the line," Grace mumbled. "Right." She pointed at me and Freddy. "Freddy, you've got a red card. Jimmo, grab a chainsaw and a Pulaski and do what Freddy tells you. Come with me." Grace had picked up a Pulaski, this ax-like thing that was also a pick, and we rushed up to the road side of that big clearing.

Someone had started up one of those feller-bunchers and slowly—it's not like they moved all that fast anyway—moved toward a line of dead trees up the road. Thick smoke rolled downhill toward us, but in all the smoke I couldn't see any flames. Maybe that was good, maybe that was bad, I just fucking didn't know.

"Might as well attack that line of trees," Grace said, pointing across the road from the camp. A standing clump of red, almost needleless trees lined the road across the way. It seemed kind of stupid, a logging camp surrounded by a dead forest. Later, Samm told me that it was a land dispute, this land owned by someone from Outside who hadn't seen the land in twenty years and didn't understand that the whole fucking forest had died and the trees had to come down. This was war. You did what you did to stop the fire and to hell with property rights.

The little forest narrowed down into a V as it came to the road. Grace explained that I should break up the grass and other ground flammables on either side of the V as she and Freddy felled trees. They began lopping off trees so they fell uphill, into the fire and a big slash pile. Even though the trees had died, they still had branches and witches' brooms and shit that could catch fire. A lot of the dead trees had punky middles, which made them harder to burn. If you could fell +em the middle wouldn't catch fire and it would slow the burn down. Mainly, Grace explained in all the chaos, in a calm voice that made me listen closer, "Mainly we don't want a crown fire, where the tops burn." A crown fire was like a whole new level of shit.

With all the smoke and the heat I couldn't tell if we fought back the fire or just wasted a lot of good burger fuel for nothing. I'd cut trenches in the dry underbrush, exposing dirt, so that if the fire burned out of the slash piles we made it wouldn't go further. Grace said we were making a back burn, creating our own little Dresden there so that the big Tokyo of a fire wouldn't have anything else to burn. You understand? Of course not, you assholes don't know history. Dresden was like this quaint little city the Allies firebombed in Double-Ya-Double-Ya Two, and Tokyo another example of 20th Century martial urban renewal.

Get into the flow of something like that, where you're not quite sure you'll live but hope to fuck you don't die, and after a while, time is nothing. Time doesn't slow down, it doesn't stop, it just no longer becomes a marker by which the universe gets measured. It isn't when it once was. What mattered to me was the dirt I exposed, the flames that didn't cross the road, and the fire that burned itself out.

You just fought. My uncle who was in the war said that once: You just fought. First came chaos and then an organization of chaos and then chaos became your local reality, and you understood it. It developed its own rules and everything and quit being chaos. I focused entirely on one task, one general series of movements: lift Pulaski, dig into ground, turn over dirt, lift Pulaski again, repeat as necessary.

Eventually, though, this new reality came into being, a new form of chaos which I realized with a start was the way the world had been some time ago. The smoke seemed thinner, the heat less. Between Grace and Freddy and that guy on the feller buncher (which I still thought was a rocket launcher), the forest in front of us turned into a big bonfire, controlled and orderly and consuming itself and not more forest. I saw around me that other workers scrambled with wet rugs or sheets stamping out fires from falling ashes that had fallen on the wind. Other than that, the fire had not crossed the road.

"We held the line," Grace said, but with a tone of voice that said she didn't believe it.

"Held the line," Freddy said.

"Did it," I said.

"Did it. Damn it, we did it!" Grace raised her chainsaw in triumph.

"Shoulda done it faster," Kyle said from behind us. "It almost got away from us. It got one of the fuel trucks."

Grace glared at him, bandana long ago fallen away, but her hair still in perfect shape, only with so much smoke and ash that it looked like a black helmet. "We held the line, Kyle."

"I really need you to listen to me closer, Grace," Kyle said. "I'm only offering criticism for your own good."

"Oh, fuck—"

She didn't get the next words out. Freddy shoved her aside and they both rolled toward me, almost knocking me down. I stepped aside and let them fall, then looked up to see why Freddy had tackled Grace. The guy with the feller buncher held a burning tree in the claws of his machine. Smoke obscured his vision and he couldn't quite see where he was going. The machine stopped and the guy let down that log, branches still on it, the crown roaring.

We later figured out that he must have seen a tree on our side of the road that caught fire, just one tree, and in our complacency we missed it. He didn't, though. Guy saved the day, he did, and what did it matter what happened next?

He dropped the tree. Just like I'll always remember that shred of metal whirling at me when the Zapata cannery blew up, I'll remember that tree falling. It came down, right on an open part of the airstrip, which was what the feller-buncher dude was aiming for, a nice open spot. All would have been well and this story might have turned out different, if not that the tree in its falling, a branch of the tree in its falling, nicked Kyle.

"I need you to step aside," I wanted to say, but couldn't. I'll always feel a little guilty forever after that I didn't.

The tree came down. The branch nicked Kyle. The tip was sharp. As it fell, it knocked off his helmet, and sliced right through his left ear, your basic Van Gogh chop job. Kyle reached up with his left hand, held it to his ear, and then looked down at a glob of blood in his palm. He didn't scream, I'll give him credit for that, but he did look mildly uncomfortable.

When Kyle's helmet came off, this amazing pouf of silver-blond hair sprung straight up, kind of a Disco Do, just whisping over his ears and falling boyishly over Kyle's forehead—over his squinty little eyes. But then a spark or a little flame from the burning tree hit his hair, and kawoosh, it went up like a cotton ball soaked in rubbing alcohol, and inside of two seconds, Kyle went totally bald, nothing more than ashes on his scalp.

He rolled forward, over and over like you got taught in grade school to put out a fire if for some chance, hey, a burning tree fell on top of you and lit your precious little Disco Do on fire. Kyle slapped at his head and his ears, or what was left of the left one. His right leg stuck out kinda funny, and for a moment I thought it was broken. It was broken, I swear. Kyle reached down and twisted and turned it, then stood up.

His right ear dangled by a little thread of cartilage, only it didn't bleed. At least, I thought his right ear had been ripped off, too. Kyle turned away from us for a second, did something to the side of his head, and turned back. He did this kind of dancing jig thing, took a deep breath, and smiled.

"Kyle, man, your ear got ripped off," Samm said. "Are you OK?"

He reached up, felt for the bloody patch, reached down to the ground and picked up something that looked like a shriveled up mushroom. Kyle smeared that thing against the stump of his left ear, then smiled.

"What ear?" he asked.

Samm looked at Kyle, over at us, back at Kyle. He started to say something, then shook his head.

"Good as new," Grace said.

Ayup, I thought.

Except he put the ear back on backwards.

Chapter 10

After two fires and damned near getting torched in both of them, I had to begin to wonder if someone had it in for my sorry ass. It could also be that life in Della was just chock full of coincidences. Like they say, try to kill me once, shame on you; try to kill me twice, shame on me; try to kill me a third time, and you're dead. Or as my Uncle Willy put it, three co-incidences is a pretty good data set for a prevailing trend.

I could see that there might be a little trend developing there. On top of almost like being snuffed twice in two days, I kept losing job prospects. At least this time I had actually worked and it looked like there would be work to come once the ashes cooled down and stuff. We weren't going to be actually clearing any forest, but we might be cleaning up a bunch of deadfall and stuff.

Samm gave Freddy and me a ride back to town. We'd all gotten pretty grimy and stuff and Samm figured that we could probably hit the showers at the high school on account of the Zapata cannery fire and all the Spit Rats still hanging out there. Freddy said she'd join us, since the water delivery truck had fallen behind on its run and her place was low on water. That seemed kinda weird: you got water delivered in Della? Didn't make sense. Grace allowed as how the high school showers had better pressure anyway and did we mind swinging by her place so she could pick up some clean clothes? We swung by Uncle Thirsty's, this liquor store on the East Road, and got us some beer and chips. I could see a party developing, uh huh.

I had just gotten all that soot and grime washed out of me and had wandered out to the front of the high school in that euphoric daze that comes with a good hot shower after a long day of sweat and being a generally stinky mess. A bunch of campers hung out on the front of the school, lounging around and more or less drifting between chaos and control. You could see people had collected their wits after a near disaster but they hadn't quite moved on to settling back in to a normal routine. That would take a few more nights of wild debauchery to celebrate the pure existence of being.

Some sunlight had snuck out of an otherwise gloomy bank of clouds, the light shining down on me and drying my dreads as I combed them out. I'd sort of zoned out, you know, when someone came up from behind me and hugged me. Her hands moved down to my crotch and I didn't quite know what to think when I got a whiff of White Shoulders. That really confused me, cuz those hands had downy red hairs on them. I reached up and back and felt a head with crisp short hairs at the nape.

"Sarah," I said.

"Can't fool you, Jimmo."

No, I thought, but your perfume sure could. I turned and gave her a light kiss on the mouth. I wasn't quite sure if we'd progressed to the swapping spit in public phase of our relationship.

"Nice perfume."

"Some woman in the bathroom let me borrow hers."

Ah, I thought. Coming out of the door I saw Freddy, her hair damp around her shoulders.

"Hey, Jimmo," Freddy said.

"Hey." I introduced Sarah to Freddy. They eyed each other cautiously and to avoid a little tiff I made it clear how I'd met Freddy. "She's on the, uh, forest rehabilitation crew I'm working on. I think."

"You think?"

"There was a little forest fire, Sarah. You didn't hear?" She hadn't, so Freddy and I had to fill her in on the big adventure. Now that I thought of it, I noticed the parking lot had filled up with a new wave of refugees, folks from East Road who didn't want to deal with the chaos and figured they'd camp in town for the night.

When I wound down, Sarah smiled, as if she'd suddenly remembered to tell me the guy from the lottery office had called to say I'd won the Powerball.

"I got the job."

"At Twee Sister's?"

"Yeah. It's pulling lattes and working in the bakery, but they're a cool bunch."

"Watch out for that Marie, though," Freddy said. "She has a thing for redheads." She winked.

"So does Jimmo," Sarah said indignantly.

Freddy eyed us funny, thought to herself, then smiled. "You guys set up for someplace to stay?"

"I have a tent." I glanced at Sarah. "We have tents."

"Tents are good. I've lived in a lot of tents," Freddy said. "Tents will work until, oh, about mid-September. So I've been thinking. We have some space out at the 'Stead—the Homestead. If you guys need a place, we could fit you in."

"We?"

"Well, the 'Stead. I can't quite remember the current count. It depends on whether or not Lisa and Doug got back together or if Laurie's kids are staying with her or the other mother. And I think Annie might be across the bay this week if John's not up on the Slope. We used to have the schedules all worked out, but then we crashed the Cray."

"The Stead?" Sarah asked.

"It's a homestead up the beach. This old hippy with a cush trust fund bought it and then went back East to close down the family law firm only he stayed and became a hot shot New York lawyer. That was twenty years ago. He rents it out at a dollar a year and then we rent rooms to whomever needs a place. You might call it a commune except that right now we're all very much into Anarchism so it's more like a Domestic Syndicate."

"And you have rooms?" I asked.

"Right now. Room, rooms. Nick and Jessie had a fight and can't stand to be within ten miles of each other. Neither one of them wanted to leave so we kicked them out until they decided who would stay. That was a month ago. Last I heard they made up but are still pissed at us so aren't honoring us with their presence. The Syndicate's idea is to lease out their rooms before they change their mind."

"Rooms?" Sarah asked.

"One has a double bed, one doesn't. You decide if you're a couple yet?"

Sarah blushed. "We sort of just met."

"That hasn't stopped anyone before."

"I think Sarah means that maybe we should take two rooms but keep our options open." I winked at her. "Give each other space."

"Well, that's what we've got," Freddy said. "House space. Come on out and stay a few days. Like I said, we just need someone to squat in the boys' space so they don't get ideas."

*

Freddy said she had to go check her mail at the post office and do some errands, but she'd be back to pick us up in an hour or so while we got our gear together. Sarah went off to see if she could find Elaine and Trish, maybe our good pal Louanne with the RV. Right, I remembered: they were supposed to head out to the Spit and get their stuff. I went to find my tent, still set up out on the ball field, and pack it up. My old orange North Face still stood on the edge of the field, out in the open so the sun could catch it.

I unzipped the front door and crawled in to grab my sleeping bag. Usually I wad up my bag in a lump in the middle of the tent and cram it into a plastic garbage bag so if it rains the bag won't wick moisture from the sides of the tent or get wet if water blows inside. Tents aren't perfect barriers against rain; they are retarders against rain, ya know? That morning, though, it had looked so nice out I hadn't bothered. I was lazy was what it was, to tell you the truth, even though I had gotten up a few minutes earlier than usual. So my bag lay out in the tent and for a moment I had to think if there was someone sleeping in it, but thought that ridiculous. It was *my* sleeping bag, after all.

Only, as I reached for the foot of the bag to yank it out of the tent, the bag didn't drag as easily. It had weight. It had resistance. It had someone in it. I reached for bag to pull it off the person—my bag, in my tent—when I noticed a shaft of light, a pinprick of light, really, pouring down from the tent. A little dot of sunlight glowed on my hand. I glanced up and saw a slight tear (just a rip, really), in the roof of the tent. When I set the tent up, I hadn't pulled the fly away from the tent itself. I'd patched the fly once, a patch on both sides, except the inside patch fell away and the surface was sort of gunky, and that got stuck to the tent. The hole went right through the fly and tent. If the fabric hadn't stuck together, I might not have noticed the light coming through.

I looked at the dot of light on my hand, up at the tent. It was as if someone had shot a pellet gun at my tent, only the hole was a lot smaller, maybe a sixteenth of a inch, if that. I moved my hand toward the sleeping bag, keeping that dot of light on it, until I touched the bag. Then I moved my hand away. On the bag was a slight hole, scorched around the edge where the nylon and synthetic filling had burned a bit. I didn't want to peel back the sleeping bag and look at the person, but I had to.

Carefully, trying not to disturb the bag much, I unzipped it, keeping an eye on that dot of light. Whoever had crawled into my bag had zipped the bag tight on the top, mummy style, and then rolled and twisted over so his head was face down. Or her head. I was jumping to conclusions there. I could reach under, grab the zipper, and open up the bag, so I did.

The guy felt cold but still rigid, twisted into how he'd last rolled in his sleep. I got the bag shucked off of him enough so that I could see that dot of light now shining on his shoulder. He didn't move. He wasn't going to move. He was dead, sleeping the big sleep. I had known that from when I saw the light, only sometimes you hope what you think you see isn't really what you think you think. You can hope.

It would take a damned good forensic pathologist to find the mark. I wouldn't have myself except that the shaft of sunlight was still there pointing it out. Right on the guy's sleeve of his long-sleeve T-shirt was a little tear in the fabric, the edges also scorched, but not melted like on the bag. Cotton doesn't melt, it scorches. If I took off his shirt I knew I'd find a little hole in his arm, just a black dot that could be mistaken for a freckle, except it was a burn mark. An entry wound and burn mark. I'd seen it before. It was how the Grays took you out when they grew weary of playing with you.

They set up an assassin-bot, a little satellite high in space that had a kinetic loader. Only, the loader packed one fuck of a punch. The Grays didn't dick around with large-caliber kinetic rounds. They thought small, real small. No one had ever actually recovered an assassin-bot round, but the Resistance had guessed they were some sort of hard substance, probably diamond, fired at incredible speeds.

That little round came screaming down out of the sky right into you. You might hear its little shock wave as it broke the sound barrier, although they said that if you heard the shock wave, it meant it had missed. It tore through anything in the way, tore through the atmosphere heating up but not burning up, and collecting so much damn energy that it burned you as much as anything. If burning was all it did you could live with that.

Think of a hot rod the diameter of a human hair thrust through your body. If it hit something vital the wound would be cauterized so quickly you might not notice it. It wasn't the heat, though; it was the shock. The round from an assassin-bot had so much kinetic energy that when it hit soft flesh shock waves rolled away from the entrance wound and all through the body. That's what killed you. Imagine getting hit with a sheet of plywood going at about Mach 10; that's what an assassin-bot round did to you.

When the cops came and the coroner looked at that body, they were going to have to figure out how every tissue in the body had been shredded and why the guy had bled to death from internal bleeding inside of about two seconds. They said that the round kept going and going, all the way through the Earth, and that if a Chinaman got in the way on the other end, it would go through him, too. There would be a hole through the Earth, too, one long extremely narrow tunnel, but only for about 15 seconds, or until the stress of the earth sealed it up. Sometimes there might be little puffs of steam as the rounds hit underground water and it burst out of the ground, superheated. If you were being fired at by an assassin-bot and could run, that's how you'd know it was targeting on you: you saw these little geysers of steam shooting up toward you.

All I knew was that I was going to need a new sleeping bag and maybe a tent. I sealed the sleeping bag back up and backed out of the tent. I didn't know who the guy was, but he'd made a mistake by crawling into my sleeping bag. I didn't doubt it for a moment. The Grays hadn't wanted to kill him.

They'd wanted to kill me.

*

So the cops came in and then the EMTs and they strapped the guy to a stretcher. Yeah, they told me he'd gotten drunk or maybe did some hillbilly heroin and passed out, but I wasn't buying that. He'd been offed, that was for fucking sure. The cops asked me if I wanted the sleeping bag, on account of the guy had crapped and pissed in it, and I told 'em to fuck the bag, fuck the tent. I let them handle it from there. I went through all the cop bullshit, you had to when a dead body shows up in your sleeping bag, only I knew after a bit of typical officer bullshit where they tried to pin the blame on the poor sucker who called in the report—me—I'd be in the clear. Didn't I have an shockproof alibi what with humping my butt out there in that fire?

So screw it, screw the cops, screw their damn report. That dead guy? He was their problem. I had new digs and a new place to sleep. All I needed was a new sleeping bag. That turned out not to be a major fucking deal, as it turned out.

An hour or so later, after the cops did their shit and they'd consented to let me go, Sarah had returned from the Spit with her stuff and then Freddy picked us up. Sarah saw me talking with some cop—a guy that looked like a Hitler Youth Cadet, spelled his name funny—and waited for me to say my tender farewells.

"What the hell was that about?" Like any good paranoid, Sarah shared my distrust of uniformed authority.

"Just a dead guy in my sleeping bag. Fortunately, I wasn't in the bag at the time."

"Huh?"

"I'll tell you later." Freddy honked in her rusty maroon Subaru—I think everyone in Della drove rusty maroon Subarus, did I mention that?—and I humped my ruck over there.

Now here Sarah said her good-byes to her loyal traveling comparisons. I s'pose had I been a more decent and sensitive guy I'd of understood that they had gone many a mile together and shared numerous adventures. Fuck, for all I knew they were old college roomies or something and might never see each other again. If I'd of been a sensitive guy I'd of seen that, only I had just found a dead body in my sleeping bag and been butt-tortured by fascista cops, so like I wasn't really in a good goddamn mood for that.

I'd regret this later.

While I tapped my heels at Freddy's car and she hung around waiting for the girlz to part tenderly, Sarah, Elaine, and Trish did the huggy and teary farewell shit. Trish and Elaine would head off to Seward and more Zapata cannery slime-line work, while Sarah stayed with this asshole schmuck guy she'd just met and pull lattes. I could see those two wanted to hang with the old Three Muskeritas shit and were a bit miffed at Sarah for falling under the spell of a good squeeze. It happens. Plus, I think they resented the fact that she had a hot new haircut while they still had these bad buzz jobs.

Looking at them hugging and doing the cheek-peck kiss-kiss thing, I had the thought that maybe I'd run into another set of Kinsey Fives, just my luck. Maybe what I'd messed with was another bit of old lesbo intimacy, three girlz out to prove that they didn't need any damn testosterone gorged penises, not as long as they had tongues. Or maybe not. I'd definitely screwed with something there.

Sarah finally pulled away from Trish and Elaine and walked over to me. I could see she had that sort of "Am I doing the right thing?" glare about her, a glare she directed at me. Hey, all I'd done was boff her standing up in an RV bathroom. She was free, Caucasian, and 18, old enough to make her own decisions.

"You'd better be damn worth it," she said to me as she passed by on the way to Freddy's car.

I had a good comeback on my tongue and opened my mouth to utter a cosmic riposte, but hell, I know women well enough to shut my mouth quickly.

We rode pretty much in silence all the way out to the 'Stead. I could tell we had become entrapped in one of those transitional moments where much worry gets expressed trying to resolve important issues. In times like this, one says nothing or as little as necessary. Driving out that winding gravel road, though, I had a thought:

It would probably be a good idea to have separate rooms for a while.

Chapter 11

Freddy got us settled in what she called "the tower annex." A former resident had taken an old radar dome from a military site and turned it into a two-story bedroom wing. I got the smaller room up top, with the skylight, and Sarah took the bigger room with the double bed at the bottom of the spiral staircase leading up to the Aurora Dome. Better yet, Freddy scrounged up a comforter the size of a life raft, courtesy of some trustafarian who'd moved on.

"Only one drawback," Freddy told me. "On a good aurora night, you gotta let anyone up there to watch the lights." Worked for me.

We'd arrived for the second eating shift, the really good one, Freddy said, for those who didn't have early morning jobs. On second shift, you had to wash the pots and pans but got to stay up late getting high and yakking. Sarah and I came downstairs just as the first shift finished clearing tables, a bunch of schoolteachers and tour bus drivers whom we'd meet later. Sitting around the big spruce-plank table sat this guy Barry, Freddy, a cool purple haired lady named Rosalyn also known as Roz, and a few of what I'd later learn were the elite of Della's TFBs, trust fund babies. You didn't think everyone there worked, did you? A huge hunk of them had decent four-figure monthly dividends from Daddy's trust fund, and a small percentage of that group had five-fig-ure dividends that so ashamed them they tried their damnd-est to appear poor as dirt. Of course they all had really great teeth and sharp haircuts.

"New blood!" Barry exclaimed when he saw us. "New students!"

"New students?" I asked. I could see maybe Sarah as the perpetual college type, workin' on the ten-year plan, only I had clearly gone beyond the university gig. "Where do you get off on that?"

Barry pointed to a neatly lettered banner hanging from the high ceiling. "The Cosmic Rational University of Della," he said: "*C-R-U-D.* You mean you haven't heard of Opera-tion Train Whistle? The Della Conspiracy?"

I wanted to ask if that was another name for the Gray Conspiracy, only I hadn't quite sussed out Barry and didn't risk betraying all. "Do tell," I said.

Barry grinned, and I could see him slip into a standard rap. You know that look? It's where someone has told a story often enough to have the bones laid down, not often enough to wear it out, and frequent enough they can lay down a few new riffs.

"I'm out of here," said one of the TFBs, a guy named Nick. "I've heard this rap before."

"Me too," said Rory, a woman with this dark brown braid going like all the way to the ground. "But you'll love Opera-tion Train Whistle, kids. Nice to meet you."

"Likewise," I said. "Operation Train Whistle?"

"Operation Train Whistle," Barry said. "Where do I be-gin? OK, start with a question. How did you two find Della?"

"Smart-ass answer?" I asked.

"'I turned right at Devil's Pass' has been used," Barry said.

"OK. Honest answer. A mental health professional in Anchorage told me to," I said.

"We get that a lot," Barry said. "Sarah?"

"I saw a Zapata ad at the Student Union at my college."

"That would be the HARD WORK CRUMMY WAGES GOOD SEX LOTSA DRUGS poster?" He grinned.

"Something like that."

"Yeah, it's some of my best work. Old, but a classic." Barry settled back and grinned. "Freddy, Roz, how'd you get here?"

"Third generation Alaskan," Freddy said. "That gonna screw up your theory?"

"Bear with me," Barry said. "Roz, tell 'em how you got here."

"Sisters of Providence transferred me up after I got my MSW. Then, uh, well, the order and I parted ways."

"So what's your point?" I asked.

"You were recruited. You didn't just arrive here of your own free will. Someone suggested you come here. Someone planted the idea in your head, however subtle. Now, why Alaska?"

"You have to go to Alaska to get to Della," Sarah said.

"Right. But didn't going to Alaska lure you to Della?"

"Sure."

"And how did the idea of Alaska get planted in your head?"

Sarah shrugged. "Jack London stories. Nature documentaries. Iditarod specials. Oh, and I read this novel once about blimps and nuclear pirates in the People's Republic of Alaska."

"Same here," I said. "I mean, Alaska's Alaska. It kinda has its own rep."

"We call it a self-replicating mythos, one that regenerates its own energy. Sort of a perpetual mythmaking machine. It doesn't need new propaganda to maintain the meme. The meme is pretty much damn near immortal. Take this big idea and let it rip."

"Sure," Sarah said. "I see that. And it sucked us in?"

"On its own. Operation Train Whistle, though, has agents. 'Conductors,' is what they're called."

"This is like its own operation?" I asked.

"To a point. You have this meme and then you want people to populate the myth, only the myth is more than a myth: it's an institution."

"An institution . . ." I could see Sarah begin to get skeptical.

"An institution," Barry said. "A social system with its own infrastructure, its own bureaucracy, its own recruiting agency that exists for a specific social purpose. That's an institution: churches, prisons, insane asylums, and universities. Alaska is a university."

"It has a university?" Sarah looked confused.

"No, it *is* a university." Barry raised a finger. "We'll need some serious drugs to explicate this point." He took out a tightly rolled doobie from one of like a zillion pockets on his vest and passed it under his nose. "Ah, Matanuska Thunder Fuck. You can't beat 10,000 years of glacial loess."

He lit the joint, inhaled on it until the end glowed like a comet, then passed it to me. As a rule I didn't do dope on account of the effects it has on my meds, but I could see this might be necessary for the sake of intellectual discourse. I took a puff and handed it to Sarah, who inhaled that puppy like it was giving her CPR.

"I continue: Why did you come to Alaska?" Barry said. "I mean, why the hell would anyone come to a place fifteen-hundred miles from the nearest state, above the fiftieth parallel, in a land that's either colder than the twat of a Plutonian ice maiden, windier than a category five hurricane, or damper than a baby's diaper?"

"Because it's someplace else," I said.

"Right. And it's not where everything else is," Sarah added. "Like you have all this space and you can get away from all that other shit."

"Bingo. Sort of a refuge."

"Yeah. Sort of."

"Only, not everyone needs that, and not everyone needs it for forever, but some do, and they stay for a dozen years, maybe only a few, maybe a lifetime. The thing is, no matter how you arrive, no matter how you get recruited, you *are* recruited. You belong here, someone else wants you here, and you can't leave until you graduate."

"You mean there's this grand deliberateness to it? Alaska, coming to Alaska—it's *intentional*?" I asked.

"Needed and necessary to the functioning of normal society, which"—Barry sucked on the joint as it came back to him for the third time—"Alaska for fucking sure ain't." He pointed at both of us. "You, Jimmo and you, Sarah, by virtue of being here, now, in this place, are here because somewhere someone has determined you should be here. You think it's accidental. No, you are threats to human civilization, the toxic scum of normalcy, a great clot of pressure that has been allowed to escape. Operation Train Whistle has seen to it that you have been allowed to escape to here."

"Only we don't know it," Sarah said.

"Now you do. Better still, the professors, the administrators, all the grunts and drones who operate the university, the CRUD, they don't know it, either. Only those of us who have been truly enlightened understand the whole purpose."

"It's not a prison, though?"

"Not a prison. Not a loony bin. Not a hospital, either. None of those things. It's a university. Think about it."

I could see Barry had turned a corner here in his exegesis, had gone into new territory. Should I pull him back? Nah. I had gotten too stoned to do anything other than let him rip.

"Think about it! A university is the perfect utopia. You have a course laid out for you—a course of instruction, things you have to do before you can graduate. Maybe you decide you like the university, The University, and so you get an advanced degree and stay in it to teach. You might graduate but you never leave. As the great cosmic genius Fredrick Pohl put it, 'life is one learning experience after another, and what you get for a diploma is, you die.'"

"But some people can leave the CRUD?" Sarah asked.

"All the time!" Barry smiled. "They come up here, get jobs, raise families, get careers, and maybe leave. Some are born here, like Freddy. Imagine that, right into the university, students for life! They can get out and go to real universities and maybe never come back. Others get to leave, except they always pine for Alaska so badly they either come back—and leave and come back and leave and come back—or they recruit for Alaska. That's almost just as good."

"And the whole purpose?"

"To keep all those people from fucking up the rest of the world. It's kind of like Operation Wet Rubber Nipple. You know that one?"

I looked blankly at Sarah and shook my head.

"Wet Rubber Nipple was this college in the 1960s "——College" (and then and there he told me the name, but like I say, I forget things, which is good, because otherwise I couldn't write about this and I'd have to be killed). "Actually, a program to recruit students in the 1960s. All these really bright, potentially dangerous radicals got lured to a small liberal arts college in Florida where they had their every demand met. Drugs? No problem? Sex? All you want.

You could study anything, do anything, and the whole point was to keep those crazies from actually getting involved in campus politics where they could seriously undermine the normal functioning of American society. It only lasted until after Kent State, and then the big foundation that funded it pulled the plug. Some of those students wound up here, of course. Thing is, that was for a few years. Alaska: Alaska is for life."

"But you can graduate."

"Maybe. You can die," Barry said.

Sarah stared at him, ran a hand through that stiff red hair, and burst out laughing, an insane, stoned laugh that grew until the very walls trembled.

"That's the biggest pile of horseshit I've ever heard," she said.

Barry smiled. "Exactly." He looked at me.

I just grinned back. Got to thinking about it, and I understood. If the CRUD was real, if there really were administrators directing the thing, people who knew the actual truth about the true function of Alaska, then they also knew about the Grays, knew about the Alien Occupation Government, in fact, had to be the Alien Occupation Government, since the whole idea so neatly fit their general plan.

Truck Stop Alaska? Hah. Escape Valve Alaska, Campus Alaska, Camp Concentration Alaska. Thing was, it was so damn perfect—that to save the Earth you had to destroy Alaska, destroy Della and turn it into a normal, boring little town. I wasn't sure I wanted to do that.

I kinda like Della. Damn, there had to be a better way.

*

Well, all that dope and that bullshit wore us out. Sarah and I moved over to the kitchen sink and sunk our arms into big vats of warm soapy water, about the best damn sexual joy medium you could imagine. Barry had gone up to his room to write down some poetry he said had come into his head during the big Operation Train Whistle riff, Freddy had gone off to her room, and Roz said she was going to practice the lead on one of her marimba songs, leaving we two little lovebirds alone.

I washed. Sarah dried. The sinks at the 'Stead were mess hall sized, big stainless steel tanks you could hide a five-gallon pot in, with enough elbow room in front to do some serious scrubbing.

Not that we had too much elbow room. Sarah stood next to me and the necessity of the particular system we had worked out required us to work closely together, very closely together. I would wash a pot, get it all scrubbed and shiny, then hand it over to Sarah. She would take the pot, turn her hips toward me as she held the pot with her left hand and used her right hand to wash off the soap, then turn back to me to take the next pot. Sometimes I'd turn to her, face to face, and hand her a dish, and we would briefly squeeze together, pelvis to pelvis. I didn't mind that cooking for an entire household of fifteen created a lot of pots and pans.

Only, eventually we had the pots cleaned, the tables and counters wiped down, the stove scrubbed, the dishes dried and put away and hanging from big chef's racks, and that bumping and grinding died down.

"I'm feelin' kinda tired," I said. Sarah had the late shift at Twisted Sister's and Freddy and I didn't have to be out on the site until midday. "Should try out my new bed."

"Make sure it's not lumpy," Sarah suggested.

"Check out the Northern Lights."

She smiled. "I'd like to see that."

"You want to come?"

"Not right away," she said, leading me by my little finger over to the tower and up the staircase.

Later, after we had caught our breath, we stared up through the skylight at the sky turning pale pink, but never dark. Midnight.

"You know," I said, "I plum forgot that in the summer it never gets dark enough for the Northern Lights."

She turned toward me and kissed me on the nose. "I knew that."

Chapter 12

The next morning, a Friday, Freddy and I went out back to the logging site to see what sort of jobs we had left. Sarah went in after we left to do the afternoon shift at Twee Sisters. We had that night all planned out, a big do, since it was the first Friday of the month, Nosh Nite, Freddy called it, time to hit the gallery crawls. I'd never done something like that but Freddy said it was like the major hipwazee thing to do in Della on a Friday night.

Headin' east we hadda hang out at Mile 7 for a bit while the firefighters sorted out all the refugees returning to their homes. It was about all the excitement a little town like Della could handle, and I could see that a long spell of utter boredom might actually be appreciated that weekend. A big burly firefighter wouldn't let us go into the scorch zone until Samm came and met us in the Ford crew cab. Freddy parked her ratty Sube in a parking lot there near this swanky restaurant, which suited her just as well, on account of her Sube had developed a pissant oil leak.

"We got a job?" I asked Samm as he drove us back out to the site.

"For now. We'll be felling dead trees to make more fire-breaks. We got some disaster money to push up that project and the fucking power-line crap can wait."

"I thought that was what we were doing," Freddy said. "I'm confused."

"Union politics. The IBEW made a stink about how common grunts like us aren't properly trained to work close to power lines. A union card, it seems, would properly train us."

"Unions are cool," I said. I thought about how some Grays ran the unions, like the Teamsters—they offed Hoffa, you know—but other unions were like a major part of the Resistance. Grays didn't like power lines or that shit. "The IBEW has done some good, uh"—I almost said 'resistance work' but held my tongue—"worker advocacy."

"Yeah, I'm not dissin' them. All I mean is that until we get certified, no power-line clearing for us. It's strictly firebreaks."

We drove beyond the clearing where old Kyle had almost bought it yesterday and up a hill toward this modern look-ing elementary school. That's the thing I liked about Alas-ka. I'd grown up going to school in old Army barracks, but they had modern shit with even art and stuff, all of it done in this sort of industrial warehouse brick look, heavy on shiny metal roofs and gable roof lines. Usually there'd be some rusty moose sculpture for art, what passed for modern sculp-ture in the fucking Truck Stop Earth. Not that it was bad, but I don't know, you see one rusty moose, you've seen 'em all.

So then we drove around that school and up to this forest surrounding the school. I could see the beginnings of a wind-ing firebreak cut through the woods. Half the woods had turned rust red and the other half didn't look so good either. Samm pointed at a row of stakes.

"The feller-buncher has enough work back at the burn," he said. "Today, we'll do it the old fashioned way."

"That's a kinda crooked firebreak," I pointed out. "Looks like a trail to me."

"Funny, that," said Samm. "There seem to be a lot of cross-country ski trails around here. You know, when that firebreak is done, it would make a dandy five-kay loop." He pulled off his hat and scratched his head. "Or so my buddies in the ski club tell me. Not that I know anything."

I glanced at Freddy and she glanced at me, then shook her head. Recreational politics, Alaska style.

*

Now, I could go and bore you with all this wonderful shit about the glories of work and how much fun it can be to fell big doomed spruce trees, but fuck if it really matters to the overall plot. We cut trees. I got paid by the hour. Now and then in the silence of coffee breaks as our ears adjusted to the lack of a chainsaw's whine, Freddy or I might say something profound. Mostly, though, while not humping that chainsaw or bucking up logs or even dropping a tree or two, I watched Samm. I had a damn good idea he worked for the local Resistance, but I couldn't yet risk making contact. Those Grays can be damned clever and the last thing I wanted was another trip into orbit. I had kinda gotten tired of that, what with the anal probes and that crap.

Anyway, the day ended and we packed up our chainsaws for the weekend and rode back to Freddy's car at that swanky restaurant. I had that good warm feeling that comes from a honest day's worth of work, good solid physical work that made you feel like you'd done something worthwhile and hadn't just put blisters on your butt. Samm had been chillin' a growler—a half-gallon—of Della's Red Knot ale in an ice chest, and we popped that and sucked it back on the ride to Freddy's car. I kinda wondered if Alaska had an open-container law, only I had long ago quit worrying about local laws the way Christians resist earthly temptations. I mean, I wuz a Christian, and I applied the same attitude toward the law and Grays that Jesus freaks did to Caesar. Render unto him, et cetera. Every law enforcement officer short of a true citizen's militia was a pawn of the AOG anyway, so screw 'em.

By the time we got to Mile 7 where some law enforcement occifers might be around, we'd polished off that growler anyway. The only way to avoid having an open container is to empty it, because then you're into recycling, not imbibing. Samm went his way—I never did figure out where he lived, and I didn't want to know—and Freddy and I went ours, back to her place she called the 'Stead, as in 'Home'. She had me drive on account for every swig I took she took two, and had gotten a bit more blitzed. We only had to make it back in sorta one piece anyway.

Now at Freddy's place I did a not-nice thing, I'm sorry to say. I would skip this over except that this is a true and accurate account of all the important events of my time in Della and it does pertain to how I kicked Gray butt and eventually found true peace and happiness, and besides, this incident taught me that in matters of fidelity, I had, as they say, some issues to work out. Plus, it involves some damn good sex, and I figure that if I got a boner off of it, you ought to as well, dear reader.

Freddy and I got back to the 'Stead, parked the car, and helped each other up to the big house. I felt steady on my feet but that Freddy sure couldn't handle her booze. Being a gentleman and all, I gave her a hand—OK, she leaned on me—to her room, whereupon she dragged me in with her. It had gotten to be about five o'clock, round about time for the big first Friday shit to happen, and everyone else in the 'Stead had hustled their way into town. Sarah wasn't gonna finish up at Twee Sisters until about sixish, and we said we'd meet her about then. So, the place had emptied out, just Freddy and yours truly.

"Jimmo," Freddy said, falling backward onto her big Swedish therapeutic bed, "Jimmo, boy, you're so fuckin' cute."

I blushed. It had been a long time since someone had called me "boy" in a nice way, and "cute" in association with that. "I bet you say that to all the natty dread loggers you know."

"Just you, stud." She wiggled a finger at me. "Come here. I need my neck rubbed."

Well, OK, I thought. No harm in that. Only, by the time I got to the side of her bed, she'd shucked off her denim shirt and wore nothing but a tie-dyed undershirt. Those big shoulders stood out, muscles hard and wiry, and she had undone her wavy red hair and pushed it off her neck. I dug my fingers into her neck, searching out knots and working on the tight cords that a day humping logs would crank up. Her skin felt soft but sweaty, with bits of sawdust dusting the line of her collar. I could still smell that White Shoulders, a stronger smell, oddly, after a day of perspiration.

"Try this," she said, and handed me a bottle of Dr. Swigg's Miracle Love Massage Oil, I kid you not, that's what it said. It smelled sort of like rose hips and sort of like licorice and a bit like wasabi. So I splashed a good dollop into my hands and worked it into her shoulders.

"Oooh," she moaned. "Yes, lower. Wait."

Freddy reached down and pulled off that undershirt, then her Carhartts, so she wuz down to just silk red panties. Silk red panties! Criminy, what kind of tough wilderness Alaskan wymmin wore silk red panties?

"Give me a massage all over, and I'll give you a blow job," she said.

I laughed. I'd read that in a book somewhere. Promise a man a blow job, particularly a man you'd never intended to suck, and he'd do anything, just on the chance, the book said, that maybe you were serious. I hoped she wasn't serious and then a part of me hoped she was, except that there was the Sarah problem.

OK, I'd only fucked Sarah twice, except our relationship had that feeling of, OK, maybe, it might work out into being something longer lasting, and wasn't that what we all sought, reliable love and companionship? Did I risk that for something else? Well, fuck yeah. I couldn't resist that White Shoulders.

Like I said, I had some fidelity problems.

So I kept smearing on that massage oil, until Freddy's back shone like the moon on a calm fall lake. The smell of it made me feel a bit giddy, or maybe it wuz the Red Knot ale, or maybe just that wild temptation that comes from exploring a new human body and wondering if maybe this one matches better than the previous one, except that, you know, they all match, they're designed that way, and the fit just differs slightly.

Then damned if when I finished and Freddy laid there relaxed and calm, calm as a cat basking in sunlight with a full tummy, damned if she didn't roll over. She did some sort of twist thing, I saw it coming but couldn't stop it, a neat roll that had me on my back, her on top and her crotch straddling my Clinton. Yes, the President would be happy to meet with you now, Ms. Prime Minister.

"You thought I was kidding," she said, as she pulled down my pants.

"I never know if a woman is kidding or not," I said. "When I think they are, they aren't, and when I think they aren't, they are. I just wait for empirical evidence."

"How's that?" she asked, pulling down my pants and yanking on my cock.

"You're a hell of a jokester," I said. I sighed, and must have done so dramatically.

"Something wrong?"

"I have to ask: Don't you have a partner?"

"Indeed." She licked my penis as if to underline the statement. "I don't have a boyfriend, though. I think a girl is entitled to a boyfriend, don't you?"

"Yeah."

"And you? What about your little love squeeze?"

"Right now I'm a bit confused about that."

Freddy stopped for a moment, looked at me. She pointed over at one corner of the room. "That's yesterday." She pointed to another corner of the room. "That's tomorrow. Live in the present." And she pointed at my chest. Her finger slid down to my belly button, those neatly clipped nails just scratching my skin, then down to my crotch, along the top of my penis, now engorged and hard as a tree, and up to the glans at the tip.

She lowered her face, mouth wide open, eyes wide and lids narrowed, and slid out her tongue. That tongue rolled up the underside of my cock, tracing out the hard blood artery there, circling it and pinching the base, then up again. Freddy licked at my skin, tight and ready to burst, until she had gotten it good and slobbery. Then she took my little devil into her mouth, all the way to her throat, her hot breath blowing on it, sucking in air with her nostrils and out through her mouth. She rode my penis up and down, faster and harder, until it seemed as if I would let loose, only of course I did not on account of that little side effect with my antidepressants.

She stopped. "We got a problem here?" she asked. I told her about the pills. "Ah: I've heard about that side effect, but never had the pleasure." Freddy grinned and went back to work.

Well, "work" was the wrong word. I had to make a slight effort and she certainly seemed to be enjoying herself. It didn't really matter to me if I came or not, since by about the sixth breath she took I'd gone through a dozen solid orgasms. Freddy seemed to want to achieve the big splash, though, and who was I to get in the way of her efforts? Finally, it seemed as if indeed I would come.

"Ah," she said, pulling off my penis and gripping down hard at the base. "Now we milk the one-eyed snake."

She pulled out a clean beaker from beside her bed and set it on my stomach. A few strokes of her hand, another quick lick of that delicious tongue, the most complex muscle in the human body, and I let loose. She steered my cock to that beaker and captured my amazing genetic potential in the glass.

"Hold it," I said, after I caught my breath. "You aren't doing some sort of sick experiment, are you?" I thought of what the aliens had done to me up on the mother craft.

"I'm, uh, just making a collection," she said.

"What, you want me to father your children? We could do it the old fashioned way." I laughed, but I could see she was serious.

"I don't want to know the father," she said. "Or rather, I want to know all the fathers. See, what I have is a bunch of beakers of jizzum, all frozen, and when I'm next fertile, I thaw them all, mix them up, and then it's turkey baster baby."

"No kidding."

"If you want, you can believe I just like to keep my sheets clean."

"I'll go with that." It was too weird to contemplate. How many vials had she collected?

"You're number ten," she said, anticipating my question. "I think I have a good sample. I like your eyes."

"So this has been really for science and the triumph of the human spirit?"

"Well, that," she said, and grinned. "Plus you give one fuck of a massage and I really wanted to blow you." She threw my shirt at me. "You get to shower first. It'll take longer to get off the smell of me."

"I'm not sure I want to."

Freddy shook her head. "Women can smell these things. Believe me, you want to."

*

So now, as they say, I had a problem and some issues to deal with. In the world where one takes responsibility for actions which can cause hurt, I suppose I had to think about how having sex with a fellow worker and housemate could complicate the budding relationship growing with another housemate. Was that house big enough? As I took a long shower, washing off the day's stink and the smell of that woman, I saw the moment pass and could see that for Freddy I might feel lust . . . but for Sarah I felt, well, the prospect of something deeper. With that thought all guilt passed and I moved on to the future, that moment there something to be treasured and not spoken of. Sometimes if you leave things unspoken they actually do not become problems. It's when you can't leave things unspoken and don't, even though you perhaps should, that they become problems. It's not so much Don't Ask, Don't Tell, as Just Shut The Hell Up.

What I had done reminded me of How I Lost My Virginity, now that I thought of it. Despite my libertine ways and a strong desire to get laid, I didn't actually complete coitus with a woman until well into my teens. Part of it was not taking advantage of opportunity. I had been scared shitless, to tell you the truth. There had been Katey, this woman with ice-blue eyes, who one night had clearly shown she wanted to have me, right then and there in the old classic '67 Ford Falcon I drove in high school. Did I take her hints?

No. I just couldn't get past the fear, whatever the fear was that held me back. Fear has often held me back, unidentifiable fear that I had to know before I could overcome it, only, like how the hell could I know it?

It had been Suz who finally deflowered me, and it took weeks of seeking the proper moment. The situation had been complicated: Suz lived with this guy named Zack, only she had grown apart from Zack and sought some distance from him but couldn't quite figure out how to create that distance, and so I had come along. I think she saw me as a way to create that distance, I don't know. We discussed my situation in open and frank terms, partly playing, partly my defense against why I didn't push her in a seduction.

I mean, sometimes when you're with a woman, and you want to have wild screaming sex with her, both of you know that this will be the thing that will happen, but before that can happen, certain rituals must be observed. Often it falls upon the guy to make the move, to initiate the process in which the end result happens. If you lack the experience in initiating the process, then out of honesty the guy has to explain why this is so, which, now that I think about it, is sort of a seduction in itself—an anti-seduction, if you must know.

So Suz and I discussed my situation like the mature adults of 19 that we were, and of course it eventually happened that one night Suz stayed over and blew my virginity. I'd like to say it was a wonderful and celebratory occasion, one that I will look back on with extreme fondness in my old age, except that that's a lousy crock of bullshit. We groped around in darkness and I found the whole fumbling experience embarrassing. Maybe I had expected that this would lead to a long and glorious affair, Suz gently teaching me the wisdom of sex, and the two of us growing closer and more fond of each other until we become partners in the glorious adventure of life.

It didn't happen.

What happened, I remembered as I soaped up my sex-tainted body a second time in that shower on the 'Stead, what happened was that I met Zan. Satisfied that I had succeeded in one of my adolescent goals, the glow of the moment still embarrassing me but also giving me new confidence, I met Zan. She had no baggage, no other relationship she had to consider. Zan set her sights on me, decided I was desirable, decided to seduce me when up until then I had thought it my notion to be the seducer.

Ah! I thought with satisfaction. That had been the code that unfolded a new world of being, just as discovering Earth had been invaded by evil alien Grays had shown me a new truth. A man didn't have to initiate the seduction, he could, in fact, be passive in the process—why hadn't that happened before? It would have made some fumbling moments less awkward. Or perhaps it had been that no women would seduce a virgin, for fear of being pushed into a role she could not occupy, but that she could seduce an almost virgin, that was OK. Fuck if I knew.

What happened, though was that I entered this long and glorious relationship with a willing and able teacher, one younger than I but more experienced, who could teach me new ways. I had become involved with two lovers, two women at the same moment in my life, and comparing Suz and Zan and Freddy and Sarah, I saw the same comparison. I felt no feelings for the former and for the latter, ah, there was the relationship to allow to nourish.

As I toweled myself off, that moment of betrayal now behind me, I understood that there could be no future with Freddy, but with Sarah, ah, the moment held great possibility.

*

Freddy and I drove back into town in contemplative silence, at least contemplative from my end. She had me drive, still a bit buzzed from that growler earlier, not to mention the doobie we'd shared after that incredible hum job, a fact I guess I forget to mention in the excitement of my infidelity. Our silence wasn't one of those bitter silences where much anger gets expressed without actually uttering words. Rather, it was one of those silences where we verified a new deepness in our relationship that would color our future together, and yet—at least this is what I was thinking—not taint relationships with others. And so we went forward into the future.

As we got closer to town, though, Freddy explained the whole First Friday thing.

"Della has this hipwazee artists subculture," she said, "composed mostly of artists but also of consumers, people who fancy themselves Patrons of the Arts, but really, all they like to do is window shop. They're classic Bobos, bohemian bourgeoisie."

"How do you tell the difference?" I asked.

"The usual: the patrons have better teeth and nicer haircuts but the artists have cooler clothes and hipper haircuts. Also, the artists have dirty fingernails."

"Because of their art?"

"Because of their day jobs."

We drove through town and down to the beach, where Twee Sisters was, on a street Sarah said everyone called Bunion Street, on account of it was the only unpaved street in downtown Della. The guy who owned the gallery used to be on the city council, Freddy told me, and somehow he pissed off the head of public works, who took out his revenge by making damn sure in his lifetime Bunion Street would never get paved. So far, it hadn't.

"The gallery crawl always starts at Bunion Street," Freddy said. "Always. It's the rule. They open at five thirty and all the other galleries open at six. Besides, Twee Sisters caters Bunion Street and they have the best nibbles, although Tarpaper will have Della Brew and the What the Hell has oysters if you get there early."

"I thought this was about Art," I said.

Freddy smiled. "It's about free food, free wine, free beer, and flirting. Art is only a by-product."

We had to park on the side of the road up the hill and walk down Main to Bunion, and sure enough, right at the corner, the pavement ended. The gallery building had a B&B, a rare book shop, some greenie organization offices in the basement, Twee Sisters, and an attached Quonset hut shop with a false front as well as the gallery itself. Freddy said that at various times the building had been a general store, a boat shop, a dance hall, a whorehouse, and a Christian Scientist

Reading Room, among other things. Across the street was an RV park with an Airstream trailer convention parked there for the weekend, a hotel down the street, and a Scotch-Irish pub called Nixon's, proudly owned by an unrepentant and distant relative of Tricky Dick Himself.

When we walked up on the porch I made a special effort to let Freddy go ahead of me and to not look too much like I was with her, although I was with her, but not With Her, because as Freddy said, People Will Talk, only the best way to make people talk was to look like you were innocent when you weren't. However, this seemed to have the proper effect on some guy with one of those hard rugged faces that was at the same time soft, and the way he put his arm around Freddy and kissed her on the ear suggested to me that maybe he had made one or two donations to her science project. After the guy finished cleaning out her ear wax, Freddy turned to me and introduced us.

"Jimmo? This is Ren. Ren's an old friend." She winked at him and he winked back. "Jimmo just got in town. He took the aurora room."

"Nick and Jessie are still fighting?"

"Fuck if I know," Freddy said, "but Jimmo and his lady friend needed some house space so we drafted them to be our new tenants."

"Hey," I said, as Sarah came up. "She's not my lady friend." I hugged her, maybe a bit more than usual, but then, our relationship had only begun. "She's my person of the opposite sex with whom I am exploring infinite possibilities."

"Ah," Ren said, "a potswwiaeip."

"How ya doing?" Sarah asked.

"Wonderful." I smiled. I did feel wonderful. The weekend had begun and I could feel myself growing ever fond of the place. "This is Ren. This is Sarah."

Ren eyed her, then smiled. "Nice haircut."

Sarah did that hand-up-the-back thing that drives me crazy and grinned. "You like it? I just had it cut but I'm kinda getting used to it." She took my hand and led me into the gallery.

*

Right off I could tell that a Gray had done the art, cuz the big white paintings on the wall didn't make one bit of sense. A lot of post-modern art—not all of it, but a lot—had been influenced by Grays, bigheads passin' for human who liked to fuck with our brains. They didn't understand art either, except that they understood that humans could create art while they couldn't. Because of that, they tried to punch the limits on art, see how cynical they could be and how much we would buy it. In my resistance cell we used to talk about this, about how Grays screwed around a bit too much with human culture—part of what we called "justification sessions," like we really needed justification for hating aliens who came down to our planet, kidnapped us, gave us anal probes, impregnated our wymmin, mutilated our cattle, and left us quivering mental cases with lifelong nightmares. I mean, on top of that, they screwed around with our art.

What I figgered out, though, was that the Grays who made the art sold their art to other Grays who passed so well as human that the Grays weren't the wiser. Grays gave the money to Grays making art, Grays owned the galleries, Grays ran the grad schools, Grays had pretty much infiltrated the artwazee, except that all they'd done was create a Gray artistic culture, and we were spectators.

WAYS OF WHITE, the exhibit titled itself; and I thought, Oh yeah, I could have fun with this. Over in a cluster of fawning art wannabees I saw the artist: big thick-rimmed black glasses with tinted lenses, the better to hide her almond eyes, and a Dutch Boy bowl cut, hair dyed so dark brown to be almost purple, dressed in tight leather jeans, a black turtleneck, and a gold lame Eisenhower jacket. Oh, and boots, big knee-high riding boots shined to reflective glossiness, the better to hide her leg servos. I glanced at her, grinned, stared right in her eyes, and gave her the sign. You know the sign: touch of the middle finger to the forehead, then tap the ears, it means, Fuck you, I know who you are. The Grays had me pegged since I'd crossed the border. Least I could do was peg 'em back.

"That's the artist," Sarah whispered in my ear. "I met her at Twee Sisters earlier. She keeps a summer place on the cove and lives in Sedona the rest of the year."

Sedona, I thought, Yeah, it makes sense: major alien base down there. "What's all this white shit?" I asked, standing before a canvas four by eight, one of four on a big huge wall.

"Not just white," Sarah said. "Read her statement."

She handed me a sheet of paper (white, of course), with lettering about a shade darker. You had to stare at it for a few minutes before the words appeared, and even then it took some intense squinting to make sense of it all. Something about "all the colors in the universe being pregnant in white" and "white being not the absence of color" (as they say, SIC), "but the impossibility of color." Lotta self-referential crap like that. The artist even had an appropriate name: Wilma White, which I believed for like about five seconds.

What you were s'posed to do, see, was stare at the paintings. Each painting had been measured off in centimeter lines (yeah, metric), each line one percentage more of the color added to the painting: "Magenta on White" or "Cyan on White," whatever. If you looked at the paintings long enough, Wilma said, you'd see the lines blurring into each other, and at the bottom of the painting the white would definitely approach cyan or whatever. So in between noshing and drinking and flirting, the people there stared at the paintings, trying to see the subtle shifts in color.

God, I hate the fucking Grays. How incredibly cynical. At least the food was good.

Chapter 13

After helping to clean out the Twee Sisters canapés at Bunion Street, Freddy, Ren, Sarah, and I made the crawl up the hill to the other galleries. Tarpaper had a show of raku sculpture that pegged the artist as a New Daddy, since every piece showed a clear obsession with infants, like all these casts of baby dolls, except that they had been fried with that quaint little raku glaze that says to me, Oh, I don't know—Dresden. Noshes were wine and discount-warehouse-store taquitos.

Across the street was the What The Hell Gallery, only that wasn't its real name, now that I think about it, but everyone called it that. I never knew its real name. Story of my life. The What The Hell had painted skateboards and foam blocks, actually kind of this hip Mayan glyph style updated for like The Modern Urban Culture, only the artist had done it with Sharpee pens.

I mean, laundry pens. Jesus.

Now, my formal artistic training only goes as far as finger painting in Miss Messina's first grade class back at Lois Elementary School, but I do know art and I do know my aesthetic theory. See, the way I get it is this: art demands two things from the artist, idea and execution. Without idea you don't have execution but without execution you can still have an idea, only the idea won't work as well if you can't tag your way out of the A train to the Bronx. Ideas have to be passable, only so does the execution. I'll take a wild and wonderful idea with mediocre execution over a lame idea with incredible execution. Craft can be acquired but ideas come from the divine.

So this like skateboard chic glyph stuff had a cool idea, although I thought that maybe the glyphs could have been taken further so that they actually meant something, you know? Like this guy had long rectangular blocks with a series of two glyphs a side on it, and I thought, OK, turn it into a game, like dominoes. Only, near as I could tell, they were just glyphs. I hate that.

And execution? You can call yourself an artist, you can draw cute little symbols, you can make quaint illusions to the repressed angst of inner city taggers, and you can even pinch a loaf on the sidewalk and call it chocolate, but if you're gonna do that, at least put some fucking effort into, put some fucking permanence into it. Use paint, I thought.

On the other hand, it was pretty spiff that the glyphs had been ripped straight from the control panels off a Gray mother ship. I stared at the artist while he flirted with some Zapata refugees—slumming Hillaries with nice haircuts—and I could see that he had been recently abducted. I mean, he walked with that pained stride of someone who had recently gotten a butt probe. Poor guy must have stumbled on some serious shit, maybe a cattle mutilation, to get tortured like that. It's why I always carry a tube of KY jelly in my backpack. The Grays might not offer you the grease, but some weird ethical compulsion they have says that if you bring your own, they have to let you use it.

For a moment I thought of maybe going up to the kid, chatting him up a bit, and seeing if he could be a candidate for the Resistance social services. See, in addition to plotting the eventual overthrow of the Alien Occupation Guvmint, the Resistance also has these like goodie-goodie causes, sort of how the Black Panthers had a school lunch program. We can do good *and* recruit new members.

A recent abductee like that kid coulda used some help. OK, you try coming down from a mother ship, ass tender like you'd gone through the cherry busting line at a hard-time prison resort, and for damn sure you'd want someone who had gone through the same hard time to talk to. The Resistance does this all the time. It's how we *became* the Resistance, you know? I was all set to help this kid out when he turned to me, hips swiveling and legs staying planted solid. Then I heard that subtle whine of his servos whirring as he brought his legs around.

Damned Trojan Horse, that was what he was. Sucker bait. The Grays do that sometimes, abduct a victim, work +em over good, and strip them of everything human. I really hated those bastards.

"Let's go," I said to Freddy and Sarah. "Is there like any real art around here?"

Freddy smiled.

"We could go to Surreal's," she said. "He's got a reception up on the Ridge at his studio. Just got back from Jackson."

*

So we all piled into Freddy's Subaru, Ren and Freddy up front, Sarah and I in the back. I took advantage of the relative privacy to swap a little spit with Sarah, you know, a deep throat kiss with just a touch of tongue. Some women hate to kiss, but Sarah there, she had the knack down pat.

"Good day?" I said when we came up for air.

"Not bad." She ran her fingers through her hair, rustling those buzzed hairs at the nape, just driving me wild. We'd fur sure have to check out the Northern Lights again that night. "Twee Sisters is absolutely a hip kind of place to work, you know? Definitely. And you had better be nice to me, because apparently I've been tagged as The New Girl in Town and about six guys hit on me."

"Must of been the hot haircut."

"You think?" She looked down at her braless T-shirt, nipples erect and poking through the fabric in the chill from the breeze blowing through the window.

Freddy took us up a long winding road, through a series of switchbacks that would make a killer chase scene in a Bond movie, and then onto a dusty gravel road. That's the thing about Della: drive five miles out of town in any direction, and toot sweet you come to a dusty gravel road. The houses along there had to be the nicest I'd seen in Della, big cedar sided chalets with those high peak painted-metal roofs and a row of windows facing the bay.

As we turned onto a side road that cut across the ridge, I realized we'd come onto the same road Lilly and Margo had taken me down when we'd first come into Della. The Ridge, right, the bluff above town.

"Surreal is this fucking fine sculptor who gets big one-percent for art commissions," Ren explained from up front. "Like the state law?" I must of given him a blank look, although how he'd tell, I don't know, cuz it's default choice with me. "The state law? One-percent of the construction cost of a state-funded building has to go to art."

"Got it," I said.

"Anyway," Ren went on, "Surreal just installed one of his famous rusty mooses down at a wildlife museum in Jackson. Heard he hooked up with like Harrison Ford's nanny or something and she's come with him to check out Della."

Ford, I thought. Secret resistance fighter. All that Star Wars shit he did? He learned it from us and spoon fed it to Lucas like as these offhand suggestions.

"Except don't go too nuts about the rusty moose stuff," Freddy warned. "It's potboiler work for him. Ask to see his backroom work and he'll be your friend for life. He's really embarrassed about the rusty moose stuff."

As we pulled up, I saw what she meant. Surreal had this big studio right on the road. It must of been a big 'do cuz there were all these cars parked up and down the road, except they parked on only one side so at least you could pass by. Fucking damn polite, I thought, one of the things I was beginning to like about Della. In a big field just mowed for hay all these life size rusty moose looked to be grazing in the grass. Off on the left, a rusty bear watched them. There were a bunch of rusty dogs around the edge, mostly beagles, yeah, a damn wildlife tableau.

"In the fall, during moose season, drunk hunters like to fire away at the moose," Freddy said. "Surreal will sometimes put blaze orange vests on them, like that works."

"What's with the dogs?" I asked.

"He had an old girlfriend who had a beagle, so he made a sculpture of it. Then everyone wanted one of their dog, so he did that for a while to pay the bills. Some people didn't pay up, and he got stuck with the dogs. Calls it his 'team' and takes +em up every year to Fur Rondy in Anchorage as this like tourist photo op thing."

We had to park about sixty cars down the road, a really big party I could see, but fuck, that was what I was there for, to hang with Delloids. Of course, fifty of the cars were Subarus. You want to be anonymous in Della, drive a Subaru, like I've said once or twice. Six of them were pale blue and all the rest were maroon.

When we got closer to the studio, I could see how the sculpture worked. What Surreal did was, he took big sheets of metal that was allowed to rust and he banged away at it until he made this like shell of a critter. He didn't do all one piece, maybe a dozen or so pieces, like a tube-shaped piece would be a leg, another the head, and so on. I could see how in twilight a hunter might shoot the moose. It looked like a moose but then it didn't, which was sort of the idea.

"See, he kinda got caught in this rut," Ren said. "It happens, like a writer will do this character, say, the Nick Hughes mystery series—you know that author—and he just means to do one book while he's working on his big novel about a kid growing up in Florida. Only, the series takes off and the publisher wants another one, and next thing you know, so much for the big novel about the kid growing up in Florida."

Right, I thought. Another example of how the alien corrupted publishing industry has fucked with modern literature.

"See, Surreal got this commission for a school up in Anchorage, sort of a joke, a rusty moose. Then he bid on another one-percent project, something to do with 'the cosmic permutations of brain folds,' and the art committee said, 'Weird, but could you do one of those rusty moose?' Well, he'd done the rusty moose, so he pitched them a rusty bear, and they went for it. He's been working his way through the major Alaska mammals since then. Right now he's been reduced to whistling marmots. That's tonight's reception: a pack of whistling marmots for a school up in Talkeetna."

As we came up the path to Surreal's studio, I could see where all the artwazee had wound up and why things had quieted down at the galleries. Everyone seemed to have come here. The party spilled out the front door of the studio, jammed these big bays where Surreal whanged away on his stuff, and down an alder-choked path to Surreal's house and the other studio. It took us about fifteen minutes to make our way to the beer and the food, which is where you always go first at a party, because Freddy and Ren kept running into people and chatting, and then they'd have to introduce us, which pissed me off, because either it was a guy, who would hit on Sarah, or it would be a womyn, who would hit on me, or maybe a womyn hitting on Sarah, but never mind, cuz I would forget their names in about a minute anyway.

On top of that, I had to challenge my fidelity issues, because some of those Delloid babes were pretty damn hot, let me tell you. Alaska is s'posed to be like this place where there are ten good men for every woman and a woman can have her pick, but no one told the Delloid women that. It looked to be the other way around. Or maybe Della was where Alaskan women went when they'd used up all the men. Freddy said that sometimes women came to Della to get away from men, and I could believe that, because I had never seen so many lezzies in one spot, I mean open, swapping spit and pawing themselves lezzies, and damn were they hot. Made me want to be a lesbian myself. We're not talking the baggy olive drab Army pants crowd, either, but lesbians in tight little biker shorts or leather mini-skirts.

Plus, while some of the Delloid womyn were a bit over 35 or even 40, they had that look that said, "Hon, don't mess with some little young tart who doesn't know her way in life. You want me." I could see it in their crow-feet eyes, their hair gone slightly dull, their faces lined with experience, and none of that mattered, because these were women who knew a good man because they'd been burned by all the bad ones. Young women don't know shit. Guys, you want a women who can appreciate you, don't mess with anything under 35.

Only, there I was, slouching toward 30 or 40 (I can't really say what with the way the aliens have scrambled my brain, body, and birth records), and I was hanging with someone

20ish. I can explain: I firmly believe in cognitive dissonance as one of life's guiding principles.

Well, eventually we made it to the bar, where we met Surreal. I couldn't pin his age down either, something I had noticed about Delloids. After 30 they hit this almost ageless period where they could be anything from 35 to 55 and more or less look the same. They had wrinkles and dyed hair and sagging butts, but you couldn't quite figure out the precise age from that anymore than you could age a big tree without cutting it down and counting rings.

It wasn't just age, though, but that some Delloids became ageless. They might have old bodies but not old minds. Maybe some of the guys had gotten in a sort of Never Never Land where they refused to grow up. Or maybe, like me, they had been abducted by aliens and been given the old cell retrofit, where you got a bit ragged and stuck at 45, and never grew older. When I say I'm in this for the long haul, I mean, The Long Haul.

Surreal had a big bushy mustache and rebar-tie hair that went every which direction but south, and he must of been sanding those rusty mammals recently, cuz his hair looked rusty, too. Just to keep Sarah flattered, he hit on her, only Freddy later told me to watch out, because Surreal had been through about six long-term relationships, although you had to give him credit because he kept his rubbers snapped tight and didn't bring in any more kids in the world. Freddy said a few Delloid guys had this like habit of knocking up women, "could knock up a lava lamp with a shit eatin' grin," was the way she put it. Not Surreal though, although he collected women the way some guys collect antique fishing lures.

"So I hear you've been workin' on some new stuff," I told Surreal, just to chat him up.

"Yeah, the marmot troupe. A couple of the gang and I are going to install it up in Talkeetna next week if you want to come along."

"Maybe. No, I don't mean that. What about your backroom stuff?"

Surreal shot a glance over at Ren. "You tell him to ask that?"

Ren shrugged, gave him that sweet boy look I noticed he'd been practicing on Freddy a lot. Practiced on a lot of women, I'd noticed, too. And men. Dogs. Slow moving moose. He was a charmer, all right.

"What can I say?"

"Well, shit, doesn't matter. I appreciate the question." Surreal looked around. "There's this dumb fuck reporter from the Trib asking me a bunch of stupid questions. He can't see the backroom stuff. OK, coast is clear. Come this way."

Surreal led us out onto the deck behind his inside studio (as opposed to his outside studio where he banged away on shit) and down a path through some alders that looked liked they'd moved in after the last glaciation, and into a clearing.

"It's still the rusty metal crap, because I really like that rusty metal crap. Love that patina of iron oxide. Only, well—look for yourself."

Surreal pulled back an alder branch, and we stepped into the middle of it. The early evening sun hit the sculptures just right, not quite shining on it, not under it, but through it, as if the steel collected the light and released it slowly. Arrayed in a rough spiral were about two dozen sculptures, some maybe ten feet across, others only a few feet wide, all of steel hammered so thin as to almost be transparent, but not thin enough that they didn't support their own weight.

The steel had been folded, hammered, folded again, and then almost shaken out into the wind, only the folds had frozen. Some pieces stood balanced on one point, a square sheet rippling out from that contact, while others rolled over in ripples and made little arches. Some seemed to hang suspended in air, and then I realized they did, on slender cables hanging from a nearby dead spruce. I had to stare at it a while until I understood what I saw.

"The aurora," I said, and then looked more closely. "Only, as seen from space."

"Yeah," said Surreal, and he gave me a funny look, then snapped the Resistance sign at me, so fast I almost didn't notice.

"But of course you had to speculate," Freddy said. "I mean, look at photographs taken from satellites, whatever."

"Of course," Surreal said, looking my way again.

I stared at him again, stared at his legs, and listened for the servos. No, I thought, he wasn't fake. He was the real thing. And so were those auroras, just like I'd seen them once, the only good thing that had ever come from being abducted by aliens. He had it dead on. It was the real thing, all right, art out of this world.

Or, at least, out of this atmosphere.

Chapter 14

Well, now that I'd seen some real art, I mean, art not created by poseurs corrupted by aliens or who *were* aliens, I could go home. Things got kinda wild and crazy up there on the Ridge at Surreal's, and as much as I hate to leave a good party—and things had developed into one kick-butt party—Sarah had to pull the early shift the next morning at Twee Sisters. Freddy and I had the weekend off, only, you know when you hit 30 or 40, weekends begin to look like time to recover from work and not time to play so hard you can't work. Old age: it's a bitch.

So Ren drove us all back down the hill and out east to the manse. Truth to tell, I looked forward to snuggling with Sarah and the way Freddy nuzzled Ren up there in the front of the Sube, I figured she might be hitting him up for a donation to her sperm collection. Hey, I could see that: he had nice bones in his face. So we dragged our sorry butts into our respective domiciles, coupling up, and went to bed.

The way the walls banged, I'm pretty sure Ren and Freddy screwed like minks. I know we did.

*

So Saturday morning came and went and just before noon, so I couldn't be tagged as totally decadent, I roused myself up and slouched down to the 'Stead great room. Sarah had already gone to work, and we weekday, nine-to-five grunts hung around in the big room downstairs contemplating adventures. Freddy and Ren had the workings of a megaomelet and a pot of home fries going, Barry had fired up the espresso machine, and all seemed well. There had been some talk earlier of doing a long beach walk on the low tide, except that most of us had slept through that, so with a huge high tide coming up that evening, the idea tossed around was to go kayaking.

The 'Stead had a fleet of kayaks out back, in a huge barn with three tiers high of them including a ten-seater bidarka made of aircraft tubing and hyplar that this guy George had built the last time he passed through Della. Most of the kayaks were singles, but there were a few doubles and one triple, either homemade of strip planking or stitch-'n'-glue marine plywood, or store bought plastic or fiberglass. One kayak broke down into three pieces and another could be packed into a big duffle bag. I mean, the 'Stead had kayaks, all right.

So the plan was that after Sarah got off work, we'd have a little snack—nothing too filling because you didn't want to kayak on a full stomach—haul the kayaks down to the beach and launch on the tide. Freddy said kayaking in the Bay, at least the north side, worked best if you had a high tide and the day breeze had slacked down, on account of, well, on account of the waves had fallen to gentle rolling swells that wouldn't pitch a kayak right over. This seemed important to me.

Now, what with that tour I did with the Seals as part of my training for Delta Force and the deep cover job that sorta resulted in me getting a red-cover passport, well, I'd learned how to be on the water. OK, I could do the frogman thing, the dashing in the night in rubber boats stuff, even the slipping into shore on a heavy surf hoo-yah. Only the Seals, or at least the unit I trained with, worked in Hawaii, on a nice warm beach with nice warm seas and even though we wore wet suits, cuz they made us look all manly and tough, we didn't need to. Well, we needed to if we didn't want our balls to shrivel up into little dried grapes, but I mean, that Hawaiian water, if you ever have to train to do secret commando-type stuff that involves a full-body immersion, take my advice: stick to the tropics.

Did I mention that in Della the water never got warmer than about 52 degrees fucking Fahrenheit?

So the idea, the very idea of putting my ass into a little boat with maybe two inches of freeboard, surrounded by scrotum-tightening cold water, and paddling out six miles from shore didn't really excite me. Never mind that that water was flat as a politician's promise six months after an election. Paddling out into it didn't really excite me. Did I say that?

Not that I admitted this, of course. Sarah was all hot to go out on the water, said she had been just dying to go kayaking since she got to Della, why, she had been kayaking all her life and a little cold water didn't bother her a bit, not at all. What could I do? I went out with her, in one of those doubles, and out of consideration for her skills and so as to avoid pulling that macho know-it-all shit, I took the bow seat and she took the stern, the one with the foot pedals for the rudder.

So Freddy and Ren went out in two singles, Sarah and I in the double, Barry in a single, and then we called up Grace from work and she came out in her own little custom single. We launched on the tide, a bit complicated cuz you have to crawl into the kayak, get situated, snap on your spray skirt, and do this all the while the damn thing is bobbing in a little surf and your paddle is hanging half on the deck. Grace proceeded to zip into her kayak without a hitch, paddle out into deeper water, and start doing Eskimo rolls, just to show off, I think. She had a wet suit top and even a cap, just to keep that 'do dry, there ya go.

Finally, though, we got everyone in the boats and lined up and began paddling across toward the Spit. Grace led, or rather, paddled ahead, and kept turning around and paddling back to keep us going, like a goddamn border collie.

It took me a while to remember how to paddle with those double-blade kayak paddles, something easier done once I remembered which side was up and which side was down. Look, those blades are sort of shaped like golf clubs, and it's not immediately obvious which end goes down. My hands got wet almost right away, but I had on these neoprene gloves that in theory kept me warm. Well, once the water and stuff in the gloves warms up to body temperature, which took a while.

Sarah paddled two strokes to my every one. I had to figure out her rhythm, was what is was, and soon we got paddling more or less in sync. She kept steering us away from the Spit, until I realized she pointed the kayak into a slight roll of waves blowing in off the head of the bay.

After all that fussing and training and stuff, I didn't even notice that we had paddled well out from shore, out there with the murres and the otters, and by the time I had, I found myself enjoying it so damn much my fear of water completely escaped me.

Except for the fact that I realized I hadn't thought of aliens ever since I got on the water, I don't want to say I thought about the AOG all the time and all that, and how the Revolution had to get its butt in gear if we were going to kick those Goddamn Grays off the planet, I mean, it wasn't like I obsessed about it every waking moment of my day. I did think about the Grays a lot, though, I have to admit, particularly since my days in Della had been taken up with trying to keep them from offing me.

Out on that water, though, I felt peace. Serenity. It was as if the flat calm of the bay calmed me, relaxed me, so that I could be there then, in the here and now, focused on a purely simple activity, not a care in the world. Isn't that the idea?

Out there on the bay, low to the water in human-powered boats, the critters accepted us. Great rafts of murres would bob around us as we paddled through, only diving if we got like a foot near them. Flying, the flocks of murres would come right up to us, a foot or two off the water, creating a ground effect where they skimmed off the water as much as flew through the air. If we got in the way of flying murres, *fhwip*, they'd part as they passed us, flying on either side, and then regroup.

We would pass by sea otters sleeping on their backs, basking in the evening sun, totally calm as we paddled by. There seemed to be a safety zone of tolerance, sort of their own personal otter space on the bay. Only once did we intrude on that, and the otter didn't panic or anything, it just rolled over and dove under the water, popping back up when we passed by.

I can't remember how long it took to get past the Spit, but it didn't seem too long, maybe half an hour. We kept clear of the harbor and all the boats and paddled on by, heading toward this island off another few miles in the bay, Gull

Island. I could see it in the distance, sort of a whitish hump. Sarah kept us on that mark, Grace leading, of course. We'd gotten out in the open water, well off shore, except that I didn't dare look back because I couldn't really turn around anyway, and if I tried, the kayak sort of wobbled.

Now I realized that kayaking became one of those methodical physical activities, like hiking or biking, where you could fall into the effort and close your mind to everything else. It became a meditative act, you know, stroke, paddle, stroke, breath, and so on. I became one with the water, one with the murres, one with the otters, my only object of focus that island ahead.

I don't know how long it took, but soon enough, I began to hear the island, then saw a cloud of birds flocking about it. I don't think I've ever heard so many birds, thousands of them, murres and gulls and puffins and cormorants, an entire breeding colony. First you heard them, then you saw them, and eventually, when you got really close, you smelled them.

Imagine 5,000 birds all nesting and eating, chowing down on little fish and krill and plants and stuff, and then shitting all that digested guano onto one huge rock and two smaller ones, no more than an acre of land with perhaps four birds to the square foot. It didn't just smell, it didn't just reek, it positively and absolutely stank. I almost gagged, but then the way you get used to a sore muscle or a nagging blister, the brain adjusts and blocks out the smell so that it's tolerable. This is the thing about human experience: even the nastiest things can be made tolerable, something which has both saved us as a species and prevented us from evolving to a higher level.

As we came close to the island, I could make order out of chaos. What seemed to be a cloud of unidentifiable birds became whirling flocks of murres, mostly, or gulls, predominantly, with a tufted or horned puffin there for some flashy color, these spots of orange whirling in the maelstrom. Long necked cormorants, elegant in their perches, awkward in flight, swooped down on us. I'd worn my gimme hat to keep my dreads out of my eyes, and good thing, too, because I got bombed twice, once on my crown and another on the bill. Our kayaks looked like we'd taken a mortar salvo, the decks splattered white with guano.

We moved silently around the big island and between one of the smaller ones, looking up at the little colonies: puffins on the grassy part, in burrows; murres on the ledges; cormorants on more prominent points; gulls everywhere. Feathers littered the water, and sometimes we'd pass by whole wings, as if a gull had flown so hard its wings had fallen off.

If the noise had seemed deafening before, all of a sudden it increased in intensity, and great clouds of birds soared up. It was as if someone dialed up the nesting switch from "mostly loud" to "garage band." Grace pointed up, and I saw the source of the disquiet: a single bald eagle, gliding on an updraft, searching for the one bird of thousands that it would take. Who knew how the eagle chose, and who knew why the Grays would abduct someone like me? The eagle tucked in its wings, dove, then spread its wings and snatched a small kittiwake gull out of midair. Even in all the chaos, it seemed that I could hear the snap as the eagle broke the bird's back. The eagle flapped away toward the other side of the bay to feed in relative peace.

It took a while for the birds to quiet down. I imagined them like spectators at a car crash, looking at the tragedy and murmuring how horrible, how horrible, that poor kittiwake, and then after the appropriate expression of sympathy, schaudenfreude, they thought, I'm glad it wasn't me.

Our little flotilla did a wide circuit of the islands, Grace leading us through a rock tunnel exposed by the tide going out. We rafted up together, our five little boats, and rested. I drank from a water bottle lashed to the deck of the kayak, the neck of the bottle salty from where spray had splashed on it, then passed the bottle back to Sarah. We chewed on energy bars or gorp, gathering our strength for the trip back. Pointed toward the Spit and Della, I could see how far we had come and suddenly felt vulnerable. Sarah pointed to her watch, and said something about the tide going out and how it would be a long walk back through the mud off the 'Stead beach when we returned if we didn't start a move on.

So once again we got back into the Zen of paddling, eyes now focused on the Spit and the buildings that seemed like doll houses. Soon the smell became less and then the sound less, and we were alone out there in the bay, back among the murres and the otters. I could hear the distant thrum of a big fishing tender heading back in. A slight swell rolled under us. Our rhythm changed to match the swell, paddling forward as it rose up, relaxing slightly as we rode with the swell and zoomed down its slight face, then paddling harder with the next wave.

Power boats passed us, water taxis making the last run for the night, or a tour boat heading back from the Cove with the passengers from the nightly seating at that little restaurant there. The bigger boats gave us room, steering well clear of us so their wakes wouldn't swamp us.

About two miles out from the Spit, all of sudden Grace paddled hard to her left. I couldn't quite see what she was doing, or why, but Sarah followed her lead. One little dot ahead became bigger, this sound like the mean whining of a mosquito preceding it. It came right on us, within ten yards, swerving back and forth. Grace waved her paddle back and forth, the white tips catching the sunlight, but the little boat kept at us. She turned harder into its wake. Between my paddling and Sarah's steering, we got turned into the wake, too. As the boat came up to us, Sarah cursed from behind me.

"Goddamn fucking jet ski," she said.

For such a tiny thing, it sure kicked up a wake. We had our bows pointed into it, every one of us, and rode over the wake. Still, the wake washed over the top of our deck and over me. I hadn't cinched my spray skirt real tight, so some of the water rolled down into the cockpit and onto me, drenching my pants and pooling in the bottom of the seat, Goddamn it.

After the jet ski motored on, we straightened out again, making our course back to the Spit. I heard the boat zoom away and thought no more of it once it had gone. We'd paddled maybe another half mile, though, when I heard it again. I saw Grace and Barry turn in the singles ahead. The damn thing was going to buzz us again. I could feel Sarah turning our boat around, but that big double didn't move as fast. I dug in with my paddle, the sun behind me and casting a glare on the water. I turned to look for the jet ski, when out of nowhere the fucking thing came, right on top of us. It must have been aikido instinct, I don't know, but that damn thing rode right up on our kayak, between Sarah and me, and as it came up, I raised my paddle. I laid the left blade of my paddle down in the water, steadying the port side, and the right blade came up and smacked the jet skier right in the throat. It took him off his jet ski and he fell backwards into the water. I heard a sharp crack as either my paddle hit the jet skier or the jet ski hit our kayak.

The jet ski kept going on its own momentum, but it had a dead-man switch and the engine shut off after the driver let go. As the jet ski hit our kayak, we rolled over to the left, then bobbed back and rolled to my right. I must have swung with the paddle when I hit the jet skier, because I then rolled toward him. Sarah had put her weight to our left, slapping her paddle flat on the water and bracing with it. That kept the big double from rolling—they're damn near hard to roll anyway—but it meant that I kept going, following my paddle forward and into the water.

My skirt should have kept me in, except that I hadn't tightened it much, or must have worked it loose, so I fell out. When I hit the water, it felt like this big frozen polar bear, fur dripping wet, had come up to me and given me a death hug. I lost my breath and my lungs went cold, my entire body went cold, and for a moment I felt as if I had ceased to be. My life jacket brought me to the surface and I got my head out of the water. I still had my paddle gripped tight in my hands, though. Off to my right I saw the jet skier bobbing in the water, his face down. I could reach him with my paddle, and empathy took over for revenge and I pushed his head back with the tip of my paddle. He then floated face up, totally out and dead for all I knew, but in no immediate danger of dying.

I sucked in big gasps of air, warm air, warmer than the water, and that seemed to get my core temperature up a degree or two. Grace had turned her kayak and so did Ren, Freddy, and Barry. I looked back and saw Sarah still in the double, paddling toward me, but she had a hard go of it. When I had done a wet exit, water had come in the bow and the bow sank under almost totally. The deck had split across the hard plastic, a gouge between the two seats. A little lower and that jet ski would have cut off Sarah's legs.

I couldn't get back to my boat, couldn't get into any of the singles of course. Freddy came up to me, though, so I held on to her stern while we figured out what to do. Ren had paddled over to the jet skier and stayed with him. He yelled something about the guy not breathing, or trying to breathe, I couldn't hear. Grace got close to Sarah, pulled up alongside while Sarah kept the kayaks rafted together. Pulling out this big hand bilge pump, Sarah started pumping water out of the bow of the double. Slowly, more stable now, the boat rose up. I remembered that it had a forward hatch and compartment, sealed off from the rest of the boat, and that gave it more buoyancy.

"Get the jet ski," Freddy said to me.

I looked up and realized the jet ski was drifting toward us. Of course, I thought. Get out of the damn water. It was a three seater, big and long, and amazingly stable, although at that point a drifting log would have seemed stable to me. I let go of Freddy's kayak and swam to it, sliding aboard without any trouble.

The engine still ran, a slight throb rumbling under the seat, some warmth from it offering me comfort. I turned the throttled and the engine engaged. I gave it a little gas, felt it shoot forward, then backed off so I wouldn't swamp anyone. I turned the jet ski back to the kayaks.

Despite Grace's heroic pumping, the double had taken on more water. We could all see that if Sarah stayed in it, the boat would go down. Maybe the airtight compartments aft and forward would keep the kayak itself afloat, but not with Sarah's weight. She'd have to bail out, too.

"Unsnap your spray skirt," Grace said to Sarah as I came up to her on the other side. Sarah nodded, pulled loose. What freeboard she had she lost when the spray skirt came undone and the water became flowing over the cockpit coaming. "Get out now!" Grace yelled.

Sarah slid out, into the water between the jet ski and the kayak, and then in one slick move, rolled up onto the jet ski. She got behind me onto the seat, totally drenched, but in the water no more than five seconds. She clung to me for warmth, not that I had anything left to spare. Out of the water, though, the foam in our vests started to warm us up.

With Sarah out of the kayak, Grace begun pumping again, and she got enough water out of it that it stayed afloat. With the bow cockpit pumped above the water, and Sarah's cockpit back above the waterline, we could see the crack in the deck was above the water now. It would stay afloat, at least long enough to be towed ashore.

"What about the jet skier?" I asked Grace.

"Leave him be," she said.

"No, we can't do that," Ren said. He looked to his right and we saw a water taxi moving along, not really noticing us. Ren reached into his life vest, though, and popped two flares. Immediately this big orange water taxi came our way, arriving in about 30 seconds.

"What happened?" the captain said, a huge guy with a salt and pepper beard and a black beret. I could read his company name then, Draco's Water Taxi. Draco glared at us, then realized by our floppy spray skirts that we weren't jet skiers, then looked at the guy in the water.

"Jet ski rode right over the double," Grace said. "Jimmo must have hit him with his paddle, and he fell into the water."

"Fucker," Draco said. "Serve him right if we just left him." But he sighed, shook his head, and reached down with one arm and pulled the jet skier into his boat. As Draco pulled the guy out of the water, I saw his stumpy legs. His chin-length wet hair had stayed plastered to his head, and it looked like the jet skier had an ear burned off. I knew better, though: A Gray.

One of Draco's passengers laid the jet skier out on the deck. I couldn't see him anymore, but the passenger motioned to Draco and said something about a crushed throat.

Draco turned urgently to the guy, then back to us. "Can you tow that kayak back yourself? I'll get on the radio and get some help, but I'd better get this guy back."

We waved him on. Sarah and Ren started rigging a line to the double kayak up to the jet ski. Sarah had gained some strength and turned to help them. We got a towing line set up. It took me a while to figure out a good speed, not too fast, not too slow, but soon enough I had the jet ski moving at the right pace and the kayak towing easily behind us. I waved back at the rest of them and headed toward the harbor.

Chapter 15

Back at the harbor, I had to deal with all that cop crap again, you know, this jet skier, when it came down upon you, split your kayak almost in half, and damn near drowned you, did you happen to notice if he looked drunk? No, but I did notice he had a mole above his left eye. Sheesh. Cops want you to be like Mr. Perfect Recall sometimes.

Anyway, we got all that sorted out. I turned the jet ski over to the authorities—Grace wanted to burn the sucker, but I talked her out of it on account of all the nasty pollutants it would throw off—and we got the kayaks and gear all sorted out. We'd wound up across Mud Bay from the 'Stead, so Barry had to hitch over and get his truck and kayak trailer, and then come back, which took an hour or so. That was OK, though, what with dealing with the cops and all.

Some EMTs had already taken the fucking jet skier up to the hospital, and then some others wanted to check us out and all, even said maybe we should go into the hospital for like a check up, but screw that. The only damn thing wrong with me or Sarah was that we were cold, and a couple of hours in the 'Stead's sauna would take care of that.

Which it did. The sauna and hypothermia, I mean.

Later that day, after we'd warmed up in the sauna and worked over the jet ski assault back at the 'Stead, I walked down to the beach to look for a kayak paddle that had gotten lost in the chaos. A good southwest blew up that evening, and I thought the waves might blow it in. OK, I didn't really think that. Truth was, I had to clear my head a bit.

A dip of land maybe a mile wide flowed down to the beach there below the 'Stead, so that if you looked at the complex from the bay, you'd see low bluffs in the middle from where the 'Stead is and starting to rise up heading east, until about 20 miles up the bay the bluffs rose a good 1,000 feet. You had great view property out there, just not good beachfront property. On the other hand, considering how fast those bluffs eroded, that might not have been a bad thing.

The Spit protected the 'Stead side of the bay from the open water, hundreds of miles of water hurtling up from the Gulf of Alaska and lower Cook Inlet. Where the 'Stead faced the bay, the lee of the Spit petered out, so anything whipping across against the Spit hit the 'Stead beach full on. The sea had to make a curve around the Spit and the bay, though, so it wasn't as if the beach got a full assault. Enough of one, though.

I worked my way down to the high tide line, that day's stretch of wrack washed up on the beach. A good beachcomber knows to walk the wrack line, on either side depending on the light, and stare down at it, not so much looking as being open to discovery. You found things that way, looking by not looking. As with beachcombing, so in love, I guess.

Not that it would be hard to miss a kayak paddle, mind. Still, when you looked for the obvious it didn't hurt to look for the mysterious. The other thing, if you look for trash, I mean, just look to pick up crap that looks like trash and you figure you'll pick it up because it is trash, sometimes you find good stuff. Some of the trash turns out to be good stuff and sometimes while looking for trash the good stuff turns up.

It's like archaeology. Back in college, I did a summer semester working on a dig somewhere in the ass end boonies of Florida, one of those rare hunks of beaches the developers haven't fucked up. A state park, actually, on the north end of—well, for security reasons, I can't reveal the actual place. You'd know it if I told you, because all these rich fart Yankees go down there every winter and clutter the place up with their stupid Mercedes convertibles and their ugly pastel polo shirts and their fake-and-bake tans they top off with a few days of roasting on the beaches in their Speedos and gold lame bikinis.

Anyway, this dig had a bunch of us college students, a few grad students as crew bosses, and some professors—"principal investigators," they called themselves—who spent the heat of the day sleeping and then who'd come out in the evening and grace us with their presence. We did all the work, the crew bosses kept things running, and the PIs got all the glory, just like in the military.

Or maybe on the plantation. Hey, it wasn't PC or anything, but since we were all lily white college students with great haircuts and good teeth, we joked and called each other "diggeroes." Get it? So the massa was the PI and we were the field hands.

I quickly learned archaeology, just like combat, consisted of hours of mind—numbing tedious work punctuated by moments of glory. The old Calusa Indians once lived on the beach site, like everywhere else in coastal Florida, and what they liked to do was fish, hunt, and eat shellfish. Lots and lots of shellfish. You could tell they had these big clambakes going for like generations, because in the middle we found a hearth as big as Detroit and around it a circle of shells like the Beltway around D.C. We even called it the Beltway. Palmettos and grasses and shit like that grew up on the huge ring, and it looked sorta neat, with a hole where you walked through it to the big firepit and this doughnut-shaped mound about six feet high around it.

We diggeroes did some test pits in the Beltway, cutting trenches into them at a few spots down to where the old ground once had been, "sterile" is what those arkies called it. At dawn we had a quick breakfast, hustled our butts out to the site, and dug until noon or the temperature hit 95, whichever came first. You hadda wear shorts and kneepads cause those shells would rip your skin to shreds, but most of us went shirtless and worked on our tans. We were s'posed to use at least SPF 25 sunscreen, but a lot of us used 15 or less. We were young. Skin cancer was but a distant horror.

No one really expected to find anything in those shells middens except, well, shells. Data is data, though, so we dug through the midden layer by layer, centimeter by centimeter, bagging all the shells in one big pile, then sifting through it later in case there would be like beads or shit in it. Each bag of shells got randomly sampled by the lab rats who sorted and identified the shells by species, and then sometimes an entire pit would be sorted and identified, kind of a random sample of a random sample. How the hell you told one species apart from another with all this cracked and broken shell, fuck if I know. That's what a PhD is for, I guess.

Sometimes, though, sometimes while digging through all that shit, with this fine white dust and sand on everything, sometimes you'd fine something really cool, I mean, just amazing. One time I had gotten all the way through my pit, I mean, a whole meter square and about three meters deep, almost to sterile, and I found this carved rock, an amulet.

I almost threw it into the discard pile to be sifted through later, only something about it stopped me. The shape didn't look right or something. That was the gift of archaeology, how you knew you could do it or not, when you could scrape away with your trowel for hours—days, even—your mind on autopilot, and then come across something that just didn't look right.

My dad used to do that looking at X-rays. He was a chest guy, a respiratory specialist, and the state would give him these fat rolls of X-rays, burned on film with hundreds of images taken at the state TB hospitals, decades of people with chests like calcified cotton candy. Dad would zip through them, whip, whip, the images flying, looking for I don't know, some white spot on a lung for some research study he did. Whip, whip, and then he'd stop, look at the image, make a note, then whip, whip, whip again, dozens of images zipping by and he'd stop again.

So there I was, peeling back shells, picking them up with fingers in leather gloves, tossing them in the pile, and the artifact popped up. I paused, about to toss it, paused again, left it in situ, as we say, and gently blew away dust and sand from around it. As I did that, the image came forth, upside down so I didn't see it right away, but I could tell, some human made this, it wasn't just a rock.

You're never, never supposed to pick up an artifact before sketching it, maybe even photographing it, and at least measuring it, but I couldn't resist. I memorized its location, gently pulled it loose from the sand and dust surrounding it, and held it to the light.

You know that game where you set up a row of dominoes to collapse in one of those complicated patterns? Pulling an artifact out of its resting place is like that. The dominoes fall, and time unfolds. In that brief moment it feels like the present and past are connected, not separate, but an entire continuum, and pulling the artifact out of where it has laid for hundreds or thousands of years stretches that continuum, and then it breaks.

Once when I was up on the mother ship the Grays explained to me that was how space travel worked. Where you were and where you wanted to be were separated in time and distance, but really, just time, and when like the hyperdrives or whatever they called it kicked in, the time between Point A and Point B got compressed, so all you had to do to get from A to B was take a little step—in the case of those mother ships the size of small asteroids, push them forward about one millimeter, which was a lot of shoving but not that much. Once you'd taken that step, you could let time uncompress again and you had moved incredible distances, and only that brief moment of time to make the tiny baby step happened, and there you were. It took care of a lot of paradoxes.

So that's what it felt like when I pulled up the artifact. I turned it over, top and bottom, back and front, side to side, looking at it until I understood what it was. It wasn't until years later, when I met my first Gray and had been abducted for the first time, that I knew what I had seen. The artifact had a woman's body, a classic Venus shape, big hips, incised V for vagina, big breasts, and on top of the Calusa Venus, the big eyes and V-shaped head of a Gray. Only back then everyone said it was a snake woman, some mystical mumbo-jumbo Calusa goddess that at least one of the grad students turned into a doctoral dissertation.

And I'd found it.

OK, beachcombing could be like that, only you found glass floats, lightning-bolt sandals adrift for years, pale orange plastic floats with Japanese kanji, or the bones of a kayaker lost at sea. The usual wrack of the ocean.

Anyways, I thought of these things as I walked up toward the head of the bay. Like I said, I wasn't thinking about finding that paddle so much as getting away from everyone and sussing out where I'd been, how I got there, what I'd do next, and how come in three days I felt like every time I fucking turned around some Gray wanted to attack me.

So I saw this guy walking my way, and right off I noticed something different about him. Maybe it was the big fawn wolfhound-mix dog loping next to him, like my old buddy Roscoe. Maybe it was the way he stared ahead about ten feet in front of him, not even aware I was in front of him. Maybe it was the shock of bright blue hair cut short on his forehead, contrasting with his long gray hair. Or maybe it was that he had like six bags of trash strapped to his backpack, including a big canvas bag on his hip belt. He had one of those high-tech trekking poles in one hand, and in the other, well, a kayak paddle. Hanging over one shoulder like a bandolier was a string of green and blue and orange fishing floats.

The dog woofed as I got nearer, and at the sound, the guy looked up. It was kinda creepy, because he had a baby smooth face, not a wrinkle on it, clean shaven and in sharp contrast to his gray hair, which made me wonder if he dyed it. Later that night, when Max joined us for a sauna up at the 'Stead and I saw the gray fuzz covering his crotch, I realized he was a natural gray. I mean, gray like in body hair, not alien.

"Hey," I said. "How's it going?"

"Cool." He looked at me kinda funny, then smiled. "Way cool."

"You find that kayak paddle on the beach?"

"About a mile up. It yours?"

"A friend's, I think. Does it say 'Fredricka' on it?"

The guy turned it up, looked at one blade, sort of blushed a little. "Sure enough." I held out my hand to take it, but he held it back. "Ah. Salvage rights. You'll have to pay my salvage fee."

"Hey, you could just be nice."

"It's a cheap fee," he said. "Tell me a story."

"A story?"

"Yeah. I collect beach junk, and I collect stories. From the junk I make, well, stuff, and from the stories, well, other stories."

"You a writer?" I asked. Crap, I hoped not. Writers were notorious liars, and I could never trust them.

"A writer is too simple a description," he said. "But it's simple enough. The name's"—and he told me his name, which surprised me, because when I was in college I had read every one of his books, which wasn't a hell of a lot anyway—"and this is my dog, Fraze." Max handed me the paddle. "Max" wasn't really his name, but for like security purposes, I'm gonna stick with that.

"Thanks," I said.

"Story?"

"I don't know—what kind?"

"You haven't been here long enough to have a bear story," Max said. Later, when I asked him how he knew that, he said, "No scars."

"You could probably tell me your 'coming into the country' story. Everyone has one of those."

"Oh yeah," I said. We sat down on a big driftwood log, and he shucked off that pack and those bags of trash and the bandolier of buoys and cracked two bottles of beer stashed in his back.

"So, I was coming down this lonely ass road in Canada—"

"Wait," Max said. "Go back farther. Go back to the point in your life where something happened that meant you knew you were going to come to Alaska."

"Ah," I said, thinking. And then I had it:

"I was riding my bicycle down the middle of this lonely county road east of Cedar Key when a deer ran out in front of me, and then this shitass Gray appeared in front of me."

"There you go," Max said. "Tell that story."

Chapter 16

I was on State 24, a long straight road grinding through cabbage palm and pines, I told Max. It was like oh-dark hundred thirty, a really insane time to drive at night, except that no one drove out to Cedar Key at night, not at 3:30 in the morning, and not in April after most of the tourists had gone north. A perfect time to ride a bike if you wanted to avoid the heat of the day, or the traffic, or the suspicions of county sheriffs who assumed anyone not driving a rental car or pickup truck had committed the crime of driving while different.

Everyone knew that DWD got you a ten-minute conversation with a redneck country sheriff and, worse, a little computer look up on the NCIC. I was one of those people who'd rather not have a cop run my name through the national crime information computer. Uh-uh.

So, for personal security reasons I rode my bike that late at night. I mean, I was also on a bike because I couldn't get a license, on account of a little misunderstanding involving liability insurance between me and the Florida insurance commission, and anyway, pumping my muscles at full throttle for hours on end used up the electricity in my body, and if I had too much electricity in my body, bad things happened.

I had an old fashioned generator light on my bike, which made pedaling a tad harder, but, see above, that was good. Some nights I liked to run with just one of those blinking clip-on belt lights, except that on some nights that really called down some unwelcome attention.

In the cool of night every damn deer in central Florida seemed to crawl out of the palmetto scrub and snack on the grass roughly mowed along both sides of the highway and in the grassy meridian. I'd counted fifty deer—usually in ones or twos but once in a small little herd of eight—before counting grew tedious.

Gliding silently by on the edge of the road, I could zip by the deer without them noticing, just the hum of the wheels on the asphalt, the whir of my gears. Now and then one might look up and maybe move away from the road, but usually I could surprise them. Not that I looked for any stealth points; I just moved so fast that they didn't see me coming until I'd gone by.

These weren't big deer, not by Alaska moose standards, more like big dogs, the sort of thing if you ran into it with a car it would be an inconvenience, not a bad situation that went to worse. On a bike, though, you didn't want to run into one. Hitting it would be like hitting a 300-pound sack of rice, and having one hit you would be like a 300-pound sack of rice running into your face. Also, they had hooves and antlers.

So it seemed like I had reached an easy peace with the deer: they'd let me ride by without noticing, and I wouldn't run them over or shoot them. I suppose now and then poachers drove those roads with lights out and a big searchlight and potted them. You could take one down, gut and clean it, throw it in the back of a pickup truck and throw a tarp over it inside of ten minutes, and who would know?

Except one deer had to run in front of me, and it wasn't a wimpy little Bambi baby, but a big buck, with antlers three times the size of his head. He just turned his head and ran straight toward me. I couldn't guess if he was going to run right into me, turn at the last minute, or stop. If I turned into the ditch, I might run into him, and if I turned onto the highway, he might turn that way. So what I did was skid to a stop, so my bike was sideways at the deer, and then grabbed it and threw it at the big buck and ran like hell the other direction. That almost worked, too, except right as my bike was about to hit the deer, everything just disappeared. There one moment, gone the next. My bike; my water bottle; my change of clothes in the panniers on the back seat; my wallet in my change of clothes; two pounds of marijuana I was running out to Cedar Key to sell: the whole thing vanished. All I had left was what I had on: my bike shorts, a short-sleeve shirt, my helmet, and biking shoes.

Then the deer disappeared, too, just as it was about to leap at me, head down and those antlers aimed at my face. Actually, one of the tines poked me in the forehead—I still have the scar here, see?—and then it disappeared. I heard kind of a humming up ahead, and I looked up and saw this weird green beam like a big cylinder of light rising up above me, the deer whirling around in that light and my bike above it.

Standing in front of me was this Gray. I didn't know of it as a Gray, of course, not then, but I'd seen pictures, because of that guy's book he wrote about twenty years ago. Big snake head, big eyes, puny little body, pallid icky skin with that talcum powder dust like it had walked through an ash tray, and, of course, that silly gee-gaw infested ray gun which Grays like to carry to impress people, but that looked so suck-ass silly you had to laugh rather than be intimidated.

I'd heard stories, of course, and knew what was going to happen. Well, two things. Either the Gray would just shoot me outright, turn me into randomly reassembled atoms, or I would get sucked up into the mother ship. I looked up again at that beam of light, saw it slide along toward me, and then it sucked the Gray up, and it went zipping above, along with the deer and my bicycle. I closed my eyes, not wanting to see the beam hit me, but I felt it, Max, oh yeah, I felt it.

Actually, it felt kind of cool once I relaxed and enjoyed it. That first second scared the shit out of me, though. You know how it feels to jump off a high tower into the water, where you just keep falling and falling? The first second of being sucked into an alien tractor beam feels like that. The following second, or the next moment after the beam pulls you up and you leave the ground, once you're in the beam, it's way cool. I don't think my bike felt a damn thing. The Gray was used to it, and the deer, well, the deer was a deer, who knows what it felt?

So I rose up in the beam, and it didn't feel like I was flying, didn't feel like I was falling. I just felt like I was standing on a big wad of jello, and then once the ride was over, there I was, with my bike, the deer, and the alien, inside a big huge room. My bike clattered to the deck. The deer stood there, too scared to move. I stood there, not so much scared to move as figuring when you'd just got sucked up by an alien mother ship, and a Gray stood there with a strange weapon, silly or not, calm and reasoned introspection and a hesitancy to make any sudden moves might be a good idea.

"Welcome on board," the alien then said with a man's voice—actually, it sounded like Jimmy Carter, because of that recording on Pioneer 10, before they started expanding their vocal repertoire. "We're just glad to have y'all visit us."

Then I looked over and saw this incredibly gorgeous woman, I mean, a flat-out, gorgeous, tanned blonde, totally naked and with her hair spreading out in all directions like she was in the middle of a hurricane. Very Cosmopolitan. If she was alien, those fuckers had done a damn good job of faking a human, and if she was human, well, she either was incredibly lucky in the big genetic beauty contest or had one hell of a plastic surgeon.

"Don't believe a word they say," she said. "They're just out to butt fuck you. And they'll probably want us to have sex."

"I can live with that," I said. "I mean, the butt fucking," I quickly added, because I didn't want to come on too strong.

She laughed at that and walked toward me, her hair still whipping around her face, except when she got close to me I couldn't feel a breeze. Her hand slid down the sides of my body, down my arms, my waist, and to my biking shorts. With a swift tug she yanked down my pants, raised an eyebrow when she saw I didn't wear underpants, raised another eyebrow when she saw my Clinton big and throbbing and ready to tutor an intern, and then whipped me around.

"Close your eyes and think of England," she said.

I don't know if it was her, the alien, the deer, or some sneaky robotic medical probe, but yeah, sure enough, they butt fucked me.

Only, well, that phrase is so harsh, isn't it? Because whatever slid up my ass, up my colon and almost up to my mouth, didn't actually hurt. It was kinda like warm jelly, oozing and sliming through my alimentary canal. The classic alien anal probe, except it didn't hurt, and even felt good in a pleasant, irritating medical experience kind of way. You know that warm goop they smear on you when you get an ultrasound? Same idea, except inside.

The probe withdrew, the last foot or so of it feeling like the most incredible defecatory experience, and then she turned me around again and gave me the best mouth sucking of my life. I'm talking tongue like a living beast, quivering lips—a kiss never equaled, and I've tried, I've tried. Then she pushed me down to the cold steel deck of that alien mother craft, the deck rising up to meet us, not cold though, warm and forgiving and soft, and curtains fell down and the deer went away, the bike went away, the Gray went away, and I was there having sex with this most amazing being.

In the dim light of our little love nest, she seemed to change before my eyes, no longer the Nordic blonde goddess, but dark skinned, dark of eye, waving brown hair falling to her hips, then short, kinky hair, and then she became olive skinned, then ivory white with red hair, then thin and lithe with short auburn hair, then blonde again, her appearance changing with every eye blink. It was as if I made love to every woman in the world, or with women I had always imagined wanting to have sex with. Old women, young women, middle aged women. When she was done, I lay back, a worn out husk.

She knelt over me, her appearance again the blonde woman I had first seen, hair still writhing around by some unfelt wind. In the quiet that comes after lovemaking, her face was calm but also looked sad.

"Who are you?" I asked. "What are you?"

"Someone lost and then found," she said. "Eve," she said, "for lack of a better name."

"Are you . . . are you real?" Not that I had a firm grasp on real right then.

"As real as possible. More real, maybe." Eve flicked that hair back. "You see me as many women, not as who I am."

I closed my eyes. "Show me that."

"OK."

I opened my eyes and saw Eve as she was. Not the roaring blonde goddess, but not plain, not ugly, not beautiful either. Except she had an honest beauty, the beauty of the unusual. Rather than a porn star fantasy, her body was slim, muscular, with strong shoulders from honest work, it seemed, a little fat on her hips and stomach, thighs a bit too large but strong, breasts neither large nor small, and a long narrow face with tired blue eyes, a strong nose, almost Roman, with a slight bump at the bridge. Her hair was no longer light blonde, no longer wavy and long, but cropped short an inch all over, and dark blonde, except for a shock of white above her right eye.

"This is who I am, as I should be if my lovers would quit trying to make me someone else," Eve said.

I smiled at her, reached up to feel her skin, touch those short hairs. I sat up, held her face in my hands and pulled her toward me, kissing her this time, then letting go.

"Who you are is perfectly marvelous," I said.

"My shipmates make me appear to be what I am not." Eve shook her head. "Am I really acceptable?"

"In all your forms but especially this one."

"Good enough to be with me forever?" she asked.

"Oh." I said. "I hardly know you."

"You could get to know me. Stay with me."

"I . . . Stay with you here, on this ship?"

"It's my home now." She looked away. "My only home since they took me away . . . many years ago. Since they destroyed my only home."

"On Earth?"

"A place on Earth that no longer exists."

She whispered its name to me, and then swore me never to say it again. I cannot say it even now, although I can say this.

Her real name is Virginia.

*

I laid there with Eve for hours, minutes, days. I have no way of knowing. I didn't feel hungry, or thirsty, or tired. I had a sense that the mother ship moved, that as I laid next to this woman who should not have existed, the aliens analyzed me, explored my brain and body, and left their mark behind.

Hours later I arose from sleep, or drowsiness, or whatever state I had been. I saw Eve looking at me, saw those visions of all those other women she could be flicker across her face and body.

"Stay with me?" she asked again.

It would be perfect love, I could see, an emotional deepness growing ever more intense as we traveled together, prisoners, though, captives held by beings we could never understand.

Stay with her? If she had a choice, I would have chosen to be with her. If they would free her, I would go with her, or come to know her better to see if I wanted to spend a life with her, but that was not what she asked.

"If I don't stay?"

"They'll return you back to where you were taken, unharmed."

I pulled her close again, and kissed her. "I have to go back," I said.

She nodded, and though I'm sure she wanted to cry, refused. "They all say that."

"If you were to be freed. . .?"

"It will never happen," she said.

The bed went back to being a floor, and we stood up, both naked. The Gray handed me my clothes, neatly folded, and my shoes and my bike helmet. My bike was there, perfectly balanced, its wheels turning although it went nowhere. The deer stood there, and I wondered if it too had met its perfect lover. The Gray waved at the bike, and I understood.

I mounted it, put my feet on the pedals. Eve stood to my right, now in her original blonde goddess form, hair streaming behind her, as if to tempt me one last time to stay. I liked the real version better, liked her imperfect beauty.

"I'll free you!" I yelled at her, for a roaring wind had risen up.

She smiled at my bravery, although we both knew it wasn't true.

A moment later, I found myself on the bike, pedaling away in that muggy Florida night, passing a startled buck that looked at me, then turned and ran into the scrub. It wasn't until later, when I got into Cedar Key and stretched out my legs from all that bike riding, that I felt the throbbing sore in my butt, and found the chip.

Chapter 17

"OK," Max said after I'd told him my alien abduction story. "Only how did getting butt fucked by aliens cause you to come up to Alaska?"

"Oh," I said. "Right. Well, the whole encounter kinda ruined Florida for me. Deer, for example. I could never look at deer the same. Nighttime bike riding and running drugs into small coastal Florida towns? Same-same. Even now, looking at really gorgeous blondes with long legs just creeps me out. You can't go to a Florida beach—well, most Florida beaches—without seeing hot babes like that.

"So what could I do? I headed north, to put as much distance from some bad memories as I could."

"And here you are," Max said.

"The short of it, yeah."

Max nodded at that. "A good story." He got this long look in his eyes, and I knew what he was doing. I'd seen it in tabloid writers back when I was stupid enough to tell 'em my stories of encounters with aliens. I'd seen it in shrinks, too. Every one of 'em wants to take your story and make it their own, and squeeze a few big bucks out of it.

"Hey, motherfucker," I said. "It's my story, so don't get any ideas."

Max looked at me, those icy blue eyes just glaring into me, and I could see his face harden, his muscles tense. He stood up, and his dog Fraze got up, and he shook his fist at me.

"No one owns stories," he said. "Stories belong to everyone. Once told, they become part of the grand human gestalt, our collective unconscious, the living legend that is the human race."

"Hey, hey," I said, seeing I'd hit a sore spot. "Dude, back off. It's cool. It's just that, well, when I've told stories before, I get ripped off."

"Oh, you're talking rights," Max said. "Now the telling of a story, that's another matter. The telling of it belongs to you." He gave me this sort of superior look, only it wasn't like he was putting me down, more like letting me know what he could do and I could not. "Of course, some can tell stories better than others."

"Right. Like washed up sleazy sci-fi writers."

"Ouch," he said. Max gave me that glare again. "And by the way, no one says 'sci-fi' a second time in my presence without getting bitch slapped."

"Point taken."

"What I mean is," Max went on. "We all have good stories, every damn one of us, because the glory of our lives is that we live, love, go on living and loving, and survive to do that day after day. And sometimes we fail. No one story is better than another."

"What we don't have," he went on, "what a lot of us can't learn to do is how to tell those stories so they make sense."

"Which is where you come in."

"Hey, it's a gift, a talent, a craft, and it's not like it came without hard work," Max said.

"And that makes you special?"

"No, it just makes me different. A writer is just some-one who has taken the time to figure out how to tell a good story. You can learn that, although some of us have a harder time learning than others. Some shouldn't bother learning, because frankly, for a lot of people, the effort is far more ex-pensive than the result warrants."

Fraze had moved up to Max and he just naturally reached over and scratched the big dog's ears. I began to realize that huge wolfhoundy-looking dog wasn't a dog, but a familiar. "Anyway, somehow I've learned how to tell a good story. So if you want your story told. . .?"

"Never crossed my mind."

"Well, we could make a deal. If you want," Max said.

"I'll let you know." I stood up, moved around and stretched, and noticed the sun had begun its long slide toward setting in the northwestern sky.

"Hey," I said. "I damn near forgot. We're having a barbe-cue and bonfire at the 'Stead. You up for it?"

Max winced, then shook his head. "Uh, I got some sort of baggage over there at the Stead."

"Old flame?"

"One or two." He held up the kayak paddle with Fred-dy's name on it.

"Oh. Freddy. Well, I bet she's moved on from whatever," I said.

"Yeah, but I'm not sure I have," Max said. He shrugged his shoulders, did this sort of clenching and unclenching thing. "What the hell. Only one way to find out."

I helped him pick up his bags of trash, took the kayak paddle from him, and we walked back toward the 'Stead.

*

By the time we got to the place, the 'Steaders had gotten a good bonfire going. Barry had hauled some marimbas down to the beach with his band, Gogogoi. There's sort of this thing about Della with marimbas, I learned later, like how come they have four marimba groups and as many ready to step in. My own personal theory was that marimbas made this eerie resonating sound that scared the crap out of the Grays. I mean, when they get going, the baritone laying in a beat over the tenors, the notes start blending together in this bizarre harmonic—only, not harmonic, cuz it's really clashing—sound, sort of like the marimbas are talking.

You know how sometimes you might be in a house, no one around, the radio off, with no sounds but the pipes squeaking or the refrigerator running or the heater going? It's quiet like, only not quiet, and then the sounds bounce off each other and you swear someone is talking? Marimbas are like that.

Only I think they are talking. I think when machines or music instruments make sounds, they become like these transistors and capacitors and what not, radio parts is what they are, primitive radio parts—accidental radio, really. Marimbas are accidental radio. And they're receiving other sounds, other voices, voices from somewhere else, like distant galaxies. So when I say that the marimbas are talking, what I mean is, they're talking.

Except Gogogoi hadn't gotten to that point yet. They were just setting up their instruments. Sometimes I get ahead of the narrative flow. It's like what Max would call foreshadowing, a lame-ass writer excuse for not putting things in order. Hey, I just tell the story. Max writes it down. If he screws it up, blame him.

Anyway, I didn't see Sarah or Freddy right off, but Ren was there with this guy who looked as fresh to Della as I was. I mean, not by the way he dressed, but the way he acted, like everything he saw and everyone he met was a total revelation. This new guy wore his clothes like they were new, too, not quite relaxed in them, but the clothes themselves weren't new. They looked like they had been snapped up that morning from the Sally Ann, although later what Ren told me was he snatched them out of dryers at laundromats and would leave $10 bills in place of each.

I kinda noticed like Ren was hanging real tight to the guy, and I sorta wondered for a second if maybe old Ren was swish. Then Ren explained.

"Yo, Jimmo," Ren said. "This here is Tim. Tim's one of my clients."

"Client?" I hadn't actually figured out what Ren did for a living, but then, I'd realized real quick that in Della, what people did for a living was always sort of a mystery. There was what they did and then how they paid their bills.

"Client. 'Get a Life.' It's my business," Ren said. He turned to Tim. "Tim, Jimmo; Jimmo, Tim. Jimmo's new in town, too, only accidental. I've got that right, Jimmo?"

"I didn't plan to come here, if that's what you mean," I said.

"Ah: but Tim did. Job, everything. Everything." Ren waved at Tim. "Am I a genius or what? Doesn't Tim look the very example of Della guyhood?"

"Yeah, he's not with a woman," I said. "Fits right in." But there was something about him that didn't seem right and got my butt chip tingling.

"Exactly." Ren smiled, then glared at me when he got the joke. "Hey, I'll hook him up with a woman soon enough."

"You should have seen me when I arrived," Tim said. "Docker's pants, Topsider shoes, the whole LL Bean look. Ren got me fixed right up."

"He had a horrible haircut, sort of a JFK mop top. Very Back East. Not Della at all," Ren said.

I stared at Tim, looked more closely. I could see Samm's hand in the style: nice clean nape, tapered up to a longish mop with some spikes to it, even some blond tipping. Short beard.

"Four D?"

"Yup. It's usually the first stop for a client. Then the Sally Ann, Gear Shed for some Carhartts and XtraTuffs, you know the drill."

"So you're like an image consultant?"

"Better!" said Ren. "A life. The whole thing. Tim here got a job—MentalHeal, if you wanna know."

"Of course. Advocate?"

"Shadow," Tim said. "I hang with the mentally deranged and keep them out of trouble."

"Yeah," I said, trying to make the word sound cold, nice and mean. "You gotta watch out for those *mentally deranged*."

"Oh—uh, no offense."

"Uh-huh," I said.

Ren took out a little tablet computer, looked over at Tim, jotted down a note. "Well, ahem. More than image, Jimmo. I took care of Tim's entire life. Got him a car—late model Subaru, natch—and a room, little cabin out East Road, and now, well, I introduce him to all my friends and acquaintances."

"He met Freddy yet?"

Tim smiled. "Nice."

Right, I thought.

"Well, you're all set then." I looked at Tim, at Ren, and realized what a great scam Ren had set up. It could work, I thought. Then again, it could totally suck. If you put a seedling into new soil, didn't you have to harden them off first? And what if it was the wrong soil?

"Yeah. And to think just six weeks ago I graduated from Harvard with a BS in psych." Tim kinda preened when he said that, and Max and I shook our heads.

"Oh, man," Ren said. "Yo, dude, how many times do I have to remind you? Hampshire College. You gotta say 'Hampshire College.'"

"Oh. Right. But I went to Harvard on a summer program."

"There you go," Ren said.

Then it clicked. I realized why Tim looked familiar, why I felt an instant loathing of him. He was the cowboy alien who'd tried to pick me up outside of Beaver Creek. Ren did good work, no shit, but not that good.

"See you around," I said, and I gave Tim that little finger-gun gesture he'd pulled on me a few weeks ago.

Cowboy, I thought.

*

Max and I wandered over to a little campfire. He set down his backpack and trash by a driftwood log, but held on to that kayak paddle, sort of like a staff. His dog Frazier clung to him, always right at his side. If Max stopped, Fraze would sit down, and if Max sat down, Fraze would lie down.

"Fraze!" a woman yelled, and the big dog turned his ears and then his eyes toward the voice, and then leapt over to her and rubbed against her. Freddy, of course. She scratched him behind his ears and he looked up adoringly at her.

"He's a goddamn chick magnet," Max said to me. "Or maybe a magnet to chicks." Max rolled his shoulders back in that gesture again, stood up straight and went over to Freddy.

"Hey," he said. "I found your paddle." He handed it to her.

"Knew you would," Freddy said. She took it from him and then laid it against the roots of a big driftwood tree. "Thanks."

"Sure."

"Oh, come here, Max," Freddy said, holding out her arms.

Max turned to me, I nodded at him, and he went to her. Criminy, it was so sickly sweet I almost puked. She hugged, he hugged, they hugged, Frazier rubbed against both of them, and then Max gave her a big sloppy kiss. Good for him.

"It's been too long, Max," Freddy said.

"I, uh, had some fidelity issues," Max said.

"Oh, sweetheart, I don't care if you screw around."

"That's not it . . . Oh." Max blushed. "It's just that—" He looked at me.

"I'm going to go see if I can find Sarah," I said.

"Right."

They sat down on that big log, shoulder to shoulder, arms around each other. Frazier snuggled up against their feet. I had to admit it looked kind of sweet—I mean, with the dog and all.

*

I left the lovey-doveys out there on the edge of the light and walked back toward the big bonfire. Barry and his marimba group, Gogogoi, had dragged their instruments down to the beach and set up there on a little flat spot. The marimbas looked kinda like xylophones, except later Barry told me that would be like so uncool to say, since marimbas were far more ancient than piddly-ass tin instruments. "We're talking Mother Africa," he'd say, which was kinda funny, since everyone in Gogogoi was like whiter than milk, definitely sans tans.

See, they had like these smaller instruments, three sopranos and two tenors, all with wooden keys and on stands, except for Dan the guy from MentalHeal, who played a low soprano that he could sit behind on account of his MS. The marimbas had big pipes, plastic, really, with holes in the sides covered with pieces of cellophane so they made this like buzzing sound.

Behind the smaller marimbas were the big machines, the engine room, Barry called them, a baritone and a bass, and the bass like so big and tall you had to stand on a bench to play it. They hustled and humped the marimbas out, got them set up. Dan sat on his bench at the soprano at the back, and then Barry stepped up to one of two sopranos perpendicular to Dan's, the lead soprano, with Grace, the logger chick receptionist, across from him, her hair still perfectly shellacked in place. Boots, the receptionist at MentalHeal, was on one of the tenors, only it took me a while to recognize her, cuz she didn't have those little granny glasses or that neat and tidy brown bob haircut with bangs. No, it was all frizzed out and spiked, and she wore this wild paisley T-shirt that was really tight. Boots had great boobs, nice firm muscles, and damn she looked hot.

Roz from the 'Stead was on the other tenor, her purple buzz-cut hair spiked out, too, and she had these cool flouncy pants and sort of a white and purple tie-dyed shirt that looked like it had amoebas on it.

Ren was up there behind the baritone, looking almost too clean cut for the group, although, well, with his shirt off he had some incredible tatts, and they didn't look clean cut at all.

And up there on bass, her long silver-and-black braids all redone into about twenty little braids, was Carol, the bike lady I'd seen on the Spit the first day, her bike propped up against a log not far from the marimbas. Carol kinda moved back and forth on the bench, her hands clutching these big ass mallets, just itching to do something.

Gogogoi didn't like cough for attention or announce a song or anything; they just laid into it. Roz started first with a couple of quick notes: ba-da bomp-ba bomp ba-bomp bomp ba-bomp, one round, then Carol came in, her arms flying high as she hit the same notes on the bass. Ren followed up, one round, two rounds, with a counterpoint, sorta filling in the spaces.

The other tenor, Grace, and the three sopranos followed up singing, no words, just a basic, "Heyyy," two more rounds until I thought they were going to run out of breath, and then they all came in with a basic pattern: bom-bom bomp-bomp, bom-bomp bom-bomp, two more rounds of that, and then when the band had been playing together and got really tight, Barry just let loose.

I could feel this like energy lift us up out there, and if we had been sitting down, we stood up, and if we had been standing up, we started shifting back and forth and then damned if by the time Barry's mallets weren't running up and down those keys, his hands whirling so fast they were a blur, we were all bouncing and swaying and leaping back and forth. I mean, you couldn't sit down, you couldn't stand still.

Carol was like this whirl of energy, her movements straight and pure and right on, the notes just booming, those big resonators booming, and the little flaps of cellophane humming. No, not humming—singing. I swore the instruments started to talk, I mean, not voices inside my head talking, but talking, communicating and saying, I don't know, words.

Only not words I knew. African words, maybe, Shona words, like where the marimba came from in Zimbabwe, I don't know, foreign words. I knew the words, though, that was the weird thing. I'd heard the words, could hear them in my head as I danced and flew about, trying to remember why they seemed so familiar.

And it struck me. That sound? It was the sound of the universe when the aliens first dumped me on the side of the road there in Florida. It was the hum of the frogs, the hum of the crickets, the roaring of mosquitoes. It was the voice of the planet, Truck Stop Earth, how the world sung to you if you listened.

It was what kept me sane, kept me alive, kept me going when the Grays first did their nasty on me. I heard the voice of my home singing to me way back when, I heard it every night when the civilized world shut up for a moment, I heard it in the surf and sea and the wind whenever I bothered to open my mind to it, and I heard it in those marimbas.

All the other voices went away, all the doubts, all the worries, all the fears, all the pain and anger and hurt. OK, it didn't go away; it just laid down low like the sea after a storm, went quiet and didn't say anything. That song became something else, more than a song, and not only did I feel it, everyone felt it.

We fell into it. Gogogoi played like they were not musicians but instruments themselves, like the song was in the wood and the mallets and their bodies, and all they had to do was let it free. Dan played with force and purpose, his ravaged, weak body somehow empowered. Sweat poured off everyone, and though it seemed like the song would go on forever, eventually it ended, as all songs do, even though the sound kept resonating within.

And then they went into another song, and another, one song flowing into the other, different tune, different melody, different arrangements and different musicians at different instruments, until finally like a good storm we were all played out, danced out, sung out, and we just had to come up for air and breathe.

But the song itself wasn't over. It just kept going and going, even though we couldn't hear it.

Chapter 18

So that party there on the beach below the 'Stead kinda got wound down. People began wandering away, practically crawling if elephants, still dancing if sober—wandering away in ones and twos and threes, coupled up or not, coupled with whom they came with or not. I could see that not just Max had fidelity issues.

Gogogoi had quit playing about a half hour ago, though the music still seemed to reverberate from the marimbas, now growing cold as the sun slid set. You think the sun doesn't set in Alaska in the summer? Oh, at 59 degrees latitude and some change, it does. "Slide," OK, I'll give you slide. The sun slides, the sun slid below the horizon.

And popped right up again.

As Sarah and I walked up the hill back to the 'Stead, I could still feel those marimbas, still hear the sound and the song, only after I thought about it a moment, realized, uh-huh, that was the ocean, you shithead. Ocean, marimbas, wind, varied thrushes ringing, glaciers growling, after a while, all nature's sound kinda ran together. So as I laid on my back, feet facing the dying bonfire, head to the south and the bay at my back, I still heard Gogogoi playing. They'd be playing a long time in my head, as long as I just listened.

Sarah and I went upstairs to the aurora room to catch the Northern Lights, hee-hee. We did a little heavy petting and some ear sucking, and we tried, we really tried to work up to hot steamy sex—which I'm sure you'd like to hear about in detail, since there hasn't been a good sex scene since Chapter 15—except that we were so dog tired we fell asleep in each other's arms.

Hey, sex doesn't always have to involve tumescent body parts, you know? It can be soft and tender, two people holding each other against the terror of the darkness. All right, quasi darkness. Maybe some tender stroking, a little neck nuzzling, some nipple biting, and lower there, darling, lower, yes, that's the spot. Never underestimate the intimacy of a good cuddle.

OK, I never bought that crap, either, but it makes a sweet little pickup line. "Oh, I'm not interested in anything hot and heavy, babe. Just holding you in my arms is passion enough. And quit sucking on my ear."

I don't know what time we all wound down. All I know is that at 9:45 a.m. on the dot I woke up and couldn't get back to sleep. Maybe I slept two hours, maybe one, maybe not even that. What? You think I checked my watch implant every time I nodded off? I felt refreshed, though, tanned, rested, and ready to rock.

Or, as it turned out, go to church. Hey, it was Sunday, the Lord's Day, ya know?

I left Sarah sleeping like, well, a Delloid after a night of marimba dancing, and snuck out of the tower room down to the kitchen. Fraze slept in front of the big ancient wood stove in the kitchen, and I thought, hmmm, maybe Max and Freddy had reconciled their differences. I'd hafta ask, having taken a personal interest in my coauthor's happiness.

Roz was up and making a latte and about to scramble up a Zen omelet—you know: make me one with everything?

"Latte, Jimmo?" she asked. She handed me a big mug.

"Thanks." I glanced down at the mug and saw she'd foamed a little yin-yang symbol.

"Omelet?"

"An omelet would be perfect. You make a mean latte, Roz—nice foam work."

"I used to be a barista at the nunnery."

"You were a barista?" I asked.

She chuckled. "And a nun. Now I teach yoga."

"Oh, well, you see ex-nuns all the time, and yoga teachers—huh, who isn't one? But someone who's pulled lattes—now *that's* different."

I sucked down that Arabian wine and could feel the caffeine work its little magic. I've tried like about 1,500 different drugs, legal, illegal, and prescribed, but coffee has always been on my top ten list.

"So nunneries have espresso stands now?"

"A little shack out East Road, you know—?"

And here Roz named the stand, which turned out to be The Best Damn Espresso Stand in Della, except I can't tell you its name, and I don't care if it did get written up in the Lonely Planet.

"You're not in the sisterhood anymore?" Heck, even though Roz wore this like skin-tight purple jumpsuit and had the body that could *wear* a skin-tight purple jumpsuit, with hair to match—hey, for all I know there was some religious order where they like wore skin-tight purple jumpsuits, St. Passionara of the Lilac.

"Not since the order closed down, sold the espresso stand, and moved out of Della. Also, uh, well, the order and

I had this little disagreement over a key matter of dogma," she said.

"Uh, anything special?" I collected religious sects like some people collected US Presidents action figures. I was curious, is all.

"The divinity of Jesus," Roz said. "I believe in Jesus, but not his divinity."

"Oh, yeah, that can cause problems. Isn't that like a major tenet of Catholicism?"

"Yeah. Pope John Paul George Ringo doesn't think highly of nuns who don't believe in the divinity of Christ. On the other hand, I think he was real. Jesus, I mean, not Pope John Paul George Ringo. One crazy twisted revolutionary who kicked Roman butt, but real."

Kicked Roman butt. I liked that. I don't think that was part of the dogma, either.

Roz flipped over the omelet, chopped it in half and slid it out of the pan and onto two plates. She gave me a plate, and for a few moments we both just ate and didn't say anything, that kind of silence you get in a meal where you're more hungry than talkative.

"So you want to go to church?" she asked me. "It's why I got up early."

I wanted to say, Yo, I'd already danced my toes off and seen the sun rise, that should be spiritual enough. Only, I don't know, ever since I'd boffed Hannah back in Beaver Creek, I hadn't had any serious religious encounters with the spiritually seeking.

"Which church?"

"Oh, *The* Church, we like to say when we're feeling self-righteous. The U-Cubeds: Unitarian Universalist Universal Life United Church of Christ. They meet in a big tent. Brother Obadiah is doing a talk today on how invoking the sacred name of Jesus can scare away UFOs. Says he's with the alien resistance."

Now *that* I had to hear.

"I'll put on my Sunday best," I said.

*

Remember those ageless Delloids I told ya 'bout who could be any when from like 35 to 60? Roz wuz like that. Sitting next to her in her Porsche Cayenne SUV—purple, natch—I snuck a glance at her face. Usually the face gives the age away. You can work out, you can have a great body, you can keep fit and trim, but when the crow's feet start getting deep and the wrinkles on the brow and around the mouth start extending around your face, that's getting old.

So yeah, Roz had the crow's feet, had the brow lines, but she still had taut skin. Maybe botox, although I didn't think an ex-barista turned yoga teacher would do botox. I couldn't tell her age by the amount of gray in her hair because, well, it was purple. Not totally purple, like streaked purple over brunette, so I dunno, maybe the purple covered the grizzle.

She had this bitchin' haircut, all spiked and short around the forehead and crown and ears and then braided in this long skinny plait that went to her waist. Oh, and she had these like dark brown eyes, so dark the irises sorta disappeared. Oh, oh, and she wore about a kilo of silver, silver rings, silver bracelets, silver hoop earrings, six in her left ear, seven in her right ear, a tasteful little silver nose stud, and a silver necklace that looked like a Calder mobile. Her Sunday finest.

Me? I put on a clean pair of jeans, my newest T-shirt, and a clean flannel shirt. Even wore socks with my Tevas.

We drove a few miles east of the 'Stead, into a big open section Roz called Church Row, one church or temple or religious establishment after another. Roz said Della had three churches for every espresso stand and two espresso stands for every bar. God, coffee, and alcohol, the three big paths to enlightenment, I guess.

That Porsche put Freddy's Sube to shame, on account of, well, it had leather seats and shocks. Working shocks. It had these leather seats softer than most major brands of toilet tissue, a seat more like a bed, and this awesome sound system that made it sound like Ennio Morricone's orchestra—Roz was a stone Ennio fan—had been locked up in the glove box and was playing its heart out.

"Sweet ride," I said. "So how come you're driving a Porsche and everyone else has Toys or Subes?"

"Clean living," Roz said. "Good investments. And no, not daddy's trust fund." Then she kinda got this far away look, and I knew that look. It was the expression abductees had when they got to thinking about their sojourns on the mother ship. "And you know how we used to not talk about the extra-spiritual adventures of perv priests? I talked. The church offered me a tidy six-figure sum to shut up, I sued, and I got a bit more. The bastard did time, too. God has her own justice, but sometimes she expects humans to do the heavy lifting."

"This before or after you were a nun?"

"Before. I wanted to give the church another chance." She shrugged. "I learned to love the church again. And God, and Jesus, and humanity, and even men. Out of all that, when I left the order, I figured I deserved a nice car. I'd donated half my award to the sisters, and put the rest into a nice little mutual fund—hey, a girl has to look out for herself in her old age. When I got out, the fund had matured nicely, so I rewarded myself with a Porsche. I would have gotten a Boxster, but Della eats sports cars for dessert."

I realized as we drove that we passed through some of the burnt forest I'd worked on the week before. Those spindly sticks of charcoal looked horrible, the ground all scorched and dry, but come the next good rain, the grass would jump out of the ground and the earth would start healing. Always did. I counted six churches, all ugly boxes sided with T-111 plywood, you know, that stuff with grooves made to look like board-and-batten siding? Then we came across this thing that looked like an undulating sheet, a tent, sorta, but not a tent.

"U-cubed," Roz said. "It used to be one of those Pentecostal charismatic fundy churches, only it went bankrupt and the U's decided to merge and bought the fundies out."

"It's a tent?" I asked. Didn't look like a tent.

"Ferrocement. The acoustics rock. Sometimes Gogogoi holds marimba concerts here, and we have to use soft knobs or we blow the audience out of the place."

Roz parked at the back of the parking lot, snout out, and I thought she'd do that obnoxious thing drivers with hot cars do, like hog three spaces sideways so they wouldn't get door dings, only Roz was like all egalitarian about it. Probably a good idea. I'd guessed in a town given over to rusty old Subes and pickups, a shiny purple Porsche would be tempting to drag a key across the hood.

We'd gotten there right at the announced starting time of noon, which meant fifteen minutes earlier, Della time, so I had some moments to like people watch and check out the congregation. Most of 'em looked like RATs—rational thinking straights—but I'd been in Della long enough to know that your rattiest looking Delloid would turn out to be not just genuinely, truly strange, but beyond genuinely, truly strange—totally strange. The folks there looked like your average gaggle of liberal, socially conscious, environmentally aware, upstanding blue state citizens. Birkenstocks. Long Indian print dresses. Utilikilts. Quartz crystal jewelry. You know, your basic Della straight, and except for Roz, this platinum blonde with waist-length dreadlocks, and me, not a weird haircut in the bunch.

"We missed you at the full moon dance," said the woman with the long platinum blonde dreadlocks said. Roz introduced her as Elly. "The cosmic energy just isn't there without you."

"I know, I know," Roz said. "Something came up, though." She gave Elly this earnest look that I read as, None of your damn business, so don't pry. I don't think Elly got it, though.

"And you weren't at the Women in Black stand in last Tuesday."

Women in Black? Roz told me about it later, this group of women and sometimes guys who dressed in black and stood on the street corner in front of the fire hall, sort of half performance art, half protest against the war, poverty, and generally evil, nasty stuff.

"Shit happens," Roz said. "This is my new housemate, Jimmo. He and his girlfriend—can I call Sarah your girlfriend, Jimmo?—have moved in."

"Sarah's a person with whom I am exploring infinite possibilities," I said. "But yeah, you can call her my girlfriend."

"This Sarah? Is it like a major commitment? I ask because I have this friend. . ." Elly said.

"Got it covered," I said. "Roz is my backup babe if Sarah doesn't work out." I winked at Roz.

"Oh. Oh!" Elly said. "Well, welcome to the Cubed. Go with the goddess."

And that was the least weird of my encounters there.

People came in, sat down, visited with each other, and after about a quarter past noon, this guy with a big bushy charcoal beard stood up, and stood up, cuz he was almost seven feet tall, and he held out his arms in sort of a hokey warm embrace and said, "Let us stand and praise the eternal wisdom of that which we cannot entirely know, that which is greater than we can imagine."

Ah, I thought. The being that which nothing greater can be conceived. A Spinozist. I liked this guy already.

"Sisters and brothers," the reverend said. "Let us sing."

Criminy, the guy was so sincerely sincere, so hip and cool and loving I thought we'd start out with one of those hip 1960s folk rock songs, you know, some Beatles number with the words slightly revised to make it quasi-religious. Only, danged if we didn't start out with "Onward Christian Soldiers," not your average hipwazee lib church song.

"The rev loves this song," Roz whispered to me, "on account of the guy who wrote it was like majorly into vampires."

Anyway, we sang a few more songs, said a few prayers, and sort of did the church thing. It brought back fond memories of church camp, when we'd have a service outdoors at like this rustic outside altar, and the birds would be chirping and the breeze rustling the trees and I'd be staring at the back of Paula McF's neck and thinking about slow dancing with her the night before and getting my first woody.

Hey, I was getting a woody right there. Religion does that to me sometimes.

Then this guy got up and did his talk. Roz said the Cubeds did that, had guest sermons or talks, and usually it was members but sometimes if someone interesting was passing through town, they'd let 'em go at it. She sorta said this I think as a warning.

"Brothers and sisters," the rev said, "we live in a great and wonderful universe, with mysteries few can know or can explain. Sometimes strange things happen to us, like we get abducted by aliens, things so terrible only our faith can explain it—and give us the strength to endure. We have today a long-time member of our congregation who will talk of his experiences. Please welcome Brother Malachi Obadiah."

Malachi Obadiah? My middle names? I started to stand up, only this guy in the front row walked up to the podium. For like half a second I worried he'd even look like me, Jimmo Variation Number Forty-seven, only, well, he had about thirty years on your humble narrator. Brother Obadiah, as Roz said everyone knew him, stood almost as tall as the rev, only half his weight, all skin, lean muscle, thin bones, and if he had any body fat, it must have been in his ass, because I sure didn't see it.

"Huh," Roz said. "I never knew he'd been abducted by aliens."

"You'd be surprised who's been abducted by aliens," I said.

But as I was looking at Brother Obadiah, and pondering the incredible coincidence that we shared part of our name, I suddenly realized why that wasn't a coincidence. I smiled to myself. Oh, I might not ever have met Brother Obadiah, but I knew him all right.

The brother began by spinning a Tibetan prayer wheel, and chanting the Om, and when he was done, he held the wheel up.

"Did you ever wonder why the Tibetans spin a prayer wheel? Did you ever think of what Ezekiel saw? Brothers and sisters, for millennia we have been visited by strange beings: Grays, some call them; aliens, others call them. I call them 'the visitors,' for I don't know if they're beyond this planet, of this planet, of another dimension, or of a consciousness we can only glimpse and never truly know. All I know is that the visitors took me away and returned me to this planet, and did things to me I am blessed to have forgotten but only know scared me beyond imagining. And they did this to me one-hundred and eighteen times."

Holy shit, I thought.

I sucked in my breath. I expected to hear titters and nervous laughter from the congregation, which is what I got the one time I dared to speak of my experiences in public; only the Cubed gang said nothing, which is how I knew they were genuinely, truly strange.

"But I have learned how to repel such attacks," Brother Obadiah said. "I have learned how when the visitors try to take me away again I can make them stop, make them whoosh away like the air going out of a balloon. I have learned how to become calm in my fears, to not let my fears rule me, to not let my fears become my power."

This got my attention, I have to say.

"And how have I done this, sisters and brothers? By falling back on my childhood faith, the faith of my Southern Baptist upbringing. I invoke the name of our Lord Jesus Christ."

Now that brought titters and nervous laughter. Mention the name of Christ at the Cubed church, hoo boy, that could bring trouble. Too, well, patriarchal, ya know?

"And Buddha, and Vishnu and Zeus and Hera and the Goddess and the Powers Greater Than We Can Imagine," he said, and the congregation calmed down a little. "But for me, Jesus works best." Brother Obadiah smiled. "You go with the deity that kicks butt."

Now when Brother Obadiah spoke of these things, I started to get nervous. My butt chip didn't burn. That would be too obvious, too simple. My whole body shook, not so much a palsy, not an epileptic fit, oh no, more like a tuning fork humming, an energy vibrating through me. My right foot started twitching, and I kicked the chair in front of me. I must have startled the woman before me, sort of a middle-aged woman with her white and brown hair piled up in a very fetching French twist, because she reached down with her hand, grabbed my foot, and started stroking it. I leaned forward to tell her to let the fuck go of my foot when she turned to me.

"Fear not," she said.

I held my tongue and felt this enormous relief wash over me, and the little St. Vitus dance raging inside me went away.

It was Carol, the bicycle lady, the bass player in Gogogoi, hair up, a touch of makeup and lipstick, in a plain blue dress, and looking normal, rational, and straight.

But, of course, genuinely, truly strange.

Chapter 19

The laying on of hands by Carol aside, Brother Obadiah's sermon totally flipped me out. Ever since I'd come into Della, I'd suspected the Grays had established like this major big time base there, which of course implied abductions, and where you get abductions, the Resistance usually follows. We're human. When evil nasty aliens assault you, you hit back, just out of instinct. I'd suspected people like Surreal and others had gone up to the big mother ship, only I hadn't quite confirmed that. You just hadda be careful in making contact with the local Resistance.

And here Brother Obadiah had spoken in public about not only what he had done, but how to defeat the sons of bitches. Jesus Christ, that took balls.

It also made me nervous as hell. See, here's the thing with religion and me. I like know that I want to connect with some great spiritual understanding, some system that will bring me peace, help me understand what the hell it all means, and maybe as a bonus lead to a fulfilling, long-term relationship with a really cool woman—or at least steaming hot sex. Only when I get into that whole Jesus Christ Our Lord and Savior, give yourself over to God stuff, it's like sticking that first needle of smack into your arm. Hey, maybe it will feel good, but maybe it will suck me into an addiction I have no control over.

If there's one thing I've learned about being butt fucked by aliens, it's that I really, really want control over my life.

Yeah, yeah, I've put on the act, I know, like when I told Hannah I was this major Jesus freak. That was to get laid, OK, God forgive me. And sometimes my quaint religious upbringing asserts itself, and that ol' good time religion pops up. So on the one hand I have this urge to like give myself over to religion, any religion, pick one and stick with it, and on the other hand . . . well, see, the big problem with religion is that I can't reconcile it with being abducted.

And here Brother Obadiah had just done that. I was havin' a crisis of faith—well, non-faith, that's what I was havin'. Big time.

Roz and I got sucked into the receiving line leaving the church, with the rev shaking hands with everyone and sometimes doing that huggy thing. I can deal with the huggy thing like at funerals and wedding and shit, but only after a few hits of some really choice weed. I kinda liked this Rev guy, so when Roz introduced me and the Rev gave me this *ursus horribilis* squeeze your fucking ribs together, but not quite, hug, I just went with it.

"Reverend Robb, this is Jimmo," Roz said. "He and this sweet young woman just moved into the 'Stead."

"Jimmo!" Reverend Robb said, and he gave me that hug. Ouch. "Are you new to Della?"

"Just a week," I said. "I'm getting settled. Got a job and everything."

"Well welcome, welcome," he said. "You'll fit right in. I just know it." He winked at me.

Well, shit yeah, I'd fit in. Hadn't Barry already explained that?

We shook hands with some more church members or deacons or deaconesses or whatever, and then made our way to the parking lot. Brother Obadiah stood at the end of our row, hands crossed in front of him, eyelids half closed over those intense blue eyes. Tall and thin, he stood out in his pale blue jeans, pale blue chambray shirt, and navy blue high-top sneakers—well, would have stood out, except he was the only person there in the row, so it wasn't like there was any-one else to stand out *against*.

"Brother Obadiah," Roz said. "Do you need a ride into town?"

"Just to my place beyond the beautiful homestead graced by your lovely presence," he said.

Roz told me later that the brother didn't have a car and walked everywhere, except that he'd developed a talent for mooching rides.

"It would be an honor to give you a ride," Roz said. "Have you met Jimmo?"

"Not in this dimension," Brother Obadiah said. "But I do believe I have known him in another consciousness."

He took my hand and shook it, one of those light, up and down, not-too-hard-a-grip handshakes, and when he did that, I felt that same calming presence flow through me like when Carol fondled my foot.

"Brother," I said. "I found your talk quite, uh, revelatory."

Those blue eyes, I thought. That voice, that nose, and that face. Oh yeah, the brother and I had met before.

"You don't think I'm crazy?" he asked.

"Crazy as a fucking loon," I said. "Which means you're sane."

Brother Obadiah chuckled, and then blew a whistle, like a long, lonely train, and of course I got it right away. Opera-tion Train Whistle, all aboard.

Elly suddenly ran towards us, hiking up her long Indian print skirt, her floppy blonde dreads flying. "Roz! Roz!" she yelled.

"Elly? What's the matter?" Roz asked.

Elly stopped, caught her breath. "My ride left without me. Can you take me home?"

"We're giving the brother a ride. I think we can squeeze in one more," Roz said.

Roz told me that Ruthie was always mooching rides, too, but she never just outright asked. Her ride always left without her was the usual excuse. That was one of the problems with having a sweet ride like that Porsche, Roz said: People expected you to give them a lift.

Elly, praise the Lord, took the shotgun seat, while Obadiah and I sat in the back. We drove in silence for a few moments, just the strains of Morricone's "Revolver" playing—my all time favorite Ennio song, by the way—until Elly started yakking about something. With her chattering away, I figured it was a good time to suss out Obadiah.

"That stuff about Jesus work?" I asked him.

"Haven't been abducted in six years," he said. "No bad dreams, no waking up with weird wounds, no repressed memories."

"Huh." I thought about that for a moment. "Do you still see Grays?"

"All the time," he said. "Della is crawling with them. That Zapata Cannery fire?"

"Yeah, they started it," I said.

"How did you know?" Obadiah looked at me funny, looked up at Roz and Elly talking, looked out both windows, and then gave me the sign, the Resistance sign.

"Brother," I said.

"Brother." Obadiah looked at me, nodded. "How many times have they taken you up?"

"Too many. At least fifteen times I know of. Not here, though, at least that I remember." I tried to think about crossing the border. Had they taken me there? I didn't think so, though I'd seen the black helicopters.

"Have you accepted the Lord Jesus Christ in your heart as your personal Savior?" Obadiah asked me. He didn't say this as like a come-on or the prelude to some evangelizing. He just said it as a question, like, Would you like fries with that?

"No. That's sort of the problem."

"That you don't accept Jesus Christ?"

"That I can't. I mean, if I said I did, I wouldn't believe, and if I don't believe, well, how is that going to scare off Grays?"

"So what do you believe?" he asked me.

"I don't know," I said.

"Maybe you do. Let's go to my house and take a walk on the beach."

*

We'd come to Brother Obadiah's house, an octagonal cabin down the street from the Best Damn Hamburger Joint in Della. The cabin sat about fifty feet back from a bluff, at the end of about a 100-foot driveway off the road. The bay side of the cabin was clad in scraps of old aluminum cans Obadiah said he found on the beach, while the front side—sides, actually—were covered with fifty-five gallon drums flattened out and turning to rust. Obadiah said he nailed the aluminum on the bay side because about ten years ago the city put big bright lights at the harbor on the Spit, and he wanted to shine the light back at'em.

Roz dropped us off and continued on the bay road to take Elly home. Obadiah stopped by his house to pick up two battered old canvas bags. He handed one to me, then picked up a straight hardwood staff I recognized as a jo.

"I tried that once," I said, pointing at the jo. "Aikido. Kendo. Martial arts. I thought I could fight off the Grays."

"You can't physically overpower them," Obadiah said.

"Found that out. No human has ever mugged me, though."

"The jo keeps me balanced," he said. "You need a staff?"

I shook my head.

Obadiah led me to a staircase going down to the beach. He said he used to slide down on a rope, but when he got older and after he twisted an ankle, some friends built him the staircase. The bluff edge in either direction had eroded, except in front of Obadiah's lots and the houses on either side, the beach had built up, a boomerang-shaped bit of land in front of it and then a lagoon behind it slowly filling up with sand and gravel.

"This is really my church," Obadiah said when we got down to the beach. "The beach, the bay, the mountains and glaciers."

The canvas bag, the staff, the way Obadiah looked at the beach reminded me of my partner in literary crime. "You know Max?" I asked.

"One of my disciples," Obadiah said. The canvas bags had big loop handles, and we slung them over our shoulders. "Let's walk. Did Max tell you how to make prayer?"

"Make prayer?"

"Pick up stuff."

"Oh yeah. He said you look down to pick up beach trash, and sometimes you find other things. Oh—" I thought of the aluminum on Obadiah's cabin."And you hang that stuff on your cabin?"

"Prayer flags, so to speak," Obadiah said.

He led the way up toward the head of the bay—toward the 'Stead, I realized. The morning tide had gone out, not a particularly big tide, but there had been some serious tidal or storm action or something, so the high-tide wrack line was particularly thick. Good pickings, I thought. Good praying. Obadiah led the way, and we walked on either side of the line, picking up scraps of plastic, cans, plastic bottles, old fishing line, and, once, a tattered tennis shoe.

"So what do you believe in?" he asked me. "I mean, just to lay out the groundwork."

"I believe in the universe," I said. "I believe in myself. I believe nasty, evil alien beings have been abusing me and screwing up my life. I believe I'm crazy as far as normal human society is concerned."

"Which makes you, of course, sane."

"As long as I take my drugs."

"Well, not even then." He reached down and picked up a turquoise blue Japanese fishing float that looked like a penis. "What is wrong with the universe, though?" Obadiah asked. "I mean, other than the aliens."

"Earth's in serious doo-doo," I said. "Global warming. Environmental disasters. Earthquakes, tsunamis, hurricanes. Plagues. Hunger. Poverty. War. The usual crap."

"Human problems," Obadiah said. "The Earth itself, well, she's OK." The way he said "Earth," I could hear the capital E. "She's just doing what she has to do to heal herself. You take a few hits from asteroids or comets over the millennia, and anything humans throw at you is small change. In healing herself, the Earth might make humans uncomfortable, but hey, that's our problem.

"No, the Earth is just fine," he said.

"Yeah, I can see that," I said. "Uh, how does this fit into some grand religious or philosophical scheme?"

"Ah. I was hoping to puzzle it out of you."

"Can we cut to the chase?"

"No. It works better if I like do the Socratic thing."

I sighed. "Yeah, you and my old man, bless his soul. Go on."

"Your old man?"

"Dad. Ignatius, but everyone called him Iggy," I said.

"Ah, Iggy." Obadiah looked out to the bay. "I had a brother named Iggy once. Long time ago, before I came into the country."

"Dad had a brother named Obadiah," I said. "Everyone called him Oby. That was a long time ago, too."

"Nephew," he said, matter of fact, like he would say, Nice Tevas.

"Uncle," I said.

"Only maybe it's better if you just call me 'Brother,'" Obadiah said. He pulled me to him, not a fake-out hug like the Rev, but one of those enveloping hugs to remind us we're all of the same universe. "Figured you'd show up soon or later."

"I knew I had an uncle up here somewhere," I said. "Everyone tells me it's a small state."

"Yeah." Obadiah let go, and we continued walking.

"So the Earth isn't messed up," he said, continuing. "And yet we feel it is. What does that say?" he asked.

"Oh, I get it. Yeah, our relationship with the Earth is like fucked."

"Yup."

"Oh, oh. I think Max talked about this, or maybe it was Surreal, or maybe I just dreamed it. We're not close to Nature is how the Greens would put it."

"We don't walk closely with Nature," Obadiah said. "We separate ourselves from Nature. We build big houses that push Nature back. We build walls, sea walls and fences and gates, that try to keep Nature out. We wear clothes that make us apart from Nature and don't let us feel Nature—let us feel the wind on our faces, the rain on our backs."

"But we do that to keep dry, to keep warm," I said.

"Too dry, too warm. Sometimes we should walk naked in the rain, walk barefoot on the beach."

I looked down and realized Obadiah had taken off his high-top sneakers, slipped them off at his cabin. I still wore my Tevas. I stopped, ripped apart the Velcro snaps, and took them off, took off my socks, and put them in the canvas bag slung over my shoulder. The sand had warmed up in the midday sun, and even though I had to pick my way over sharp rocks, I got Obadiah's point. Close to Nature.

"So how do we get closer to Nature?" I asked. "Is that it—just take your shoes off?"

"It's a start. What's cool about Della, about Alaska, is that by necessity we live close to Nature. I mean, Nature is like so in your face, so big, so powerful you can't fight her. You have to work with Nature, or you die."

"Or become extremely uncomfortable," I said. I thought about going into the bay after that Jet ski rammed into my kayak.

"We need to become more aware of Nature, though—even in Alaska," Obadiah said. "Which is really what knowing Jesus Christ as your Lord and Savior is all about."

Obadiah didn't say that with his "You want fries with that?" voice. He said it seriously, like he meant it.

"Knowing Jesus Christ is like knowing Nature?"

"Uh-huh. Set aside all the dogma, all the church teachings. Get to the bone and what you get is like this guy who said he was the son of God, which is sort of like saying, OK, the Big Cheese himself, only Jesus is really an aspect of God, God as man. So if you know Jesus, understand his nature and his Nature—" And here Obadiah said "Nature" with this like inflection in his voice, so I got the capital N, too, just like I got the capital N when Old Man Tom in Anchorage said "Native." "If you know his Nature, then you see that the whole point of the Jesus thing is that humanity is not separate from Nature, humanity *is* Nature. And the whole point of Christianity as a religion, in my humble opinion, is to get closer to God—closer to Nature."

"And that scares off the aliens?"

"Yeah. Aliens, I think, are this force that wants us to get away from Nature," Obadiah said. "I mean, they're an advanced technology, with powerful ships, able to control great forces. But do you ever see them smelling flowers, walking barefoot through the grass?"

Of course not, I thought. I'm not even sure they had toes. "So by invoking Jesus Christ, I dunno—I'm invoking Nature?"

"Gaia, if you want," Obadiah said. "Getting closer to the Earth. All that Mary stuff—I think that's sort of saying, Hey, Jesus came from the Earth." Obadiah stopped, picked up a ball of monofilament and started unraveling it from a piece of driftwood it was tangled in. "One more thing. Who reveals this truth? Priests. Shamans. Ministers. But also artists, musicians, sculptors, poets, writers. You. Anyone who has figured this out and tries to make humanity more aware of the universe. It's a sacred calling."

"Huh."

"So, again, I ask you? Do you believe in Jesus Christ as your personal Lord and Savior?"

"I believe in the Universe," I said. "I believe in the Earth. I believe in Nature."

"There you go," he said. "Walk with Jesus."

Chapter 20

In our philosophical discussions, Brother Obadiah and I had wandered along the beach toward the 'Stead. As we came up to the driftwood logs and fire pit where the party had been Saturday night, we came across Sarah walking down the path to the beach.

"Jimmo," she said. "Roz thought you might be down here."

"I went to church with her and met the brother there. We've just been walking the beach from his cabin. Sarah, this is Brother Malachi Obadiah. Brother, Sarah."

"Obadiah," he said. He took both of her hands and held them, I guess like the chick version of his handshake. "We've met before."

"We have? At Twee Sisters?"

"No, not there. Not Della. You just don't know it." Obadiah looked at me. "You've met Sarah—it's Sarah for here, right?—you've met Sarah before, too, you know."

Well, uh, yeah, I thought. Known her for almost a week.

"Uh, OK," she said. "Good meeting you, Brother. Uh, Jimmo, Roz is making a bit pot of halibut chowder. She said to invite the brother if I saw him. Brother, you want some chowder?"

"I ate a large breakfast," he said. "I should be moving on. I still have some prayers to make." He lifted up his sack and headed east.

"Weird guy," Sarah said as Obadiah disappeared around a little point along the bluff.

"There's weird and then there's weird," I said, thinking still of what he'd said. "Maybe some people are so weird that by the time the world catches up with them, they're normal."

Sarah gave me That Look, the one that sorta said she'd cut through my bullshit and didn't exactly find a shiny pearl.

"Let's eat," she said.

*

That Zen omelet still lay in my stomach, and I didn't think I was all that hungry. You'd think I might have had enough to eat for the day, except that with the churchgoing, the making prayers on the beach, not to mention like all the cerebral exercise—which really burns up the calories, ya know?—a third meal of the day by two in the afternoon sounded like a good idea. OK, I'd have a light supper later that evening, maybe just some tomato soup.

Even though I'd lived at the 'Stead like three days, I hadn't fully explored the compound. If ya ask me, I think Barry—alleged to be the master architect—stole his plans from *He Built a Crooked House*, that story by what's his name, Bobby Heimlich? Right, Heinlein, my co-author Mighty Mike tells me. Some scienterrific story about a guy whose house went into the next dimension.

What with two eating shifts and all those rooms and cottages connected willy nilly, I couldn't be sure if I'd met everyone. It would also explain like how come all these damn people showed up for halibut chowder, although, you know, that was some kick-ass chowder, now that I think about it, so maybe they didn't like live there and had just come for lunch.

Not that I consulted a seating chart or anything, but between Max and I, we figured out that dang near all the 'Stead rezidents, partners, and hook-ups du jour were there. As I came into the big kitchen, I saw Barry and Roz, of course, Lisa, Doug, Laurie, and Annie and John, whom I think I had met the night before. Freddy, yeah, and, sure as shit, Max, thus explaining Fraze's presence lying there on the kitchen floor guarding the back door. A squad of rug rats ran all around the house. You think I even tried to get their names? I couldn't even count 'em.

Oh, and a couple of new dogs had shown up: this wired Jack Russell roaring around the place, an old husky with one blue eye, one brown eye, and a big charcoal dog lying next to Fraze.

Wait a second: I'd seen that dog before, another wolf-hound mix, slightly bigger than Fraze.

"Bobo?" I said.

The big dog lifted an ear and raised an eye, woofed in kinda a sigh like, Oh, I suppose you want me to get up out of this nice patch of sunshine and come over and greet you? But he did, along with Fraze, about 200 pounds total of mean, lean, alien-sniffing canine machine between the two of 'em. Bobo stood up on his hind legs, paws on my chest, and gave me a big floppy tongue kiss. I would have fallen flat on my ass, except Fraze leaned against me from behind.

"You have this effect on every dog you meet?" Sarah asked.

"No, no, Bobo and I have met before."

I looked around the kitchen, at the table, out the window at the parking lot. No, I didn't see them, didn't see that VW van. Then I looked out on the deck.

Sunday had turned into one of those rare, spectacular Della days, although what did I know, having been in Alaska less than a week? Clear skies, blazing sunshine, and temps in the like mid-seventies—for Della, you're talkin' a heat wave. Out on the deck, Grace, her big frosted 'do lookin' a bit frazzled after the party and playing the marimba, talked to a woman with deep auburn hair pulled back into a braid. The woman reached up with her left hand in that sort of un-conscious gesture people with long hair make to push back a stray strand of hair, only as she touched the left side of her head, she paused, then rubbed the bristles of hair cut short around her ear—around the whole top of her head.

I noticed her earrings when she did that, four hoop ear-rings, a small hoop in her ear lobe, and each hoop after that getting slightly larger. In the afternoon sun she had stripped to an undershirt, a little camisole top with roses embroidered around the edges.

"Lilly?" I asked.

Lilly turned around suddenly, then stood up. She smiled and ran toward me and gave me a hug not unlike that of the Rev.

"Jimmo!" That brush of hair tickled my face. "What the hell are you doing here?"

"I live at the 'Stead. Uh, are you here now?"

"Friend of Grace," she said, waving over at her. "We hooked up in town last night, and she invited me to come out for the party, and then I spent the night on account of uh, well, Margo and I split up and she got the van." She pointed at Bobo, who'd come out on the porch with Fraze to check out the commotion. "Bobo stayed with me. I think I got the better deal."

Lilly stood back from me, but still holding me with her hands on my waist. I looked at her again. Sometime since I'd last seen her, she had cut her bangs and the hair around her ears really short, a bit longer on the top, buzzed around her ears. If not for those earrings, I might not have recognized her right off. From the front it looked like she had this kinda shaggy crew cut, but she still had that long braid—a haircut like Roz's, I realized, only without the purple coloring.

"You got your hair cut," I said. I mean, duh.

"Grace talked me into it," she said.

"I couldn't convince Lilly to go short all the way, but doesn't the crop bring out her eyes?" Grace said.

"It looks great," I said. "Sort of like her mom."

I don't know where that came from, but it did. In saying it, I realized, ho-ho, Roz *was* Lilly's mom—a young mom when Lilly was born, if I had Lilly and Roz's ages figured out right.

"My mom?"

"Roz," I said, jerking my head back at the kitchen.

Lilly's face went a little pale, and she stepped back from me. "How did you know?" she asked quietly.

"You just told me."

"Oh," Lilly said. Grace came up to her and hugged her. "I guess I've been outed—I mean, not like that." Lilly rubbed the stiff hair on her head. "You think it brings out my eyes, Grace?"

"And your ears." Grace nibbled on Lilly's ears. Hoo-hoo, I remembered that little trick.

Sarah came out onto the deck then and put her arm around me. OK, it was a possessive move, but hey, you think guys are the only ones who do that piss-marking stuff?

"New friends?" Sarah asked.

"You know Grace, from Gogogoi? This is Lilly. Uh, Lilly picked me up in Tok and gave me a ride to Della."

Sarah nodded at Lilly, squeezed me a little harder. Dang, how did woman pick up on these things? Did I mention that Lilly and I got that VW van a rockin'? Besides, there I was standing next to her and not to Lilly, who, I should point out, had her arms around Grace, not to mention an ear in Grace's teeth.

We all sort of stood there, feeling a bit uncomfortable the way you do when you're in the room with ex-lovers. It reminded me of my going away party when I left the old Shoeshine State and set forth from Florida on my grand adventure that sucked me up to Alaska.

OK, like I have to admit that after all those years in Florida I'd created some baggage. Hey, it happens. I'd invited pretty near all my friends and anyone else who wanted to come, and sometime in the evening, it happened I was hanging on the screened porch, drinking what really ought to be my last beer, considering how hammered I'd gotten, and I realized there I was in the same room alone with four of my ex-lovers and my current squeeze, the one whose heart I was breaking by going away. Things got a little awkward until Suz—remember? the one who deflowered me? —shut the door to the porch, walked over to me, pulled down my pants, and all five of them proceeded to screw the stuffing out of me.

OK, well, that didn't happen. But a boy can dream, can't he? What really happened was we stood there in awkward silence, then "Rock Lobster" came on the stereo, and we all danced. And then I left for Alaska.

Lilly, bless her heart, broke the ice. "So, uh, Margo headed south, but I got a job at Four Dee Stylz, you know that salon? Said they need another stylist on account of Grace quit to work on this logging project. I kinda got a makeover as part of the job interview. And, well, I met Grace there when she was getting her hair done."

"Really?" Sarah asked. "Gregg cut my hair just last week." She turned around, sort of fluffed up the nape of her neck.

"That's a sharp haircut," Lilly said. "Gregg said I should cut my hair like that, but I decided to go with just half a buzz-cut."

Great, I thought. We were heading into girl-talk territory. Haircuts. Styling tips.

"Gregg's right," Grace said. She waved over at Sarah. "You see that nape, Lilly? You've got a neck that would carry off the look, too."

"No," Lilly said, all of a sudden getting quiet. "I've worn my hair long all my life."

She stood there, holding onto her long braid, getting even quieter. I felt like a shit for tricking her into revealing Roz was her mom, but hey, with those floppy bangs out of her face, it became real obvious: they had the same eyes and nose and mouth.

"You really think I have the same haircut as Roz?" she asked me.

"Uh, yeah, except for the purple hair. That same buzz-cut, long-braid thing," I said. "Kind of a cool look, that ultra-short, ultra-long contrast thingy going on." Criminy, I was babbling away. Shut up, Jimmo. Shut up.

Shit, why did I say that? Now Lilly would feel really self-conscious. Not only had I blown her cover, but I told her she looked just like the woman she might not have wanted everyone to know was her mom. Time for a distraction.

"Hey, chowder's getting cold," I said. I put my arm around Sarah and steered her back toward the kitchen. "You ladies coming?"

"I'll be right with you," Lilly said.

As I turned to go inside, I saw Lilly reach into a pocket on her shorts and pulled out something shiny. We went inside and lined up for chowder. When Grace and Lilly came in a few moments later, Lilly was rubbing the back of her neck and tugging at the short hairs there.

Nice try, I thought. Even with the braid whacked off, she still looked like Roz.

*

You know how sometimes people think something's a big secret and like nobody could possibly guess, except, well, it turns out the secret is so obvious everyone knows anyway? I knew this guy in college, Pete, big lanky dude, grew up in the Deep South, like Alabama or Georgia or something. Smart as a whip. He wound up being like a major public advocacy lawyer, ACLU or something. Anyway, on account of his upbringing or maybe the progressive culture he grew up in—yeah, right—Pete was like way discreet about his sexuality. On matters of sexuality it should be not only, don't ask, don't tell, but none of your fucking business, which is easy for those of us batting point-oh-one on the Kinsey scale to say.

If you were like not only gay, but way-gay like Pete, and came out of a culture where shitheads would beat you up for acting metrosexual, not to mention even possibly swish, you kept your head low. Or dick low, I guess. Pete put on this big tough football player act, and if he even liked show tunes, he was going to whistle "Camelot" in the shower. Quietly. Alone. And no playing with the soap.

In those days when I went to college, not only had it become cool to sway into Kinsey Four territory, it had even become hip. These really choice babes you thought might be a fuck-buddy would turn out to be lesbians for four years, you know, hook up with your roomie and her friends and don't bother with a man. Sexual exploration. So it wasn't like anyone would slam you for being gay. I mean, hell, it had become way cool. Sort of a white guilt thing, I think, like you couldn't be white and experience oppression, but if you were gay, hey, there ya go.

Pete laid low anyway, and went through college like hyper discreet. If he hooked up with somebody, it was like a major deep black operation, leaving separately and closing the drapes, all that stuff. But all his friends knew. Don't ask me how. We just knew. Finely tuned gaydar, I dunno. Pete eventually got involved with this guy who would turn out to be the love of his life, so when it became too hard to be discreet—actually, I think he just got tired of being sneaky—Pete came out to us. It was like, I have something important to tell us, like he was dying of cancer or he was secretly a Republican, and then he says, "I'm gay."

Well, duh. We knew that.

So when Lilly came in for chowder and we all sat down at that big spruce plank table, Lilly at one end, Roz at the other, Lilly tapped a knife on her glass and got our attention.

"I need to announce something," she said. Lilly ran a hand across her head, tugged at those short hairs where her braid used to be. "Uh, I'm sorta new to town, and maybe not everyone here has met me, but, uh, I feel like I belong."

"You're GETs, all right," Barry said.

She grinned. "No, not that. Something else. I don't know—how do I say this?"

"You're my daughter," Roz said.

Lilly sighed. "Yeah, there you go. I'm Roz's daughter."

We all looked at each other. I'd already figured that out, of course, but hey, once she got those bangs off her face and got rid of those dorky retro glasses, it was like way obvious to anyone. Same eyes, nose, mouth, ears.

Well, duh, we knew that.

Chapter 21

I'd like to say the reunion between Roz and Lilly turned out just peachy that afternoon, with mother and daughter reconnecting and discovering a bond lost long ago, but hey, this ain't no sweet-hearted family drama, this is real life. Well, never mind the aliens, the RATs, the GETs, Operation Train Whistle and all that. Real heartbreak, I mean.

When Roz had told me about joining the sisters after that little encounter with the perv priest, she sorta let slip that there had been "consequences," as she put it. I think that's maybe why I figured out Lilly was Roz's daughter. If you're talking a good Catholic girl who joins the sisters right out of high school, what sort of consequences could there be? Uh-huh, I'd guessed that priest had left Roz with more than screwed up memories. So what do you do when you've been impregnated by a priest, you're not even eighteen, and you can't quite find it in your heart to keep a being who came out of that mess? You do what Roz did: give up Lilly for adoption. I figured Roz left open the option for Lilly to get back in touch with her, which is how she tracked her mom down.

Not for a minute did I buy that impregnated priest business. I mean, yeah, I'm sure Roz thought that, and I'm sure the perv who poked her was a priest, only I didn't think he was actually a priest priest, if you know what I mean. Woo-hoo, long before the Grays took over the world's governments, they had pretty much corrupted the Catholic Church. All that hoorah about priests running amok among altar boys and girls had nothing to do with men unable to control their earthly desires. Not earthly, mind you. Out of earthly, yeah.

So the way I figured it, Lilly had come about because, well, what else, some sleazeball Gray had done a little genetic mixing. Same old story. In her heart of hearts, I think Roz knew that the Grays had messed with her just as they'd messed with me, which was why she had taken me under her wing at the 'Stead.

But enough about my problems. Suffice to say, with the kitty out of the sack, Lilly and Roz had gone public with their relationship, and let the healing begin. It would be a long healing.

Well, so much for family revelations and gorging on the best damn halibut chowder I'd ever eaten. After a great meal and one too many awkward silences, Sarah and I went upstairs to the aurora room and laid down for a nap. Well, I tried to. Just about when I started to drop off to sleep, Sarah snuggled up next to me and started nibbling on my ear. I think I've made it pretty clear by now how much that particular little act of foreplay drives me nucking futs.

"So did you sleep with Lilly?" she whispered in my ear.

"It was raining," I said. "She and Margo had a fight in Anchorage. Margo stayed at the hostel and Lilly and I went camping. Yeah, so I slept with her in their VW van."

"In the same bed?"

"Hey, the top bed was broken and didn't slide out."

"Side by side?"

"Yeah, but Bobo was at the foot of the bed. You ever try to get laid with a ninety-pound Irish wolfhound mix on your feet?"

"Did Lilly tell him to get down?"

"She might of."

"And did she do this?" Sarah sat up and slipped off her long sleeve Della Shorebird Festival T-shirt, the one with the Pacific golden plover, you know?

"First she took off those dorky black retro glasses."

"What about this?" Sarah unzipped my jeans.

"I think I might actually have done the unzipping."

"Surely not this?" she asked. Sarah took a firm grip on the base of my cock, and then wrapped those sweet lips around it, gently nibbling on Mr. Jones while she stroked it with her tongue.

"Oh no," I said. "Not like that at all."

Sarah smacked her lips, took a deep breath, and dove back under the sheets.

*

Sunday at the 'Stead went on like that, lots of naps, probably more than a few couples having screaming sex (or at least, soft moaning sex), Roz puttering in the garden, Lilly puttering in the garden, Barry reading last week's Sunday New York Times, people wandering in and out of the kitchen snacking, and then the overnighters slipping off to go home and feed the cats or maybe remind their spouses of their existence—Grace, for example. I mean, to feed her cat. I don't know if she had a spouse, male or female, but if she did, Lilly was going to be a surprise.

Ya know, a usual Della Sunday afternoon.

After a bunch of us polished off the last of that halibut chowder, I found myself in the kitchen with Freddy, Max, Sarah, and Lilly. Lilly and Roz had been playing this little dance all afternoon, sort of avoiding each other and not avoiding each other, each wanting to say something and catch up on all those years and grief, but neither knowing how to do it. Roz finally gave up and went off to her room to do her yoga.

My whole week in Della had been one kick ass adventure after another, and sneaking off to bed and snuggling with Sarah before going to work the next morning sounded like a good idea. Day of rest and all that, ya know? Then Lilly hadda pop off her mouth.

"Hey, what time does the sun set? We should go watch it set," she said. "I hear up on Baycrest at the turn out there's like a little party every night, you know, Mallory Square, Della style?"

"Oh, that is so lame ass tourley," Freddy said.

"The sun'll set about eleven-thirty," Max said. "Hey, wait a second—"

Max stood up suddenly, went to his pack, pulled out a little journal and flipped through it.

"Huh. I thought so. We should do it."

"Do what?" I asked.

"Go see the analemma at sunset."

"The anna-huh-uh?"

"Analemma," he said. He did this little mock professor shtick then. "Ahem: the analemma. The graph of the sun's movement as it appears in the sky."

"Yeah." That jogged my memory. Those little figure eights on globes? That thing. "Well, not-yeah. I'm not following you exactly."

"The analemma. This guy up on the Ridge made an analemma, traced out the sun's position at solar noon every other day for a year—marked it on the ground."

"Even on cloudy days?" Sarah asked.

"OK, he skipped a day. Sometimes two. Sometimes three, but that was OK. He could go back and measure, do it the scientific way if he had to."

"Anal little cuss," I said.

"Well, thank you." Max grinned at me. "But tonight when the sun sets, as the analemma goes, it's important." He grinned again. I knew he wanted someone to ask him the question, so I indulged him.

"And why is that?"

"Because today the Equation of Time is damn near zero."

Oh right, I thought. I knew that.

"Is this analemma the thing up on Oly's Mountain? Like a Little Stonehenge?" Freddy asked.

"Except it's not a Stonehenge," Max said, defensively. "Not even close. But yeah, that one." He reached down and pulled Freddy up. "It's an important astronomical moment. The analemma. Zero time. Come on."

"Where is this again?" I asked.

"Up on the Ridge. Oly's Mountain—that big flat table-top mountain? There," Max said.

"Oh," I said. Oh, I thought, realizing which mountain he meant. That mountain. The one I'd seen when I first came into Della, the one the aliens had taken over for their base, the big fat mean mother of all alien bases. *That* one. My butt chip burned like crazy, so, oh yeah, you betcha, was I ever up for seeing the analemma.

*

So we all piled into Freddy's rusty maroon Subaru, Freddy driving and Max up front, me in the back seat next to Sarah and Lilly on the other side, Fraze in the front, and Bobo in the back. We drove down East Road toward—I love these inspired, creative names—East Hill Road, and up toward Skyline Drive. As I said earlier, I think those are the names, but hey, you know, so many psychoactive drugs, so few neurons. I tend to remember descriptive names, and everything else is who the hell cares? Max thought to swing by Surreal's place over by his sculpture studio on the Ridge and enlisting him in our cause, but when we called him on his cell phone, the dude didn't pick up.

As that kick-butt 2000cc Sube engine whined and we drove up the hill, Max told us all about the analemma. It's not like I remember this shit, but when Max wrote up my grand adventure, hey, he'd even written a fucking article on it for the Della News and said he could put it in as a hyperlink.

Look, there ain't gonna be none of that fancy techno crap in this book. We're talking straight text, ink on paper, and if one of those shady e-book publishers picks up the rights, they better not dick around with the Bodini Garamond Light Sans Serif, shaken, not stirred or whatever font some hotshot New York book designer chooses. OK? We got that clear?

Anyways, Max turned around in the shotgun seat, Freddy driving, and said, "So, this analemma thing. Here's how it works."

"You're not going to do footnotes, are ya?" Freddy asked as she turned the wheel sharply to take a hairpin turn halfway up the hill. Freddy apparently had long experience with Max's quaint conversational style.

He gave her a glare. "*The analemma*: OK, so up on Oly's Mountain, I put this like way cool big post that Surreal built in the middle of an old hay field. This was in my Get Out of Dodge days, when Della had lost a little of its charm and I hauled tail to the hills to get away from certain, uh, relationships." He glanced over at Freddy when he said that, and she grinned.

"So anyways," Max said, "I lived in a little cabin on the edge of the field—that one Walking Juan later took over before he shot up Siouxsie and Abe's place and got sent to Spring Creek for fifteen to twenty-five, with time off for good behavior?"

Siouxsie and Abe? A shoot out on Oly's Mountain? That got my butt chip humming, but Max went on.

"I needed like a ritual, something to do daily to keep me focused on my craft. So every day, I set my alarm at fifteen minutes before solar noon, using the Naval Observatory's tables for lat fifty-nine degrees—"

"Ahem," Freddy said. She took a right at the top of the hill and onto Skyline, this winding road at the edge of the bluff looking down on Della.

"—you can look it up at *www.usno.navy.mil*. Although, well, there's this Canadian site that actually is a bit more user friendly."

"Land the plane," Freddy said.

"OK. Uh, so at solar noon each day, I put another way-cool Surreal-designed rod in the ground—all right, a piece of rusty rebar—at the tip of where the shadow hit the ground. Like I said earlier, some days I had to skip this, on account the weather sucked. Mostly, though, I got the rods in and the pattern worked out. Later, after the spruce bark beetles killed every damn huge tree from Della to We'll See Ya, I planted little nursery trees at the rods marking the beginning of each month. Oh, and at significant dates."

"Like today," I said. "Zero time."

"Zero Equation of Time," Max said. "Thanks for mentioning that."

In the rearview mirror, I could see Freddy roll her eyes and shake her head.

"See, those rods measure the position of the sun as seen from Della or wherever. And, yeah, I know the sun itself doesn't move, so don't anyone be a smart ass." He glared over at Freddy.

"Did I say anything?" she asked.

Max continued. "If the Earth didn't tilt on its axis, or if the Earth moved in a perfect circle around the sun, there'd be no apparent movement, and the analemma would be one big dot."

"Only the Earth moves," Sarah said. Max smiled at her; good little student.

"Ayup. If you graph out the analemma—I have one for Della right here in my journal if you want to see it." He started to reach into his back pack.

"Later," Freddy said.

"OK, OK. Anyway, you have an X axis and a Y axis. The Y shows the sun's altitude as seen from Della or wherever. That's the effect of the axial tilt. The X axis shows the sun's declination. That's the effect of the Earth's elliptical orbit."

"Uh, hang on there," I said. "What does that matter?"

"The earth moves faster at certain points in its orbit. In January, we're cruising, and right now, in June, we're slowing down. Kepler's Second Law."

"Oh, Kepler," I said, like I knew what he was talking about.

"Trust me on it," Max said. "It's like a spinning ice skater. Pull in your arms and you move faster. In the Earth's case, it's enough that on some days, the Earth moves so fast the sun arrives sooner at solar noon than it did the day before, while on some days, the earth arrives later. You'll see, but on the analemma I built, it's fatter on the bottom—the winter months—and thinner on the top. At some points, the sun's position is right at zero on the X axis. The equation of time is zero."

"Here we are," said Freddy. She looked over at Max, and gave him a big smile. "Nice landing."

"Dog is my copilot," he said, and scratched Fraze's ears.

*

Now, of course the trip up to Oly's Mountain didn't take the whole span of Max's exegesis on the Equation of Time and all that crap, so let's just say that interspersed in that trip up the hill sometimes nobody would say anything, or I'd be thinking and not paying attention to what all went on, or that there would be like gaps in the conversation where Lilly would go, like, hey, look at that moose, or Sarah would lean over and give me some tongue action and whisper, OK, when we get back, let's check out the Northern Lights again.

See, what Max told me about fiction, and how come I can't write it worth a crap and he can, is that in your basic flow of the novel, stuff just goes on to fill in space. You sort of want to give the lay of the land, or maybe write about personal mannerisms to develop character and stuff. In a novel you can do that, unless you're like Ernie Shot His Mouth Off The Hemingway, and things are like sparse and everything. You know, It was a Subaru like any other Subaru, maroon and rusty and true.

Shit like that.

So what I didn't write, in that scene above, about that drive up to Oly's Mountain and the Big Gray Redoubt was how my butt chip just burned the whole way. You know how you get this itch, say, in your balls or up your ass, but you're on a long bus trip or maybe strapped in your seat during takeoff and you can't like politely scratch it? But it still itches like a few dozen fire ants have taken up residency in your crotch, and they're testing out their new formic acid Uzis? That's what it felt like driving up to the analemma.

The road wound along the bluff there, real close to the edge at times, which is why I'd taken the driver's side back seat, not just so I could stare down Freddy's neck and smell her White Shoulders, but because I wouldn't be sitting on the edge side. I am fucking afraid of edges. Not heights. Edges.

After a while, the road turned into the forest, or the remnants of the forest, past this sort of nature center, with a big gate and some tourley buses there waiting to scream down the hill back into Della to pick up blue hair eco-tourists. Someone had put up a little shrine on the gate, those things you see at Death Spots where people crash and their survivors get all morbid to honor the dead, only I think it's more to parade their grief. You wanna honor the dead, do it like walking the little man, in quiet and wash your hands afterwards. Although, well, the Day of the Dead thing is kinda cool, now that I think about it, like with those skeleton dentists, skeleton auto mechanics, skeleton masseuses, and skeleton prostitutes.

Max told me later though that the shrine didn't honor some drunk teenster flung out of a pickup truck at 88 mph, but this like alky kid who got popped in the face there in the parking lot by this other drunk who just happened to have a .22 five-shot derringer under his seat. That might have explained the broken bottles of Jim Beam stuck on the branches of an alder bush.

A little ways along Skyline Drive, Freddy hung a Louie toward Oly's Mountain. I could see Skyline went on for a couple of miles or so, but we weren't going to that end of the road, not that day. Pretty soon the dead spruce forest got spindlier and spindlier, and we rose up into alder and elder-berry country, alpine taiga. The little GPS chip the aliens put in my head told me we'd gotten to altitude 1,343 feet and rising.

When Freddy said, "Nice landing," her quaint little way of telling Max that he'd wrapped up his lecture sweet and tidy without getting too professorial—although, dude, you do run on, did anyone ever tell ya that?—well, we'd come to the flat top of the mountain. I don't know what geological forces slice off the tops of mountains, but now and then you find these like high plateaus where you could put in a landing strip or, in this case, an alien Zod class fighter base. Acoma Pueblo. Macchu Pichu. Places like that.

Sure, Max told me he'd lived in an old Quonset hut left from when the Air Force had a radar site there during the Cold War, one of those White Stripe things. Or Alice. White Alice, OK, that's it. You know, big dome dishes, lots of an-tennae, hulking metal buildings, Quonset huts out the wa-zoo. I didn't believe it, though. Zod fighter base, you betcha.

It had all been torn down years ago, and Max said some homesteader got the place cheap from the guvmint on ac-count of it had sort of these toxic waste issues. You know, as-bestos, PCBs, used condoms. The guy sued, though, and the guvmint took it back and made it a Superfund clean-up proj-ect, which was how Max got such a cheap cabin. Someone had to keep an eye on the place, is how he put it.

OK, OK, I know. Land the plane.

We drove through an old busted gate, ignoring the chain link fence with the RESTRICTED AREA DO NOT ENTER sign, the barbed wire, and the goat skulls strung on it, and pulled up next to Max's old cabin, or the concrete pad where his old cabin had been.

Max said after that little incident with Walking Juan, some town vigilantes burned Juan's place to the ground—as well as a metal building could be burned. Surreal salvaged the steel and, a couple of thousand hammer blows later, there you go, rusty moose, beagles, and whistling marmots.

Freddy parked next to a brown Toyota pickup truck, the second most common vehicle in Della, and like all late model Toys, the truck bed and fenders had rusted away. A bumper sticker on the tailgate said NICE DOGS STRANGE PEOPLE, which kinda jogged my memory and then Max said, "Hey, Surreal showed up," and I realized I'd seen the truck at Surreal's whistling marmot party.

We piled out, Fraze and Bobo bounding off into the waist high grass, and saw Surreal standing in the meadow, facing about northeast. Max led the way. As we got closer, I saw those rusty sticks of rebar poking out, just like he said, only on top of them someone had stuck rocks and seashells and birch burls and every now and then those glass floats you sometimes get lucky enough to find on the beach.

"Thought we'd find you here," Max said to Surreal.

"It's Zero Time, homey," Surreal said. He kept staring off at the horizon and didn't turn toward us.

He stood at the northern end of the analemma, kinda where the figure-eight of sticks circled around and then headed to the south. The sticks got taller or shorter depending on where they had been set in the circle—tall at the summer end, short at the winter end, except with the high bluejoint grass, only the summer sticks pointed up.

Surreal stood behind one tall stick, a series of sticks growing taller as they went around the circle, with the tallest stick about eight places away, OK, the solstice stick, right.

"How long to sunset?" Surreal asked.

"Fourteen minutes," Max said.

Damn, we'd timed that well.

*

Now, I'd like to say we did some sort of cosmic ritual for saying farewell to the sun on Zero Time day, except, yo, uh-huh, I *am* an ordained minister from the Universal Life Church—it took me all of five minutes to download my certificate off the Web—but ya think this means every frigging chance a spiritual moment comes up, there I am, like a SWAT team of preachers and I spring into action? No, sweetheart, some days I just lay low and don't do any preachifying. Or shamanizing. Whatever.

Nah, all we did was stand there around the June 13 analemma post, still hung over and lack of sleep catching up with us, until the sun set more or less in line of sight with that post. I mean, that was it. Max said if we had been there about noon, we could have seen the gnomon cast its shadow on the post. As if.

The setting of the sun over the Zero Time on June 13 post wasn't all that spectacular. Sometimes a sunset is just a sunset, and if you wanted to get down to it, I thought Max was being kinda arbitrary and all about that. On the other hand, June 13 had one bitchin' sunset.

See, like to the northwest there of Oly's Mountain and Della these like other mountains spread out across the inlet, a couple of volcanoes and the like. One of them, this four-peaked mountain called Really Am, No? or something like that, sorta steamed a bit. Max said it had done that for decades and every now and then it would steam some more and people thought for sure it would blow, but it never had—not like this other volcano that the sun set near, Very Doubtful or whatever is was called. That one had blown like a baby with the trots, Max said, dumping inches of thick gray ash all over the place.

Alaska being Alaska, you'd think, OK, lots of snow and ice, even in the summer, and like up there on that ice field and in those mountains the snow would never melt. Uh-uh. Most of the mountains across the inlet from Della had turned green in the summer, fuzzy patches of viridian, vibrant and alive for like eighty-five days of pure chlorophyll excitement. In shadows and cracks, OK, a patch of snow or maybe a hanging glacier would give like some relief.

Even with global warming—an alien conspiracy to jack up the planet's temp more to their liking, by the way—not every glacier melted, not completely. Some of those big glaciers lost part of the winter's snowpack, and what had been white became blue. Glaciers, Max told me, got the air compressed out of them, and when that happened, they turned blue. Kinda like old people, glaciers turned blue after a couple zillion decades.

Down south, your basic sunset goes like this. Big orange ball goes down to the horizon. Flash of twilight. Dark. Really dark. Kabbam! Sunset over. Not in Della, not up there at Latitude 59 degrees and some change. The sun takes its own sweet time, kinda, OK, maybe I'll set, I guess, but slowly, thankew. So while Max and Surreal stood there probably pondering the whole astronomical significance of Zero Time and all, I just watched that sun ooze its way over the horizon, over those mountains, over those gleaming patches of deep, teal blue.

A little band of cotton-ball clouds spread across the horizon, sort of these wispy stratocumulus thingies, and the sun set below the clouds, through the clouds. It was like the sun laid out a palette of oils. You gotcha quindacridine red-orange, you gotcha rose madder, you gotcha jaune brilliant, you gotcha shell pink, you gotcha puffs of eighty percent white, you gotcha phatalo blue, good-bye, good night, see ya later.

I squinted in the glare, watching the top of the sun, cuz sometimes on a sunset you can see the green flash. It happened quick, just this little burst of green, add a touch of sennelier yellow light, OK, more like turquoise, and no sooner had I thought, Way cool, the green flash, that blob of green separated from the sun, moved sideways, and quick as mercury, slipped away to the south. Maybe someone not as sophisticated in the ways of the universe wouldn't have noticed it, but hey, when you've been yanked up to orbit by aliens, you learn a few things.

Uh-huh, that was it. I'd just seen a fucking Gray mother ship orbiting on a low polar circuit.

They were back.

Chapter 22

So anyway, even though we were like way bushed and tired and dead on our feet, Surreal got this idea that maybe we should celebrate Zero Time Day with a little project, sorta something to honor the equalization of cosmic forces.

"Let's make a crop circle," he said.

Oh man, I wasn't too sure about that. There's this like obvious association between crop circles and aliens, on account of that stupid movie—I mean, if the Grays *could* be destroyed with water, I'd of been packing a Super Soaker long ago—but the thing is, what with all my abductions and little trips up to the mother ship, I'd never really ever seen any crop circles from where it landed. Not that the ship really landed. Sort of hovered, is what it did, and that big elevator beam just sucked you up.

Still, you've gotcha well known alien conspiracy theorists who go, like, crop circles equals aliens. Maybe. Maybe so. I didn't consider myself a grand expert on the complete structure and complexity of the alien occupation and its millennia long tampering with human affairs. All I know is what happened to me and others in the Resistance. Crop circles weren't really part of our experience.

Still, they gave me the creeps.

"It's still light. We could get caught," Max said, like they'd done this before. Make crop circles, I mean.

"Hey, just something simple," Surreal said. "A quick spiral. We've got a good crew, and you and Freddy know the drill."

"Uh—"

"Jimmo?" Max asked.

I wanted to say, make a crop circle and you sure as shit would be inviting the Grays to check it out. And then I thought, crap, what's another spot on the leopard? Maybe it was about time I started calling the shots, yo, here I am, bring it on.

"Sure. Why the heck not," I said.

"Cool," Surreal said.

He walked over to his truck and started yanking equipment out of the bed. A 100-foot tape. A couple of stakes. Two five-foot boards with rope loops. Surreal and Max looked around that big grass field, then walked over to the Zero Time post.

"We'll start here," Surreal said. "Seems appropriate, eh?"

He took out a sharp knife and cut seven stalks of bluejoint grass, and began shaping them into little human shapes—part of the ritual, Max said. Surreal had studied with a group of British circle makers who passed through Della once, and they said the ritual was very important, I think because it fucked with the heads of the woo-woo conspiracy theorists who studied crop circles.

As Surreal prepared the center of the circle—the nest, he called it—Max told me about the first time they made a crop circle.

"This was a couple of summers go," Max said. "In August, when the days got shorter and we had a good, dark moonless night to pull our prank. I was up at Surreal's studio on the Ridge helping him move another band of rusty mammals, and to stretch our legs, Surreal suggested taking a hike on the trail across the street. I thought that was kinda weird at the time, since moose hunting season had started and no one short of a death wish went walking in summer-high blue-joint grass during moose hunting season."

"Only," Max said, "as Surreal pointed out, it was night."

"Surreal led the way, and when we got to a big open field on the side of a hill facing the Ridge Road, Surreal stopped by an alder bush just off the trail and started yanking out boards and a measuring tape and a grass roller. I figured Surreal had stashed it there a day or so earlier, which made the prank not just a spontaneous act, but a deliberate and conscious conspiracy to commit, well, art," Max said.

"Surreal had sketched out the whole project, right down to how to make the circle without leaving obvious foot prints in the grass. I couldn't tell what we did," Max said. "I just followed Surreal's lead. Hold this. Step over there. Trample this down. Push the roller here. After about an hour or two of trampling and measuring and at one point delicately bending blue-joint grass at precise intervals on the stalk, we were done. Surreal and I went back to his studio, had a couple of beers, and I wound up passed out on a couch in the studio. I woke up the next morning to someone banging on the door.

"It was some red shirt from the Trib," Max said.

"A red shirt?" I asked him.

"Like in Star Trek," Max said. "Trek Classic. You know how in almost every episode, an away team goes down to some mysterious planet, and there's a security officer in a red shirt? And the red shirt dies? The Trib has reporters like that, usually young punks right out of college, and they last like about 20 issues and then disappear."

"Anyway," he said, "someone had called in the crop circle to the Trib and the News, but the Trib red shirt—I think her name was Noomi, but I could be wrong—beat the News out to the story. Had Max or Surreal heard anything strange the night before? Seen any weird lights? Noticed anything unusual on the Ridge?"

"Noomi stood right next to the lawn roller we'd used the night before, grass stains still on it. I told her Surreal and I were working on one of his sculptures and hadn't heard a thing," Max said.

"I woke Surreal up and we went down to that little view—you know, where you can see across toward Oly's Mountain?"

I nodded; I knew that view all right, my first sight of the alien Zod fighter base.

"A bunch of cars had pulled over on the side of the road, including a state trooper," Max said. "A stringer for one of the Anchorage TV stations was there, taking videos of the crop circle. Some woman had knelt down in the grass and was praying and burning sage. You'd have thought a fire had started up, but no, it was just a dang crop circle."

"And it was gorgeous, like a maze, with all sorts of twists and turns in one huge circle—a design Surreal said he'd learned from the Brits." Max chuckled. "It even had a code in it, in binary and ASCII, a reference to this British crop circle in Hampshire—the big-head circle?"

Right, I thought. The Crabwood Farm crop circle. It was a hot topic in abductee circles.

"I've heard about it," I said.

"Later, Surreal and I tried to tell the Trib reporter we had made the circle," Max said. "We showed her the tools, Surreal showed her his sketches and measurements, but she totally blew us off. Hell, she'd even figured out the code. 'Beware the bearers of false gifts and their broken promises,' something like that. The Trib reporter said she'd already talked to a noted crop circle researcher, and that guy—someone named Silver or Mercury, one of those metal names—said to expect a hoaxer would try to take credit. Surreal took great offense at that. 'We're artists,' he said."

"Wankers," Surreal said. He'd finished with the ritual. "We *are* artists."

"That red shirt from the Trib didn't even quote us, didn't even try to consider the obvious explanation," Max said. "She was all into our crop circle as like a manifestation of sacred meridians or some sort of unconscious projection."

"The collective unconscious," I said. "Yeah, what Carl Jung said. Mandala symbolism and all that shit."

"There you go," Max said. "I tried to lay Occam's Razor on the reporter, told her the best explanation was the simplest explanation. And she said, 'While there is a rational explanation for everything . . .'"

"'. . . There is also an irrational one,'" I said.

Max stared at me kinda funny, and it was then our relationship turned a corner, and he started to believe what I'd known all along: Crazy fuck that I might seem, I could actually be right.

Or at least highly entertaining.

While we were yammering, Surreal got Freddy, Lilly, and Sarah together at the center. He teamed me with Sarah, Max with Freddy and Lilly, and gave the women each the zero end of a long measuring tape. Sarah and Freddy would hold the tape and Max, Lilly, and I would follow them, stomping the grass flat with the boards. Surreal held on tight to the measuring tapes at the center. The idea was that the women would walk with the tape, Sarah clockwise and Freddy counterclockwise, and periodically Surreal would let the tape out some, so that as they walked they moved in ever increasing spirals. Max and I would follow behind or help lift the tape over them as we crossed paths.

For the first few passes, we got in each other's way, constantly getting tangled up, but as the spiral got larger, our teams would be opposite each other. Surreal had 100-foot tapes, so with us more or less measuring out the radius, we'd wind up with a 200-foot crop circle.

"This is pretty goofy," Sarah said.

"Yeah." I smiled at her. "I like goofy."

"Me too."

The thing I liked about this project was I got to walk behind her and stare at her cute little ass. I'm not normally the kind of guy who gets off on women's butts, only some women—I thought fondly of a girl I knew in college affectionately called Jane Swivel Hips—merited closer attention.

"I don't think I've done as many goofy things in my life as I have here," Sarah said. "This is a pretty goofy place. Goofy people."

"You think?"

"Not that I've noticed." Sarah looked back at me and smiled, a nice leering smile, actually, and I found myself again thinking of the Northern Lights. Surreal was shouting something and then I saw him waving at us to get down.

"What the heck?" But I laid down. My butt chip sort of throbbed, too. I scuttled up next to Sarah, and we made ourselves invisible in the high blue joint grass and fireweed.

From the northeast I heard a thrumming, sort of a persistent, irritating whine, you know, fresh cut lawns on a summer evening, the roar of a John Deere tractor, the smell of a cheap two-cycle engine. Only as near as I could tell, no one in Della cut their lawns, on account it was neck-high blue-joint grass, so why bother? I parted the grass a little to see, and coming up over the river valley flew this like kite thing. I blinked, on account of I'm a bit nearsighted, and looked again, and saw, yeah, this like kite thing, two big fabric covered wings with a little cart and a little engine and this person sitting in it.

"Ultralight," Sarah said as she crawled next to me.

I couldn't see the person in it, two people, actually, now that it got closer, not that I would have recognized them anyway, but as the ultralight came up on us, my highly honed instincts about aliens went on overload. There was some serious mean nasty alien on that little idiot plane. Only, at the same time, I felt like, whoa, against the forces of evil stood one brave person, dedicated to protect the planet, committed to resist the Grays and the Alien Occupation Government. Like me, but with some kick-butt weapons.

That ultralight came closer and closer, the whine louder and louder, and I knew if it headed straight toward us, we were busted, cuz even hugging the earth in that high blue-joint grass, hey, from about twenty feet up, we were toast.

Only, like at the last possible moment, just as the ultralight came across the flat little top of Oly's Mountain, and thus us, the ultralight banked to the south and headed back to Della, flying through a notch on the Ridge and down to the bay. I wanted to say the pilot tossed us a little salute, but I also wanted to say that I was home at the 'Stead, sleeping off what was turning out to be a bitchin' hangover, and looking forward to another round of screaming sex with Miss Sarah.

"That was close," Sarah said.

"Close only counts in buzz cuts and tactical nukes," I said. "Who was that?"

"Northern Flights," she said. "This ultralight tour outfit. If you've got the gonads to strap in, Marie will take you up. I met her at Twee Sisters the other day—she works part time, but who doesn't? She offered to take me flying, but I think she was hitting on me."

Surreal stood up from the middle of the crop circle, and I saw Max and Freddy getting back to work on the other side of the circle. Took 'em a while, I thought. Surreal waved at us and then shouted.

"That's my girl!" he said.

"Surreal's daughter?" I asked Sarah.

She shrugged. "Or sister or niece or whatever. It's kinda hard to suss out familial relations in this town, you know?"

Right, I thought to myself. Lilly. Roz.

"Let's hustle!" Max yelled. "The early morning flight from Anchorage is due in about two hours, and then the tourly flights get going."

Sarah took up the tape again and I got back to stomping the grass behind her as she measured. We'd pretty much reached the end of the tape and had maybe another twenty feet to go.

"So Marie hit on you?" I asked.

Sarah smiled, and it made me think for a second, OK, I might not be the only one with fidelity issues. Not that there was anything wrong with that.

"Right off. Freddy was right: she does have a thing for redheads. After Dohna hired me and introduced me to Marie, she gave me this look—That Look: you know, the one you gave me when we first met?"

"I did?"

"Oh babe, absolutely. You were almost leering. It was really cute."

Sarah winked at me, and I thought, Uh-huh, the Northern Lights were looking good.

"So Marie gives me That Look, and then she runs her hand up the back off my neck and says, 'Sharp haircut, sweetheart.' Only she said it sorta, well, sexy."

Sarah paused then from her measuring, and looked off toward the bay and I thought to myself, OK, a Kinsey three, maybe a four.

"Not that I noticed," she added.

"She's a redhead?" I asked, teasing.

"Could be, but yesterday she had a platinum blonde buzz cut. I could check if you want." Sarah winked at me, and I hate to admit it, but I blushed. "Hey, we're done."

She held up the end of the measuring tape and waved at Surreal. On the other side of the circle, Freddy held up her end of the tape, too.

"Stand right there," Surreal said. "Freddy, Sarah, measure out ten feet and give the ends to the guys. Max, Jimmo, make a little circle around the ladies and stomp it in the same direction as the grass in the spiral."

We did that, putting in two circles at the ends of the spirals.

"Now walk back the way you came and meet me at the center," Surreal said.

As he wound the tapes back up, we walked around and around the spirals, like coming in out of orbit, I realized, remembering that one time the Grays abducted me in a Zod fighter ship and didn't bother with the elevator beam. That had been one kick butt ride. Took me about a day to unretract my balls from my stomach.

Back at the center, we joined the rest of the guerrilla artists. Fraze and Bobo had been bounding after us, but early on they realized we weren't playing with them and went back to snoozing next to Surreal. In the little clearing I couldn't see the spirals, just the beginning of 'em winding out. The way the grass flattened out, though, swirling like a wave, it looked kinda cool. OK, spooky, like these blobs of some unknown force had wound around and around knocking down the blue-joint. The prevailing irrational theory had it that ultrasound did the trick, and you could tell because the grass stalks had been snapped precisely at the same height, as if some unknown force had been dragged across it—a force so great, so powerful, and yet so restrained, it didn't break the stalks, but bent them.

Wow.

"Looks good," Max said.

"It'll look better from the air," Surreal said. "I'll get Marie to snap a shot on her next pass." He smiled. "Did you see that flying? She rocks. I told her she shoulda gone into the Air Force."

We all laid down at the center there, Sarah's head on my lap, Freddy and Max side by side, even Lilly and Surreal kinda cozying up to each other. One or two of the higher magnitude stars had popped out, but other than that, the sky remained a deep, dark blue, kinda cerulean, ya know? Darker but not really dark, light enough to see these big huge lenticular clouds looming on the horizon.

Now Max swears none of what happened next really happened, and Sarah, Lilly, and Surreal said they might have seen something weird, but hey, it's Della, you know, like the bumper sticker says: KEEP DELLA WEIRD. All I know is what I saw and did.

So we were lying there in the high blue-joint grass, in that circle we'd stomped down and eventually we'd have to walk out of without leaving footprints, sorta blissing on the cosmic fun of it all, and I heard that whine of Marie's ultralight again. Only, yo, that whine went from like a puttering lawn mower sound to something louder, tougher, we're talking V-12 engine or something. Then it became this like jet sound, then more than a jet sound, rockets roaring and then not even rockets.

I stood up, damn near dumping Sarah off me, and looked to the south. It came in fast, that delta shape, and yeah, Surreal swore later it was just Marie doing some fancy flying, buzzing us after she had dumped her passenger at the airport, but uh-uh. Surreal was just covering up what we both knew we saw. I knew that shape. I knew that sound. Zipping right over the edge of Oly's Mountain came a Zod fighter, no more than fifty feet off the ground, so close the grass flattened, almost ruining our hard work. A foo fighter, as they said in the Big War.

I wished Grace had come with us then, that she hadn't gone home to feed her cat, because I think even a whiff of the fluorocarbon drenched hair spray might have sent that Zod fighter scattering. Only she hadn't come, I didn't have a can of hair spray with me, and I knew I was royally, totally fucked.

Well, I did when that big lenticular cloud came over me. Against the darkening sky it would have been hard to see, except like lightning shot out from above it, little bouncing balls scuttling around the big cloud. I could smell the ozone, feel every little hair prickle up and stand straight with goose bumps. And my butt chip? My body quivered again as it had when Brother Obadiah spoke of the aliens at the U-Cubed church. No Carol the totally weird bike lady was there to lay on hands. No Uncle Oby was there to get my ass out of this jam. I began to shake, whether from the wind, the lightning, or the utter terror of it all, I don't know.

Another Zod fighter whipped around us, two now, then three—they always came in groups of threes—buzzing us and tormenting us. I couldn't see Sarah or Freddy or Lilly, just Max and Surreal sort of off to the edge there looking the other direction, at one of the Zod fighters or something.

This big light came down from the cloud then, a column of light; and oh yeah, I knew that light, that cloud: the mother ship come to take me away, maybe for good this time. Down that light a woman descended, her long blonde hair whipping around her. She wore that skin tight silver suit the aliens made humans wear when on the mother ship, silver to the hands and feet, and showing off rather nicely that woman's hot little cleavage.

She came down then, yeah, Venus on the half shell: Eve descending, all right. Eve, that other worldly woman I'd seen when I was first abducted. Her feet touched the ground, that column of light still around her, and she reached out to me.

I stood, terrified, shaking, knowing that they'd come for me, that this time I would not resist Eve, that I would take her hand and go up in the mutthahship with her and leave this planet, this earth.

Earth, I thought, remembering Brother Obadiah then, remembering what he'd told me on our walk that morning, what he'd said at church. Earth, Nature, Jesus.

"In the name of Jesus Christ our Lord and Savior, I command you to return!" I yelled.

Eve pulled back her hand, her hair settling down, no longer a wind to whirl it about.

"In the name of Mother Nature, I command you to leave!" I yelled again.

Eve's hair grew shorter, her skin darker, and the silver suit moved up to her neck, her breasts growing slightly small, but still, hey, pretty damn sweet to look at.

"In the name of the Goddess, in the name of Gaia, in the name of the Force that lives within us all, I command you to end this!"

The light in the column grew dimmer, no longer a whirlwind, no longer a thick shift that sucked up blue joint grass and twigs and fireweed. A fierce wind blew off it still, whipping off my hat, my dreads flying back. Bobo and Fraze stood to either side of me, their fur flattened, and they both growled that wolfhound growl, rising from their throats and sounding like steel being sundered. The growling of those two big dogs, one light, one dark, sent a calming energy into me.

"Leave," I said calmly, holding out my hand to Eve.

Her hair had turned dark blonde and cropped short, her features now interesting, but not unworldly beautiful, and that shock of white appeared over her right eye. The silver suit fell away, and she walked toward me, naked but for a spirally etched shell on a thong around her neck.

"Virginia," I said to her, and she took my hand. "Virginia Dare."

She came to me, left that column of horrid light, walked out of the mother ship's embrace and back to the Earth.

And as she did that, I saw her turn into a whirlwind of golden motes. The column of light became narrower and narrower, until it was but a rope of light rising up to the lenticular cloud, the rope winding back up as if being winched; and it disappeared, the cloud disappeared.

The whirlwind swirled before me, separating into two little tornadoes, then three, and perhaps I blinked, perhaps in the dim light I had never seen the whirlwinds at all, but one moment I saw these clouds of golden motes that had been Eve, also known as Virginia, and in the next moment, there stood Lilly, Sarah, and Freddy, naked and glowing in the fading light. I saw in them the face of Eve, as if she looked out from their eyes, and then Eve disappeared, faded—absorbed, I like to think—and became Lilly, became

Sarah, became Freddy. Some essence of Eve, long ago taken from this Earth, had moved through time and generations of women not quite of women born to find herself in those three women—those three women I loved, or at least with whom I'd had really hot, screaming sex.

Those Zod fighters disappeared, the clouds went away, the lightning quit, Fraze and Bobo went back to sleep, and I found myself lying there, as calm as I'd ever been, with Sarah sleeping quietly, her head in my lap. You would have thought nothing unusual or strange had happened. And maybe you would have been right, except that when I looked down at Sarah, looked over at Lilly and Freddy, they all had this shock of white hair over their right eyes.

Explain that, you rational, thinking straights.

Chapter 23

And so the Grays left Della, every little stinking one of them, Zod fighters, kinky servo assisted legs, ugly ears hidden by ball caps and hideous hair styles, big eyes and all. Kyle, the boss of the logging operation? Got transferred back to Oregon, Samm said. Tim, the Zapata Rat Hole camp boss? Skipped town after his name showed up on the state sex offender list. This city council member with a big pot belly? Took a job with a Washington big box chain store.

All of them, gone.

Max told me later there had been this moment when Della looked to shred off its protective code of genuinely, truly strange weirdness, that maybe the aliens would win, but after that night we made the crop circle—which Max and I called The Incident on Oly's Mountain, original, huh?—things settled down in Della. Canneries didn't blow up. Wildfires didn't flare up. Big huge tsunami waves didn't roar in out of nowhere. OK, that didn't happen, but it could have. Yeah, shit continued to happen, but Shit didn't happen.

Surreal and the women didn't think anything weird had gone on up on Oly's Mountain. Yeah, the next day that Trib reporter called him up to ask if he'd seen anything strange up on the ridge. Marie, bless her heart, took a photo of the big spirals, a little bit flattened by a freak thundershower, but still impressive, and the photo made the front page of both papers and got picked up by the Associated Press, CNN, and the Weekly World News, of course, which meant it had to be true.

Max and I knew the real truth, of course. Oh, and those big wolfhound mix dogs, not that Fraze and Bobo were talking. Something in the way they walked, something in how the dogs carried themselves, I dunno, they just had this attitude about them that, Yeah, uh-huh, we whipped alien butt. For weeks afterward they did that little superior dance dogs do when they catch a rabbit or chase off a moose raiding the sugar snap pea vines in the garden. Uh-huh. We kicked butt.

Otherwise, everything seemed perfectly normal, and the idea that single-handedly and with the power of the Lord, Gaia, the Goddess, and Mother Nature, the idea that I had kicked alien butt—well, who'd believe that? Certainly not you, dear reader, cuz the spine of this book says "Fiction." Everything weird and unusual and strange that happened in Della my first week in town has a rational, logical explanation.

And an irrational one, of course.

Still, one thing struck all of us as kinda unusual. Lilly, Sarah, and Freddy all had that little shock of white in their hair. Sarah tried to cover it up, but no matter what red dye she used, it didn't take. If she buzzed it back or shaved away the patch of hair, it would grow back within days. When people saw them together, they'd accuse them of trying to start some sort of trend, you know, Susan Sontag of the North or something. Do you think they tried to say, Hey, we went up to Oly's Mountain not looking like this, and when we came down, Hey, shock of white? OK, Lilly tried to say that until

Roz told her, sweetheart, just give it up, even in Della some things are just too weird.

The days grew shorter, the nights longer. The logging job ran out and then I got another job and one after that. Sarah and I moved in together into the aurora room, with Lilly taking the room downstairs. Grace went back to her husband. Bobo went on long beach walks with me, and sometimes we'd run into Max and Fraze and Brother Obadiah, and we'd go off making our prayers.

But after the Incident on Oly's Mountain, I never, ever saw another alien, not in Della anyway. Lenticular clouds would be just lenticular crowds. A man with a hat with floppy ear muffs would just have cold ears. People with big sunglasses just had big sunglasses. People wobbly on their knees just had bad knees.

And if sometimes a cloud seemed more than a cloud, and my little butt chip got burning, I would whisper to myself what Brother Obadiah taught me.

In the name of the Earth, of Nature, of the Goddess, of Gaia, in our Lord Jesus Christ, I command you to leave. A peace would descend on my heart, and all would be right with the world. I would take off my shoes, and walk barefoot in the sand, closer to Nature, closer to the Earth. Or, as Brother Obadiah would say:

Walk with Jesus.

Acknowledgments

If you lived with me, worked with me, talked to me, or were otherwise some part of my life from 1999-2005, you helped write this novel. That's how art works, and I thank you.

In particular, I'd like to thank several organizations and people without whom this novel would never have happened, or at least taken a whole heck of a lot longer.

The Seaside Institute's Escape to Create artists residency in Seaside, Florida, provided me the time I needed to focus on and finish Truck Stop Earth. I'm grateful to the Escape to Create directors, Marsha Dowler and Karen Holland, for making that happen, and for their support and friendship during our common creative endeavor, I thank my fellow Escapees, Eric Gansworth, Leslie Neumann, Alex Freeman, Ian Ingram, Kristine Robinson, Lisa Endriss, Stephen Ingle, and Jenny Krasner. My hosts, Jim Nedohon and Steven Golsch, graciously allowed me to stay at their Watercolor vacation condo.

The Alaska State Council on the Arts provided financial support for me to attend Escape to Create through its career opportunity grant program—i.e., they helped pay my airfare down there. Despite frequent budget cuts, ASCA continues to support Alaska's artists. If you're an Alaska legislator reading this, hey, how about giving them some more support, OK?

My fellow members of Science Fiction and Fantasy Writers of America, as always, provided a vast cultural support group for those of us wonky enough to explore realities beyond. And to my marimba group, Shamwari, thanks for helping me blow off steam every Monday night.

As always, my wife Jenny Stroyeck has given me her day-to-day support of my creative endeavors. Mostly, she puts up with my strangeness and keeps me grounded in reality. My sisters, Helen Armstrong, Janet Shook, and Marcia Armstrong, and my mother, Sylvia Jander, are the other rock-solid women in my life.

Throughout this novel, Dana Stabenow and Chris Bernard have kept me going when I began to doubt my abilities. I am blessed to know them as editors, fellow writers, and friends.

And finally, the beaches of the Gulf of Mexico and Kachemak Bay have offered me solace and inspiration.

— Michael Armstrong, Homer, Alaska

ABOUT THE AUTHOR

Perseid Press is proud to present the new novel from Michael A. Armstrong, award-winning journalist and novelist.

Michael Armstrong was born in Virginia in 1956, grew up in Tampa, Florida, and moved to Anchorage, Alaska in 1979. He has lived in Homer, Alaska, since 1994. He attended the Clarion Science Fiction Writers Workshop and received a bachelor of arts from New College of Florida and a master of fine arts in creative writing from the University of Alaska Anchorage. His first novel is *After the Zap*. Michael's short fiction has been published in Asimov's, The Magazine of Science Fiction, Fiction Quarterly, and various anthologies, including *Not of Woman Born*, a Philip K. Dick award nominee, and several Heroes In Hell anthologies. His other novels include *Agviq, The Hidden War,* and *Bridge Over Hell,* part of the Perseid Press Heroes in Hell universe.

Michael has taught creative writing composition, and dog mushing. He is a reporter and photographer for the Homer News. He and his wife, Jenny Stroyeck, live in small house they built themselves on Diamond Ridge above Homer, which they share with an incredibly adorable labradoodle.

www.ingramcontent.com/pod-product-compliance
Lightning Source LLC
Chambersburg PA
CBHW031208020726